All
DIFFERENT
DIRECTIONS

DAMIEN MINNA

PAGE PUBLISHING, INC.
New York, NY

First originally published by Page Publishing, Inc. 2018

ISBN 978-1-64350-883-2 (Paperback)
ISBN 978-1-64424-848-5 (Hardcover)
ISBN 978-1-64350-884-9 (Digital)

Printed in the United States of America

This book is dedicated

2

All elements of *Creation*
involved in making this I AM process available
for individual self-expression,
I offer to you my *Love*, *Thanks*, and *Praise*

2

My *Soul Mate*, who rescued me from myself,
who gives me *Inspiration* to *Be a Better
Man* with every breath I take,
I offer to you my *Love*, *Thanks*, and *Praise*

2

My *Faith*, *Family*, and *Friends* both near and far,
from the *Past*, *Present*, and *Future*,
I offer to you my *Love*, *Thanks*, and *Praise*

2

All *Experiences*, *People*, and *Situations* that have
painted the canvas of the masterpiece,
I am *Honored* to call my *Life*;
I offer to you my *Love*, *Thanks*, and *Praise*

2

The Almighty Creator, the Alpha and Omega,
the *Process* that embodies the
I AM and **WE ARE**,
I offer to you my *Love*, *Thanks*, and *Praise*

2

The ***Unity*** of **All there IS**,
Now and *Forever*;
I offer to you my *Love*, *Thanks*, and *Praise*.

Backward

L *ife's a Trip.* Where you end up depends on where you've been. How you get there is entirely up to you. *Purpose* isn't a destination; it's a practice that unfolds like a well-composed symphony. Every action that takes place is etched in time forever. Once something is finished, that's it. We co-create memories with everything available to us, leaving our mark masterfully woven into the fabric of *All there Is*. Every "thing" defines itself as itself in the *Process* of *Understanding* existence.

I AM no better or worse off than any other person. Good and bad are labels that we all give meaning to in reference to what we have perceived. *Perception* is merely what we make of the conditions we are exposed to. At some point, we were taught the difference between right and wrong from other versions of *Ourselves*. WE ARE reflections of a *Source Energy* that is so complete that it seems futile to labor over the trivial details. Our reality is an elaborate construction of suggested ideas that give us the impression that we know what we're talking about.

I've done my best to learn from my experiences, and in doing so, I created a *Life* worth *Living*. I utilize my free will to make mistakes worthy of *Suffering* in an effort to *Understand* my meaning. Free will is a gift given to everyone willing to express their individualized *Self*. Within this earthly reality, we may never understand the secrets of the universe. That's why it's of paramount importance to dive deeply into the exploration of *Self*.

Each *Soul* existing in this space-time continuum has a *Responsibility* to express itself as an energetic particle of the greater whole. Upon completion of this life, maybe, just maybe, we will get

5

a chance to experience the *Wholeness* of *Creation*. Until breath no longer permeates our body, it is important to focus on the only thing we truly have control over—our ability and willingness to explore *Ourselves* in observance of the *Great Unknown*.

Belief is a concept that challenges everything about the way we think. The mind's ability to create *Value* out of the human experience is dependent upon the way we react to *Life's Happenings*. *Believing* in possibilities beyond what we can understand opens a portal to self-exploration. This book is nothing more than my best recollection of what happened around me and how I chose to react to it. My response to the subtle nuances suggested by possibility is uniquely my own. I'm motivated to share *Lessons* I've *Learned* with the specific intention of shining *Light* upon common stumbling blocks. If my travels can illuminate the path of self-awareness for just one person, I have found *Success* in my efforts.

There are **2** ways to read this book. Since I see the world *Differently*, I chose to write this book a bit *Different*. If you don't like the style, I beg of you to ask yourself why? I feel there is no better question. Is it because at some point, somebody said it should be another way? What happens when something you believe in turns out to be completely *Different* than anything you understand? Trying to figure out why you feel the way you do is often an uncomfortable process. So too was owning up to the problems that taught me some of *Life's* most important *Lessons*.

I invite you to use your free will to enjoy this work in any way that pleases you. My intention is to tell the story in a way that's interesting and entertaining. I also chose to write in a way that reflects my search for *Deeper Meaning*. I *Believe* there are no accidents, only opportunities to *Learn*. I've learned that there are undeniable *Truths* that can easily go unnoticed in everyday life. Most of the time, we are so involved with what we think matters, the *Essence* of our existence goes unnoticed. If you pay close enough attention, the answers we are searching for are often right in front of *Us*.

If there's something here for the curious onlooker, I AM *Grateful* for the *Opportunity* WE ARE able to experience *Together*. If this work proves to have no inherent value to the reader, please discard it and move forward with whatever makes Your Life worth Living.

Mirage

I was sprawled out on what appeared to be an operating table in an eerie dark and cold room. Nobody was in the room, but I could see silhouettes just outside the door. I heard voices feverishly muttering medical terms, but I couldn't exactly make out what they were saying. All of a sudden, I was no longer in my body. I had an aerial view hovering over what seemed to be a lifeless vessel. I saw my body lying on the table, but I was overwhelmed by a drastic sense of polarity as my *Essence* was slowly floating away. As I ascended, the subtle glow emanating from my skin began to fade.

It was like a scene from a Hollywood movie, and I was all too familiar with how it was progressing. Without the presence of an actual voice, I shouted out, "I'm not done yet! I'm only twenty-four, and it can't end like this. I haven't accomplished what I'm here to do. Put me back in my body! PUT ME BACK IN MY BODY!"

Suddenly, I was back in my body, staring up at an *Abundant Being of Light* suspended just above me. At first, I was franticly repulsed at the potential of my life coming to an end. Then a soothing warmth radiated through me which created an instant calming effect. Unsure of what was happening, I cried out, "Am I going to be able to return to my life?"

The response I received echoed deep within my *Soul*. A body without form answered me in words beyond space and time. "If you return to your *Life*, it will be *Different* than anything you have ever known."

I replied automatically, without processing the information I just received. I answered clinging to the only reality that made sense to me, "That's fine, please just let me go back to my life."

The *Voice* then said, "You can return to your *Life* if you agree to three things. First and most important, you must work to find *Oneness* within *Yourself*. Second, you have to *Live* the example of what it means to *BE* in an effort to positively influence your *Friends* and *Family*. Finally, get to work on accomplishing your *Purpose*. If you agree to these three things, you may return to your *Life*."

It didn't matter if the *Voice* told me I needed to backflip through six hula-hoops with my hair on fire, I wasn't ready to let go of my physical existence. When I agreed, there was a blinding flash, and the luminous presence above me filled the room. The warmth I felt is simply indescribable. Rays of light, like the kind one sees when the sun pokes through the clouds after a rainstorm, plunged into my motionless vessel. Once the ethereal glow filled my body, a wave of serenity flashed inside me, and I opened my eyes.

The American Dream is filled with opportunities that are often difficult to understand. At a young age, the happiness equation is presented in a manner that represents equality, hard work, and freedom to pursue dreams. If you fill in the blanks correctly, then the sky is supposedly the limit. *Illusion* and reality are oftentimes cloaked in an ideology that seems fair and just. The impulse to pursue what makes one comfortable is fueled by high-rise cities and corporate propaganda. Hollywood renditions of real life are often disguised as untapped potential just beyond people's fingertips. The tendency to get ahead often derails the *Soul's* path in a way that makes material gain look like the forefront of all good adventures. This is a story about how *Life* works itself out even when the road map goes up in flames. Every moment offers a chance to experience the *Divine*, while free will guides each individual toward self-expression. With every end comes a new beginning, and each *Life* has a unique *Responsibility* to make sense of its happenings. Since I *Learned* these *Lessons* after years of hapless meandering, I'll back up a bit in an effort to paint a clearer picture.

When things didn't work out the way I dreamed they would, I had to come up with a new plan. I poured my heart and soul into a high school football career that ended with the first championship in the school's history. I was decorated with many honors, including having my jersey number 2 retired. My grades weren't the best, but I was one of the best linebackers in the state. I thought this would be enough, but the universe has a funny way of working things out.

I wasn't big enough, strong enough, or fast enough in the eyes of major college recruiters, and I definitely had a "unique" way of getting things done. My game was incomplete, and I needed to polish it if I was going to find success. Highly discouraged, I turned to a mentor to comb through my options. Time was running out when it came to getting a football scholarship, and I had a bum shoulder that required a fairly serious surgery.

Junior college plus reconstructive shoulder surgery meant I'd have to take a year off in my hometown to recover. This was an unacceptable option in my eyes, as I watched all my friends that actually did their homework go off to major universities. The first two doctors I saw would not grant me medical clearance to play football, so I went for a third opinion. The third doctor confirmed that I needed surgery but added that I couldn't really damage my shoulder much more. It was a clean tear, but I could play through the pain if I was willing. My heart hurt much more than my shoulder, so my teenage brain saw an opportunity among the wreckage.

I highly valued the opinion of a mentor I became close with in high school, so I listened carefully when he offered an option I had not heard before. He told me of an athlete that had graduated a few years before me who had found himself in a similar situation. The athlete decided to go to a prep school on the East Coast and completed a postgraduate year at a Connecticut boarding school. Each boarding school was allowed three such athletes to boost the morale and talent level at each school. The process enabled the smaller boarding schools to even the playing field against some of the larger schools in the area.

The following morning, I went to the library at the junior college I was supposed to attend. My mentor gave me a stack of papers containing information about the boarding school attended by the athlete. One of the papers among the lot was a football schedule. I investigated every school on the schedule and reached out to each of the football coaches detailing my interest. By the end of the day, I received three responses from coaches asking to see game film.

When I broke it to my *Family* that I wanted to move to the other side of the United States to attend a fifth year of high school, they were shocked to say the least. Sunday dinners usually dealt with a completely different type of excitement. I was the oldest of four crazy boys, which meant I was the ringleader of all the nonsense. Moving to Connecticut meant I would be breaking up our California version of an *Italian Catholic Family*. Being the first to graduate high school meant I was the pace car for all future *Brotherly* endeavors.

My *Dad* served in the Air Force Special Forces and then became a cop and then a lawyer. So to say he is detail-oriented is an understatement. My plan to go to prep school was like telling him I was going to fly to the moon with a jet pack I made in the garage. Once I explained that the opportunity would expose me to an Ivy League education, his wheels began to turn. At the end of the day, *Dad* was my number-one fan. He also saw merit in the potential of the experience itself. I needed him to buy in. Without the support of my most valuable asset, my *Family*, I couldn't confidently move forward. My *Dad* gave me much-needed insight and understood that if a few critical pieces fell into place, the idea wasn't all that bad. He did mention that he thought I was crazy nonetheless. *Mom* was another story. She always got behind my crazy ideas. Since I was young, she had an unwavering *Faith* that I would *Find My Way*. But her first baby was now leaving home. This was a tough experience for her, but she had *Faith* in my ability to accomplish *Great* things.

At home, we all shared something special. Our *Family* was *Different* in that our home was our sanctuary. The entire bunch was a bit hyperactive, and *Family* events resembled a sandbox jungle gym instead of formal get-togethers. During Sunday dinner, you were more likely to get beaned in the head with a grape than see silverware in the proper order next to the dinner plates. Fine china and roasted duck were often substituted with paper plates and a large bowl of

Mamma's pasta. The Peter Pan mentality was often embraced, as the Lost Boys would have nothing to do with growing old, and neither would we. Despite the insanity, *Unconditional Love* was always present in the most mysterious, elusive manner.

The following week, critical pieces started to fall in place, and the great adventure began to take shape. Three of the coaches that saw film of my senior-year football season were quick to offer me a fully paid opportunity to play for their team. I received their offers on Monday, spoke with all three coaches on Tuesday, and committed to one of the schools on Thursday. I was in pads, practicing with the team by Sunday. I went from being depressed, confused, and not knowing what to do with my life to being on the other side of the United States, practicing with a new team in ten days.

I wasn't a naturally gifted athlete, so football never came easy for me. I had developed a formula to be *Great* though. If I trained harder, studied longer, and practiced as though I were preparing for a championship every day, game day became an opportunity to perform at the highest level. Football is a game that pushes physical limits in an extreme manner, and playing through injuries was part of the gig. Having a banged-up shoulder meant I had to adjust my strategy a bit, but I accepted the challenge and found a way to get it done. I always took pride in my ability to find a way to make things happen despite the circumstance. I didn't travel all the way across the United States to be average, and I took the commitment that I made to the coach and team very seriously. I was there to be a *Leader*, and that meant giving everything I had on every single play.

The football season was a success as the team went 7–2 and was crowned co-league champions. I was again blessed with many individual honors, but none sweeter than being part of another championship team. When the season was over, I flew home to California and underwent surgery to fix my shoulder. When I returned to school, I began the recruiting and rehab process. It was a long, painful journey getting my shoulder back into playing shape, but something happened during this time that would define my *Purpose* in a way I never could have imagined.

I received interest from Harvard, Yale, and Brown and went on recruiting trips to see each school. I really buckled down in the classroom and received decent grades during my time at prep school. It was much-needed scholastic discipline, and I learned that there are things in life more important than hitting people on the football field. Unfortunately, it was too little too late. The combination of my high school GPA, my SAT scores, and my prep school scholastic efforts fell just under the bar for an Ivy League education. Amherst and Wesleyan offered me an opportunity to receive an incredible Ivy League caliber education, just on a smaller football stage. Since I had my eyes on playing in the NFL, my dreams overtook my reasoning process, and I accepted a partial scholarship to a state university in California. It gave me a chance to play football on the grand stage and prove myself alongside the best football players in the nation.

One day after therapy, I met an interesting character on the table next to me in the training room. He had blond hair and blue eyes looking the part of a California surfer dude, so I struck up a conversation with him. It only took seconds to realize my first impression was way off when he responded to my greeting with a firm German accent. I stuck with my original profile and asked him if he surfed. Surprisingly, he said yes. He explained that his mom lived in Germany and his dad lived in Bali, Indonesia. I was immediately drawn to his story.

I asked him, "You mean Bali, Bali? Like, the best-surfing-spots-in-the-world Bali?"

He said, "Yeah, my dad owns a village there. I'm Jasper, the friendly ghost." Convinced that he misunderstood me or maybe his English was off, I attempted to clarify again by asking, "You mean a villa, right? He owns a villa."

He said, "Well, kind of. It's more like a little village. There are five small bungalows on the property he owns, and it's at the edge of cliff that looks over the ocean."

Baffled, I jokingly said, "Bro, you're my new best friend. My name is Damien. When we graduate, can I please do a surf trip and stay with you?"

Little did I know this was the beginning of a relationship that would extend far beyond the confines of the training room. I experienced many significant relationships during the short time I was at prep school. There was something significant about living and learning together at such an influential time in our adolescent lives. It added a dimension of camaraderie to high school that you just don't get when you leave campus and go home to Mom and Dad. The prep school experience broadened my horizons and added an element of discipline to my young life that was critical for my future success. There was a component of my personality driven by EGO though, and it clouded my decision-making process. Not only did I pass on an opportunity to earn a private school education at a pristine school, I also chose to leave prep school early.

Graduating with my friends was not a priority to me as I already had a high school diploma. Against the advice of my football coach and advisers, I elected to spend five months in California, beefing up for the upcoming season of Division 1A football. As I look back, I truly regret this decision because I didn't finish what I started. I didn't realize that there was more to the experience for people who had invested in me. I robbed them of seeing me finish, and it's something I have to live with forever. No take-backs. No do-overs.

The irony in it all is that I missed the fun part of my senior experience at prep school—that time when kids get to be kids, knowing that they have their whole life ahead of them. I missed the time when teachers ease up a bit and the teenage experience dares to unfold its ridiculous happenings. And I missed it all because I thought I knew what was best. I wanted to be comfortable and move forward with what I thought I knew. Oh, what I thought I knew.

Dreams

W hen I showed up to training camp, I was ready to go. My shoulder was all patched up, and I was beyond excited to earn a spot on the team. Division 1A football was the real deal. Everyone on the team was athletically gifted in some way. Though our team wasn't nationally ranked at the time, we had a preseason schedule that was packed with some of the top teams in the country. This meant we had an immediate opportunity for national exposure and no time to waste. At the conclusion of rookie camp, I had proven that I deserved to be there. I was excited to see where I fell into place once the veteran players showed up for full training camp. During rookie sessions, there were plenty of chances to get reps and learn the system. When the other guys showed up, the game started moving faster, and the veteran players got most of the reps with the rookies being left to catch up or get left out.

The pace was grueling. Our day started at 6:00 AM, and we were on the field practicing by 7:00 AM. We then lifted weights, watched film, and had a mandatory team meal before we got about an hour to rest. Then it was back to the field for another practice, followed by another film session. After a second team meal, we had a few hours of downtime before another film session and one final practice, followed by our last team meal. We had to sign in and out of all our meals and some of the guys were on a strict calorie count. We usually finished our days around 8:00 PM and got up the next morning to repeat the process. This went on for a month straight with no days off. Living my *Dreams* had become a pretty regimented ordeal.

Since I didn't have a full scholarship, I had a lot to prove and very little time to do it. Realistically, if I didn't do something special in camp the team was not obligated to keep me. As a partial scholarship athlete, I was subject to roster cuts each week. There was an extremely talented athlete trying to make the team that pulled his hamstring the first week during conditioning. He was black and blue from his butt to his knee, but he pushed hard to work through it. By the end of the week, his locker was empty. I'd never seen anything so cutthroat. I was simply a number, and I'd either rise to the occasion or I'd be another common student walking around campus.

The intensity of football at this level left no room for bullshit. If you were late, you got punished and did extra conditioning after practice. The same applied if you forgot your playbook, got caught sleeping in film, or skipped reps in the weight room. The coaches would run your tail off until you got the hint. If you did something devastatingly stupid like fail a drug test or get caught partying during camp, they simply dismissed you from the team and dropped your scholarship. Most of the players didn't have the money to continue, so it was the end of the road for both their football career and their college experience.

I was so stoked on being there that I would never challenge such a great opportunity with utter foolishness. I did come up with a pretty fancy idea though. Since I was a partial scholarship freshman, I rarely saw the field even during practice. It wasn't necessarily because I was a bad athlete; it was simply a numbers game. There were six linebackers in front of me. Most of them were upperclassmen, and the freshmen were full scholarship athletes in the same position I was. This meant if there were any reps left after the starters got in, the freshman on a full ride got the call before I did. They rarely saw the field either, but their future was secure because they signed four-year scholarship contracts.

Since I was getting so few reps, I was afraid that I wouldn't be ready if I did get my number called. I needed to find a way to maintain a competitive edge. I decided that I could do so by staying in superior condition, and that wasn't happening with my butt on the bench. After practice, I decided to do extra conditioning with all the guys that got in trouble. Day after day, I did this until one afternoon a coach noticed I was running with delinquents all the time. He said, "Minna, what the hell is your problem? How come you can't pull your shit together? You're in the dog pound every day! I thought you Catholic school boys were smarter than that."

I didn't say a word, and I just kept running. A few days later, I got called into the head coach's office for a one-on-one meeting with the head honcho. An assistant coach did some research and found out I had never been in trouble. Not once. He went to the head coach and told him what I was up to. The head coach explained that as the seventh string linebacker, it didn't look like there was room for me on the defensive side of the ball. He asked me if I would be interested in moving to offense to play running back. He mentioned that we only had a few fullbacks and I'd have a much-better opportunity to make the team this way.

I left his office glowing. I didn't care what position I played, I just wanted to make the team and help them win in any way I could. My strategy to stay in great shape showed the coaches how serious I was about being there. It caught their attention and let them know I meant business. I learned the entire playbook in four days, just in time for our final scrimmage. When my number was called, I was ready. I squeaked by the final cuts and was officially part of the team.

I was happy about this, but I had another goal in mind. Eighty-five players made the team, but only fifty-two got to travel. In order to travel with the team, I needed to earn a starting spot on special teams to be added to the official roster. I had two weeks to prove myself before the actual season started.

I showed up early, stayed after practice to ask questions, and continued to run with the dog pound. When it was all said and done, my *Greatness* formula paid off again. I was one of only three freshmen to make the traveling squad, and the only one that was on partial scholarship. By the time game one rolled around, I had earned a spot on the kickoff and kickoff return teams.

The sense of euphoria that crept down my spine as we took the field for our first game was electric. I had done it, somehow I made it. I might have taken a dirt road instead of the highway, but I still figured out a way to get it done. When the whistle blew, my nerves calmed, and it was back to playing the game I loved so dearly.

You'd think I would have been grateful for what I had in the moment, but one of the oddest occurrences rattled my bones. I looked across the field and saw one of my high school teammates playing for the other team. He was on a full scholarship and started on special teams. He also got an opportunity to play offense and defense. I don't want to take anything away from his efforts or abilities; he is a great guy and an exceptional athlete. It just got me thinking.

He was a senior when I went to prep school, and his team completed an undefeated championship season. He did things the right way. He stayed out of trouble and worked harder than everyone else, on and off the field. I wasn't a bad kid in high school, I just wanted it all. I played by my own rules, and the books fell pretty low on my priority list. My *Dad* warned me about this, encouraging me to take school seriously, but partying and girls were much more important. Having fun kickin' ass was a far better time than tests or homework.

I felt like a fool. I was supposed to be living the *Dream*. Instead, I couldn't stop thinking about all the self-imposed speed bumps I kept putting in front of me. I was happy for my high school teammate, but the entire flight home I thought about where I would be if I had just done things right the first time. When I returned to school the next week, my rose-colored glasses were a different shade. I had a renewed sense of focus, and though I was happy about making the team, I knew I was capable of much more. School became a priority to me as I realized that an education was the most important part of being in college. When it came to football, I approached my *Dream* of being *Great* with a sense of fury beyond any effort I had previously put forth.

As the weeks went by, I continued to climb the depth chart at running back and had earned a starting role on almost every special team. Playing in front of fifty-thousand-plus people each week was everything I *Dreamed* it would be. I honored each moment with grace and enthusiasm. I gave everything I had every single minute I was on the field. Once I made it to third string running back, it meant I took almost every repetition on the scout team. The first and second-string running back practiced with the starters, which meant I was next in line.

The scout team consisted of the best remaining athletes that were not starters. Our job was to run the opposing team's plays against our starting defense to prepare them for the upcoming game. One week during drills, our senior all-American safety came off the edge on a blitz. At the last moment, he slowed down to avoid a major collision. I hit him so hard the back of his neck hit the ground before the rest of his body. The entire team erupted in laughter as one of their best players just got clowned by some punk freshman. It was as if he got caught with his pants down in the middle of the final dance at the prom. He was furious.

After practice, he approached me in the locker room and asked what the hell did I think I was doing? He said, "Look, superhero, it's practice. There's no need to go full speed. You're going to get someone hurt, and then what will we do come game time?"

I looked him right in the eyes and said, "First of all, I didn't come here to sit on the sideline to watch you play. If that was my intention, I would just buy a ticket, it's much easier that way. And secondly, I go full speed to give you the best look possible so you're ready on game day."

He followed by saying, "Okay, rookie, it's on! You just put a target on your back for the rest of the season."

I said, "Good, bring it."

He tapped me on the shoulder, gave me a half-cocked grin, and walked away. As I sat in front of my locker, part of me felt quite accomplished. The other half of me was wondering what the hell I had just done. Every day after that moment was like stepping onto a battlefield. Play after play, everyone on defense took pride in the opportunity to line up across from me. I got everything they had on every play.

This resulted in me losing far more battles than I won. It also meant I spent a lot of time picking myself up off the ground. My efforts did something awesome though. The other guys on the scout team started to rally around me, and the team's collective effort got a little nastier. As time went on, the intensity stayed the same, but some of the guys on defense started to help me up after hitting me so hard I saw stars. I began to gain the respect of the veteran players, and it was an incredible feeling. Not everyone was a fan though.

One day our six-foot, seven-inch three-hundred-pound defensive end took a cheap shot at me after the whistle. Once I was on the ground, he put his knee in my stomach and used my face as support to help himself up. Nobody saw, but it pissed me off so much that I got up and fired the ball at the back of his head as he was walking back to the huddle. He turned around with a look of fiery vengeance in his eyes and took pursuit at my life like a runaway freight train. One second before a devastating head-on collision I thought to myself, "That was a horrendous decision, and now I'm going to die." Right before he removed my head from my body, all five of the scout team linemen came to my rescue. A full-scale brawl broke out between the offense and defense. Some might view this as savage debauchery, but this is not unusual; it's just football. The feud was broken up, and practice went on like nothing happened. If you think about it, we were a bunch of grown men in the best shape of our lives, with plastic strapped to our bodies running into each other at full speed. A little scrap is bound to happen every once in a while.

After practice, the Sasquatch that tried to behead me passed by while I was taking off my cleats. With an ear-to-ear grin, he chuckled and said, "You're one crazy white-boy rookie. You're all right with me."

Despite all the awards, trophies, and accolades I'd received in my football career, what always meant most to me was the respect of my teammates, *Family*, and *Friends*. It was a big deal in my eyes, and it's something I will forever hold close to my heart. It turns out that not only did the team respect my efforts, but the coaches also saw something special about my character.

The following week we had a home game, and the town was painted red as our arch rivals flew in for battle. We kept the ball on the ground in an attempt to control the game clock. It was a tight one, and both the first- and second-string running backs were rotated in and out. Late in the fourth quarter, the ball was pitched to our second-string back as he dashed toward our sideline, attempting to turn the corner. As he planted his upfield leg, he took a nasty hit right around the waistline. His cleats stayed firmly stuck in the ground, and his body buckled over itself. I'd never heard a grown man scream like that.

The stadium was so silent you could hear a pin drop. When the ambulance carted him off the field, it was like our entire team had been punched in the stomach. What we had just witnessed was every football player's worst nightmare. Each time we stepped onto the field and strapped on our helmets, we knew the risk we were taking. When we saw one of our own go down, the terrifying possibility became a gruesome reality. We lost that game, and I have no recollection of what the score was. I just remember the sound of him screaming in agony.

On Monday, the bad news got worse. He sustained a dislocated hip, ending his season and career. It was extremely polarizing for me because I had just lost a teammate and friend, but this meant there was now an opening at the running back position. Though I was next on the depth chart, I was informed an open competition would be held for the second-string running back duties. I found this to be a bit odd because I was next in line for a shot to show my stuff. Nonetheless, I saw the challenge as an opportunity to clear all doubt in everyone's mind that it was my spot.

I put forth a solid week of practice and outperformed all other backs during an intersquad scrimmage held days before our Saturday game. The night of the scrimmage, the team was informed that our starting running back had a death in the family and he would most likely miss the next two games. It seemed as though a black cloud was hovering over our season at the worst possible time.

For all intents and purposes, I thought I would be a shoe-in starter for the week's upcoming road game. The evening, before we boarded the plane, I was called into the coaching office to meet with my position coach. I was asked to close the door behind me and to have a seat at his desk. He said, "There's no easy way to tell you this, but we are going to start the guy below you on the depth chart. He's a junior with game experience and has been on full scholarship for three years now. The university has invested in him, and his number

20

has been called this week to start at running back. You will travel as the second-string guy, so be ready for when your number is called. I know this might seem unfair, but that's football for ya."

It was around thirty degrees come game time, but it seemed much colder to me. I felt robbed of something I worked hard to earn, and it hurt. I resumed my role on special teams but never saw the field on offense. We lost the game, and the starting running back had eighteen carries for thirty-three yards, missed multiple blocks, and also dropped a couple of passes. I was speechless. I just didn't understand how politics could stand in the way of hard work. It was an extremely tough pill to swallow because I cared so deeply. But like the coach said, that's just football. It was what it was.

The next week when practice resumed, my name was at the top of the depth chart. I was told that I would work with the starting offense all week and that I was the number-one guy going into Saturday's game. After practice, I raced home to call my *Family* to share the news. My *Dad* was elated. Though the game was an away game, it was just up the freeway from where I grew up. Pops called up the box office and bought a ridiculous number of tickets. I think he was more excited than I was. Everyone we knew was invited to come watch my first game as a starting running back for a Division 1A football program.

Thursday night during our last practice of the week, we were running a full contact drill against the scout team. The quarterback called a run play to the left side, and I was getting the ball. The ball was snapped, and I got the handoff going full speed to the left when I saw the linebacker fill the spot I was supposed to run to. A huge hole opened on the right, and I saw nothing but open field on the backside of the play, so I planted my left leg to cut back. I was going so fast that my knee couldn't support my weight, and I heard a loud pop when I went to change directions. I fell to the ground, and three guys jumped on top of me. From the bottom of the pile, I heard a scream that sounded similar to the one on the game field a few weeks before. When everyone got off the pile, I realized the scream that I heard was my own. The trainers were called onto the field, and the drill was moved up ten yards, and practice continued.

The lead trainer gave me a series of tests, but after one such movement, he looked into my eyes, and I could see his heart drop. My heart immediately followed. I asked if it was bad, and he mentioned there was no way of knowing until we had an MRI to confirm the damage. A few of the assistant trainers helped me onto a golf cart, and they took me to the training room. They gave me a brace and said there's a chance that it was just a bad sprain. They told me not to worry too much and that I might be back in a few weeks. I knew by the look in the lead trainer's eyes that he had treated an injury of this magnitude before. I tried to remain positive, but I knew. I went home on crutches, and the first thing I did was pick up the phone to call my *Dad*. We cried together like orphans in the rain.

The next week, the MRI confirmed my worst fear. I had torn my anterior cruciate ligament, and it would require full-blown reconstructive surgery. The team doctor cut right to the chase. He said, "I can fix your knee, but if it was an A+ before, you can only expect an A– from here on out. Your knee will never be the same."

I was devastated. Instead of taking a plane to a crowded football stadium full of fans, I drove home with my *Mom* and *Dad* to have my second reconstructive surgery in two years. When I returned to the team in spring, I was unable to practice as I had months of recovery ahead of me. I was shuffled to the side with a group of guys that were also recovering from injuries. All the hard work I had put forth meant nothing now as I was a total question mark for the future. During my season review meeting with the head coach, he told me the team had planned on offering me a full scholarship, but now the risk was too great.

I went home over the summer to continue rehab and passed on voluntary team workouts. This just dug an even deeper hole for my planned ascension back to the top. At the end of summer, when I returned to camp, the team had recruited a handful of new running backs. In all honesty, the doctor's diagnosis was pretty spot on. My knee was never the same. I didn't have the speed or size of the new guys, and my knee wasn't even fully recovered. The coaches realized this and asked me to take a year off to rehabilitate my knee. This meant a year on the practice squad with no scholarship and an uphill climb after that.

This forced me to face a few harsh realities. Football at this level was a brutal, cutthroat, violent game. I was undersized, and I just had my second reconstructive surgery in two years. What if I got hurt again? The odds were not in my favor, and I needed my body to last the rest of my life. These guys were so big and so fast, it was hard to fathom that I passed on a private school education to expose myself to such torture. I did some *Soul-searching* and made a very difficult decision. I called my *Dad* and told him I was done.

He said, "Damien, are you sure?"

I said, "Yeah, *Dad*, it's over."

Hustlin'

I was lying in bed when the rumble of the U-Haul came to a screeching halt outside my window. Shortly thereafter, I heard a knock at the door. I knew it was my *Dad*, but I let my roommate answer the door. A large part of me didn't want to let go of what I put so much force into creating. Despite the disappointment, I never doubted my decision. I knew in my heart I was making the right choice for my future. Together, my *Dad* and I loaded up everything I had and began the long journey home.

It was a five-hour car ride, but we didn't talk too much. There were no perfect words; I had to completely start over. My *Dad* was a master at tiptoeing around life's peak experiences. He was just the right amount of sunshine in the middle of a downpour. I was so bummed that I had to go home to junior college—the same junior college that I had avoided like the plague. Pops encouraged me to look at this next opportunity as a stepping stone in the great adventure of life. He said, "In life, everybody gets knocked down. A man shows his true character by the way he chooses to get back up. So get up, dust yourself off, and get back to work."

The advice needed to be put in motion rather quickly as I had to make a decision on what to do with my football career. Part of me wasn't even sure I wanted to play anymore. The silly game had brought me as much turmoil as it had glory. I definitely did not want to sit out a season. I was sure I would lose my focus and passion to play. So I took a few days to think things over and then met with the coaching staff at the junior college. They were happy to have me, and I was in pads, practicing the following week.

It was so different than what I grown accustomed to. The effort, the pace, the intensity, all of it seemed to lack a sense of urgency. The entire team felt like they had their own agenda, even the coaching staff. The school had just brought in a new head coach and his staff mixed in with a few older coaches that had been there for years. There was no status quo or tradition. The entire program was in the process of rebuilding, everything needed to be started from scratch. It almost seemed fitting that I landed there because everyone had something to prove.

The veteran coaches remembered me from high school, and they had interest in me playing linebacker. The new head coach was an offensive guy who needed help at running back. Since I played both ways in high school, I thought I'd give it a shot. I had no idea how much of a physical demand I was putting on my body. Both positions were high-impact roles, and the collisions of the college game were much more severe than the high school level. There was also more actual football to be played at the college level than in high school games. College quarters are fifteen minutes long while high school quarters are only twelve minutes. Coming off a serious knee injury, I had bitten off more than I could chew. I was a step slower, and I wasn't in the same shape as when I showed up to camp the year before. I spent far more time doing rehab and not enough time on the field doing football-related activities.

The coaches had a two-year plan to get me back to the Division 1A level, but I had other ideas. I was still interested in playing football, but I was more concerned with getting into a good school close to home. I only wanted to spend one year playing junior college ball. I was looking to take my show on the road as soon as possible. The coaches and I never saw eye to eye with this strategy, which created a service mentality to my efforts. Since it turned out we were both using each other, it solidified our separate agendas. Wins were tough to come by, and with only about one hundred people in the stands each week, game day had a much different face. My effort, on the other hand, did not. I gave everything I had each and every time I stepped onto the field.

Even though junior college football was different in many ways, there were special moments during the season that restored my faith in the game. With very little at stake on the final scores and overall record, the players and coaches continued to show up. Week after week, everyone gave their best effort because they loved being there. Sure, a few players would move on to big programs to continue their careers, but it was the love of the game that brought us all together.

When you're a kid in front of the television and you see the guys playing ball on Sundays, the seed of mysticism becomes planted in your *Soul*. You see gladiators battling it out on the gridiron, and young minds become entrenched in possibility. The first time you strap pads to your little body, the fantasy of reenacting your Sunday hero's movements begin. "I wanna be just like them when I grow up."

Somewhere during the heavy conditioning, broken bones, and three-a-day workouts, the fun gets lost. Games are meant to be fun, but the nature of football pushes extremes in a way that emphasizes exploitation. Every time the game levels up, for example from high school to college, there is more at stake. The added pressure stimulates the competitive aspects of the game but also adds the cutthroat nature of Wall Street. It's kill or be killed—no prisoners, no survivors. It's Rome that caters to PETA. Junior college football was different. The carnage was still there, but it was more like backyard ball with a bunch of buddies. The intensity resided and fun was reintroduced to the game.

With less focus on football, it left time for me to put more emphasis on my studies. I had a top-rated private school in mind, and if I was serious about attending, I really needed to pull it together in the classroom. It was no longer about just passing. I needed exceptional marks to show this school that I was worthy of a top-notch education.

When I visited my college counselor, I was given an articulation agreement that the junior college had with all the private schools. It was simple math. If I passed X number of classes, I would be an eligible candidate to apply for all the private schools in the nation. It was no horsing around though. Nobody was going to hold my hand and if I really wanted it I needed to prove it.

The football season gave me faith in the game again, but the increased effort in the classroom helped me find *Faith* in myself. When it came to the field I always found a way to get things done. In the classroom, I often doubted myself. My hyperactive nature translated well to the field in sports, but not so much in the classroom. Sitting still and focusing on things that didn't interest me was always a struggle. I was also scarred by the private Catholic school approach toward education. Coloring outside the lines was frowned upon in the private school agenda, and I wasn't the best at following directions. Educators were either patient with my learning process, or they thought I was a demon brought to this earth to make their life difficult.

My first year in college, I took a sociology class that broke the education system down into several parts. At the end of the summation, it covered about 85 percent of the general learning styles. If you fell into this continuum of understanding, the education system worked well for you. If not, there were extended variations that were not covered in the general curriculum. Since there was limited time and funding dedicated toward these *Different* understandings, it was left to the student to reach out for further help. This never made sense to me. If a kid had trouble learning, why was it their responsibility to figure out a way to fit the square peg through the round hole? The system was flawed, but it made the struggling student feel like it was their fault. This damaged my psyche, and I didn't figure it out until I was in college. My frustration with being labeled *"Different"* lead me to believe I was doing something wrong or that I was a bad kid. Failure to diagnose this wrinkle not only put me at a disadvantage learning, it submerged bad habits into my processing system that I had to learn to unravel.

If I wanted to achieve at a level beyond my understanding, I needed to find a way to overcome these obstacles. The articulation agreement helped me do this because it was a black-and-white game plan that helped me develop a strategy. It would be tough, but how was it any different than the framework of accomplishing something on the football field? Physical adversity is something I became very good at overcoming. Now it was time for me to do it from the mental perspective.

Since I was at a disadvantage, it meant I needed to study harder, stay after class to ask questions, and smash the project and essay portion of each class. Test taking wasn't exactly my strong point. When I could control the time and effort that went into outside work, I could exploit the opportunity. In addition to these strategies, I also had a few compensation skills that carried over into my higher learning approach.

I was always a bit of a social butterfly. If I could find a way to tone it down a bit, a balanced interpersonal approach could actually benefit my efforts. There was psychology that went into my slippery slope approach toward excelling in the classroom. The educators at a junior college were very similar to the coaches. In my view, there were three types of higher learning professionals:

LECTURERS. These were your egomaniacs who used their authority to jam information down the throats of students for future regurgitation. They were usually categorical extremists that saw education as a point value matrix. The more answers properly barfed up, the smarter the student was. They were easy to hustle as the game was pretty straightforward. They didn't really care much as each student was simply a number that needed to be guided through the system. Generally lacking personality and often military-style academics, they were pretty easy to manipulate. Just give them what they wanted or needed, and flying under the radar was a piece of cake. I generally tried to avoid these types if I could because wiggle room was limited, but at least I knew what to expect.

INSTRUCTORS. These were your overly emotional, underpaid academic enthusiasts. *Instructors* were so deeply entrenched in their own world of personal interest that it drove them toward education. Some of them cared passionately about what they were teaching. This was the Achilles' heel toward passing the class or hustling the system to get a grade. If they did care, it was usually a quirky, interesting character that responded well to personal interest in the material. Since most students didn't care about their junior college classes or education facilitator, a personal attachment to the material and *Instructor* could often benefit the final outcome.

The other side of this coin was the difficult hermit that had lost their interpersonal communication skills long ago. So often victimized by students' "grandma death" and "dog ate my homework" stories, they had become hardened by the profession. For these lost souls, the feeling of saving a misguided youth can remind them of why they got involved in education in the first place. Either way, *Instructors* were a unique bunch that required a fine sensitivity when analyzing their teaching style. Settling for the wrong one could mean trouble if I needed to catch a break at the end of the semester.

TEACHERS. *Teachers* are my personal favorite. These are the individuals who truly teach knowledge to the world. Beyond all reason, these people cared specifically and entirely about students that were interested in *Learning*. They would adjust their approach as needed for those seeking a deeper understanding of the material. They composed their knowledge as though it was a finely tuned symphony. They knew how to break it down into building blocks palatable for any type of student. They could appropriately speed up or slow down their approach so that an entire lecture hall of students could absorb the material at their own individual rates. If a student had questions and showed genuine interest, *Teachers* would go to the ends of the earth to aid in the *Learning Process*.

I was a slow reader and sometimes had difficulty processing large chunks of information. Details give me a better understanding of how the small parts fit into the greater whole. Sometimes there was so much material covered in a short period of time that *Instructors* didn't slow down to answer questions. *Lecturers* didn't really care if you were listening to them or not. *Teachers* helped make learning possible for everyone.

School is like a knowledge gas station. Your mind consumes gas so you can travel to greater places with the knowledge you buy. One of the most interesting components about college is you don't have to be there. You're paying for the opportunity to educate yourself. Some of the material was really interesting, and for the first time in my life,

I developed a deep thirst for knowledge. *Teachers* shined light on the potential for broadening a deeper understanding.

I would often lead with the troubled-athlete, bad-kid approach. This is what people saw when they looked at me, so that's where I would start. With the *Lecturer*, it didn't matter. They didn't care. If they did, it was of no consequence because they were lost in the structured clutter of the system. As I mentioned before, it was a straight hustle. I was familiar with this angle, so I understood it keenly.

I had fun with the *Instructors*. It was like a well-written drama or a partnered golf match. I would let them take the lead so I could figure out what par for the course was. Then I would follow the flow and see where it took me. My final play would depend upon the personality of the relationship we created. With the *Instructor*, it came down to the material covered and the final outcome of our interpersonal communication. If there was something to learn, I held it close and took it with me. If the happenings became sour, it was all about finding a way to salvage the best potential grade.

Teachers motivated students and fueled the fire of *True Learning*. They kept knowledge within reach and constantly stimulated the consumer to come back for more. Learning became a grand undertaking with the final destination unveiling untapped potential in each student. It left each wisdom-seeker with a redeemable gem for the future. *True Learning* enriched the value of knowledge by creating a personal experience that encouraged each student to dig deeper into themselves.

One of my *Teachers* explained that education should be seen as a knowledge exchange. He said semester after semester it was the questions challenging the material that made teaching enjoyable. A sharp mind is a potent weapon that can create significant change for the future. Great minds need to be challenged by other wisdom-seekers. It sharpens the sword of creative ideas.

My *Dad* was right. The junior college experience was an important stepping stone in my great adventure. Football had become the vehicle I used to unfold *Dreams* I didn't even know I had. In two semesters, I earned a 3.5 and 3.7 GPA—all As and Bs. I also did well enough during the season to capture the interest of the coach at the private school I was targeting.

For the final touch, I created a convincing entrance application essay and was accepted by the school I had worked so hard to impress. The time I spent praying ended up paying off too since the football program found a way to cover almost the entire tuition. The school didn't offer scholarships, but somehow they found a way to float the bill. I didn't ask questions. I packed up my stuff and headed south for the next leg of my journey.

Transition

Football was back in front of me, and I understood exactly what I needed to do. I was in good shape, and my injuries no longer affected my ability to perform at a high level. Even though I came in with the eligibility level of a junior, I was still required to participate in rookie camp because I was new to the team. Turning heads wasn't hard because of my successful experience in multiple training camps. It took a week to fine-tune my skills, and by the time the veterans showed up, I was ready to rock.

The competition level was a mix of all the schools I had previously played for. The skilled positions were stacked with above-average talent, and the linemen were a bit smaller. The game was slower than Division 1A football, but that was to be expected due to the smaller size of the school and funding behind the program. The level of competition changed nothing for me. As far as I was concerned, my job was to smash the dude in front of me and find a way to win no matter where I was on the field.

The head coach decided to play me at linebacker, the position I excelled at in high school. Playing two positions most of my career offered a competitive advantage because I understood both sides of the ball. I enjoyed playing running back, the potential of being the glory boy and scoring touchdowns was always fun. But there was something about being the show stopper at linebacker that really tickled my fancy. Completely shutting down another team's game plan by the use of brute force was pretty cool.

At the end of the day, I just loved being out there playing the game. Junior college taught me that it was about more than just tackles, touchdowns, wins, and losses. I enjoyed coming together with a group of guys and setting our sights on a common goal. Each day, we would bust our tails to work out the kinks in our game and come together as a team. I loved the struggle, the smell of the grass, the awkward headaches we got after the first week in a helmet. I enjoyed getting my ankles taped and accessorizing the uniform with wristbands and gloves. One of my all-time favorites was the sound of cleats on the pavement as we would walk down to the field on game day.

When I left Division 1A ball, I pretty much let go of my dream to play in the NFL. At some point, I needed to say enough was enough, and I swore that my body would be the breaking point. After multiple surgeries, I needed to be realistic with how far I was going to push myself playing this silly sport. I made a promise to myself that when my body told me to stop, I would listen. Until then, I vowed to enjoy every single moment.

The week before school started, the final depth charts were posted, and the team was eager to play ball. After a successful training camp, I had earned a spot as one of the first-string linebackers. I knew the defense well and couldn't wait to line up against our first opponent. The first game of the season always coincided with the first week of school. The buzz of everyone showing up on campus was accompanied by the excitement of another game one with a new team. Everything felt so positive and full of potential. Football was fun, school was challenging, and every time I walked out of a classroom, I was treated to panoramic views of the Pacific Ocean. Life was good.

When I packed my stuff and drove to training camp, I did so without much of a plan regarding living arrangements. I had just over two weeks to make friends, scout the terrain, and find a place to call home. Luckily, I had a few luxury items to barter my roommate leverage with. My *Dad* had just settled a case and bought the *Family* a new couch and big-screen TV. This meant the old gear needed to find a new home, and what better place than a college apartment an hour up the road from *Mom* and *Dad's*? It was just my luck that two juniors on the football team were in the market for a roommate, a couch, and a television. Both guys were cartoon personalities equipped with appropriate alias nicknames. Bano and Lamb are the two dudes responsible for showing me the ropes of the private school social scene.

To this day, Bano and Lamb both swear the only reason they considered me for a roommate was because of the couch and television. College is known to be a place where lifelong friendships are forged. Up to this point, I made some decent buddies, but I was never in one place long enough to let my relationships grow roots. The two characters I was paired up with were rascally socialites accustomed to a routine of respectful chaos. They were just the right amount of spice for me. They walked the line by celebrating good times with the right amount of academic discipline sprinkled in. I didn't see the potential when I first moved in, but the relationship I developed with these two chance bozos turned into a *Friendship* that would extend far beyond the structured learning environment.

When I met with my guidance counselor for the first time, he offered me a roadmap to guide my scholastic efforts. When we were locking in my first few classes, I was given a blueprint detailing which courses I needed to graduate. It was very similar to the articulation agreement I used during junior college that landed me this amazing opportunity. This roadmap was gifted to me with a piece of advice that would govern every scholastic maneuver I would make for the rest of my college experience. My counselor said, "A lot of time, money, and effort will go into the next few years of you being here. If I were you, I would take full advantage of the people and resources within these walls. Get to know as many people as you can and be genuine with your efforts."

Learning is a delicate process for all parties participating in the knowledge exchange. Every interaction has a subjective and an objective point of view. The understanding of each piece of advice depends very specifically upon the manner in which it is received. I was damaged by the education system, so my understanding of it was skewed to reflect my odd experiences. I found ways to get by, but my emotional scars became deviations, making simple advice hard to understand. My college counselor had over one hundred students that he would advise to help them maximize their college experiences. By the numbers, that meant he was very effective for 85 percent of them. I was part of the 15 percent that understood his advice a bit differently.

My college experience to this point was focused on accomplishing general requirements. My counselor mentioned that I needed to start thinking about what I wanted to major in. I had no idea where I wanted to focus my studies. School to me was very similar to football. Show up. Get work done. Find a way to win. Don't ask questions; do your job. Now I got to choose what I wanted to study? I was so flabbergasted by this overwhelming opportunity to guide my own life that the decision seemed futile. It made sense that college was a place where people could take their educations where they wanted to, but why did I have to take all these classes I had no interest in?

I had already stumbled through more than half of the prerequisite classes that were on my graduation blueprint; 140-plus credits were needed to graduate, and I transferred in 72. I came to find out that even though the school viewed these as acceptable transfer credits, they did not consider them fit for their private-school curriculum. Some of the classes were the exact same; they even used the same books, but it didn't matter. Only twenty-nine credits transferred toward my degree at this private school. Even though I had been passing college level courses for two years, in the eyes of the administration, I was a second-semester freshman. As if reading and processing information much slower than the average student wasn't enough, now I had to retake entry level courses with incoming freshmen.

This didn't sit well with my already damaged view of how my learning style fit into a misguided system. Private colleges used these classes to not only broaden the spectrum of general knowledge but also to weed out slackers that were not serious about their education. This meant more busy work, lame extended projects, and detail-oriented homework material. I petitioned the classes pleading to the deans that I not only proved that I deserved to be there but I already passed the courses. My request was scoffed at, and I was sent back to the drawing board with all the drunk teenage frat boys and sorority girls.

I was pissed. There was a loophole in the system, but it meant I would have to go to the special studies department and take a bunch of tests that made me feel like damaged goods. I made it all the way to a private university flying under the radar, and I'd be damned if they were going to put asterisks by my name come diploma time. Besides, the real world doesn't give you extra time to finish quarterly reports or let you opt out of training seminars. I was against the wall again, and I had to find a way to get it done.

When it came to choosing a major, I found myself a bit lost. I thought, *What am I majorly good at?* Communication always came pretty easy to me, so I wondered if they had a major that dealt with that. I went back to my counselor, who happened to work in the communications department, and asked him how to major in communications. He said I needed to decide on a media or speech emphasis and choose a minor. It seemed reasonable that I would communicate in a business environment moving forward, so I chose business with a marketing emphasis as my minor. The difference between a media or speech emphasis was only a few classes. Since most of my life I had been told that I talked too much, the decision seemed inevitable. I chose to fine-tune my squawking skills, and speech communication felt like the perfect place to do it.

For the first time in my life, I was excited to go to school. I was deeply interested in the subject matter, and as it turns out, the major I chose was predominantly female. There was a 70:30 ratio between females and males. I guess the macho thing to do was major in business or economics. That was fine by me. I thought to myself, *I'll learn about great thinkers and speakers, persuasion, and propaganda. And I will do it at a school by the beach, surrounded by women.* Not a bad deal. Let's just say I had a bit of extra motivation to get to my 7:00 AM classes.

As the first semester came to a close, I found myself getting into the swing of things at this new school. I really enjoyed the *Learning Process* in the classroom, and I enjoyed myself just as much when I wasn't at school. I lived right across the street from campus, which made everything almost too easy. I could roll out of bed and be at class before my coffee buzz even had time to kick in. I'd skateboard all over campus and, when school was out, cruise down to the locker room for practice. If the surf was firing, it was a fifteen-minute drive to the beach, and after all the football games, our pad was the party place to be. In most circumstances, this amount of extracurricular freedom would derail even the most focused college student, but I had developed such an appreciation for the struggle that I just enjoyed the ride. It was everything I could have ever wanted out of a college experience.

As classes came to an end, so did the football season. We won more games than we lost but not enough to claim a title. I had some decent games and a couple pretty good ones, but none that had the NFL beating down my front door. I finished second on the team in tackles, but my body took a licking in the process. I was about twenty pounds undersized for the position I was playing, but I made up for it with spit and vinegar. There were times when other teams would make fun of me during games because a guy my size seemed out of position. Then I'd smack 'em in the mouth a few times, and it all made sense when I would shut down my entire side of the field. It took its toll on my body though.

In the last few games, I started to experience some problems with my knee and shoulders. Every once in a while, I would hit someone and get what the football world calls a stinger. This meant that after a collision my entire arm would go numb, and I'd have to leave the game for a few plays. This was a fairly common occurrence for most football players. It felt like your arm fell asleep, and once it woke up, it burned like a son of a bitch but then returned to normal. That was when it was considered okay to return to the game.

In hindsight, it didn't make much medical sense, but I'm not sure football in general does. It's a battle game where each player is expected to act as a warrior, and warriors fight till the death for their team. I played through sprained ankles, broken bones, concussions, lacerations, dislocations, and so much more. If you can you name it, I probably played through it. It's just part of what you do as a player;

it's the nature of the sport. Everyone knows the possibilities, and there is a 100 percent injury rate in this game. Injuries are just going to happen. It's a question of how you will react when it does. Most of the time, after I was injured, I needed to be physically dragged off the field or carted off on a stretcher. Those were the only two ways I was going to leave. There was one occurrence when I sustained a concussion, and the trainer hid my helmet in the equipment box. I couldn't even remember my name, but I convinced one of the guys on the sideline to let me borrow his helmet and ran back onto the field.

Toward the end of the season, X-rays were taken on my neck to try to determine the source of the stinger problem. I was told I had spinal stenosis, which meant that a portion of my spinal canal was narrowed and was pinching nerves. The doctor said there was a chance it was genetic, and I might have had it my entire career. He mentioned the wrong type of blow to my head could result in some very serious consequences. There were two games left in the season, so I decided to wear some extra padding and sort it out when the season was over. Because I could have had this injury for years, I didn't see it as an immediate threat.

When the season ended, I also had an MRI on my knee, which acted up a few times during the year. It seemed like nothing major, but I thought it was a good idea due to the severity of the previous injury. The MRI discovered a small tear in my meniscus and some built-up scar tissue that the doctor said required a mild cleanup surgery. It was only a two-week recovery, and I was able to walk on it days after my third football-related operation.

Football was the purest logic system I had ever participated in. It moved fast and had a clear sense of direction. It was black and white between the lines, and if you worked harder than the next guy, there was always a way to win. You didn't have to be the biggest or fastest if you played the smartest. Knowing the rules and angles made preparation a key component to strategic advantage. At the end of the day, it was the only thing I was ever great at. It was the only place I found a platform to give everything I had. I was confused by slow-moving things that I didn't understand. The real world offered angles that seemed unfair, and the playing field was never equal for all parties involved. Strategic advantage was often manipulated outside the confines of the rules. The systematic process of life was very much like a battlefield, but things were not black and white like they were in the game of football.

After the surgery, I had some *Soul-searching* to do. I only had one year of eligibility left to play ball, but my body was telling me to hang up the cleats. Adhering to the promise I made to quit when my body told me to isn't something I was ready to do. Football had become a part of who I was, and letting go was much more difficult than I had anticipated. The team was poised to return almost all the starters on defense and we looked strong heading into the next season. The linebacker below me on the depth chart was a talented underclassman that was bigger than me and, in my assessment, a better fit at the position. Our offense graduated most of our starters, and we looked young and inexperienced at some of the key positions. This got me thinking, a tendency that sometimes got me into some pretty precarious situations.

I had an idea that I thought created a loophole in the promise I made to myself about walking away when my body told me to. I saw championship potential in this team if we just shook a few things up. As a leader, I saw an opportunity to be a veteran presence on an offense that obviously needed help. I played running back at the college level before, and I was willing to do whatever was needed to help the team win. I thought what better way to ride off into the sunset than to cap off a blessed football carrier with one more championship ring.

Just before spring practices started, each player had a one-on-one meeting with the head coach to discuss the previous season and plans for the upcoming one. I took this opportunity to talk to the coach about my bright idea. I brought my high school championship ring with me and explained to him that I would do anything to get another one. I had practiced my speech over and over in my head and couldn't wait to see the look on his face when I suggested this act of valor. I was sure he would see the merit in my sacrifice and would truly understand how special of a leader I was.

When I finished unfolding my plan to him, he leaned back in his chair and gave me a cold dark stare never once breaking eye contact. He was unimpressed by my independent thinking and noticeably offended by the presence of my high school championship ring on his desk. He said if I did this, I would be jeopardizing my starting position on the team and my traveling status. I was so convinced that I could prove myself to him that I ensured him if he just gave me a shot that I wouldn't let him down. The meeting ended with the coach saying, "Fine, do whatever you want. Don't say I didn't warn you."

The knowledge exchange is a delicate process, but it can also kick you in the teeth if you're not paying close enough attention. I was on the wrong end of this one, and I let the idea of being passionate stand in the way of my better judgment. I was confident in my skills, but again, my unique way of doing things had caught up with me. Sometimes well-intentioned objective thinking is outweighed by the subjective reality of another perspective. At the end of the day, his job was to coach, and mine was to play. Once the rules of the game get altered, anything goes. I'd love to complain and point fingers in this situation, but the reality was I made the bed. Now I had to sleep in it.

Flawed

I spent the spring semester grinding the studies hard in the classroom. The graduation roadmap I was given didn't specify an order in which I needed to take my classes, so I chose to first take courses related to my major. I was so intrigued by enjoying *Learning* that I was eager to dive into the thought-provoking classes. Historically, I wasn't exactly the most dedicated scholar, so I threw the concept of letter grades out the window. I was more interested in the subject matter than I was about competing for a grade. This didn't mean I wasn't trying hard; it was actually the exact opposite. When I stressed myself to push for points and percentages, my focus wasn't in the right place. When I was able to relax and absorb the information, I was able to infuse it into my everyday life and actually *Learn*.

I liked the idea that I didn't have to go to school if I didn't want to. It was a very different approach than the high school concept where a student is required to be there. I was in college at this point because I chose to be. Most of the *Teachers* in the communication department were brilliant and earned the right to be at a prestigious university. They wanted to *Teach* as much as I wanted to *Learn*. This was a huge advantage for me because half the students were there on Daddy's dime and were expected to do well. The pressure created by this expectation played a strange psychological role in their learning experience. They expressed their freedom in strange ways that usually included drugs and alcohol outside of school. I'm not saying I didn't enjoy the occasional tasty beverage; I just didn't feel the need to push the limits of being away from home to such an extreme level. I was more interested in making my *Family* proud that their firstborn son was going to graduate from a prestigious college.

As far as football went, I was on a naive road to self-destruction. It only took a few weeks to recover from surgery, so I was back on the field by the time spring practices started. The knee felt good, and I was playing running back as I requested in my meeting with the head coach. The coaches on the offensive side of the ball were actually pleased that I was there to fix their problem with lack of depth at the position. They saw potential in me being there and knew I could get the job done if given the opportunity. The problem with this particular coaching staff was simple. It wasn't a democracy; it was a dictatorship. The position coaches were extremely helpful in teaching me the offense and getting me up to speed. Unfortunately, they were not in charge of making the depth charts, and I had made Hitler very unhappy. The signs were everywhere. I just chose not to see them.

When summer came around, I extended the lease on the apartment and took a few classes. This enabled me to stick around the school gym and enjoy the beach life of Southern California. I worked hard in the weight room, gave school my undivided attention, and went to the beach as much as I could. I had a deep connection with the ocean. Most of my life had been spent in cleats, so finding the time and balance to appreciate the surf was awesome. There was something unique about the tides that calmed my *Soul*. I was a hyper kid who was always involved in highly structured activities. The ocean was a free-flowing experience that I always felt brought me closer to *God*.

I had a certain respect for the ocean that was much bigger than anything I understood. It was the only place I could go where I would find peace in stripping myself of all earthly belongings while *Surrendering* to something out of my control. It was a way to put everything on pause for a few hours to clear my head. I was never any good at surfing, most of the time when the waves were big I would just bodyboard. It didn't matter to me what I was riding as long as there was a wave under me. The extremist in me liked the thrill of finding the biggest wave I could paddle into and just let go. Letting go was something I struggled with in my life, and sometimes it got the best of me. The ocean demanded it. If I let the outside world get into my head for even a second when I was on a wave, I found myself at the bottom of the ocean.

When summer was over and training camp started, I found myself at the bottom of something else, the depth chart. Two incoming freshmen, a sophomore, and a junior were all in front of me while I held down the fort as the senior fifth-string running back. I spent three weeks of camp riding the bench, only getting reps when the others were injured or needed water. I developed so much rage that I turned each opportunity I got into highlight reel. If I was blocking, someone ended up on their back. If I got the ball, the defender got run over, or I'd break a long touchdown run. I did most of this with the third-string offense against the starting defense I used to play for. None of it mattered. Each day the coach found something wrong with what I was doing and had me run with all the guys who had discipline problems.

I was devastated. The game that had been so good to me had become tainted in a way that changed things forever. The hardest part about it was that it was partly my fault. If I would have kept my mouth shut and just played the game that I worked so hard to be good at, things would have been so much different. Instead, I was the product of a political power struggle, and I had become an example of exactly what not to do.

When game one rolled around and all the students flooded the campus, I found myself in a position that I had never been in before. I was a common face among a crowd of students that were simply there to go to school. I had been a starter on every team I ever played for since I was in the seventh grade. Usually, week one of school was filled with excitement and anticipation. It was traditionally time to go to war after countless hours of preparation that soaked up most of the summer. This time, I knew there was no chance I would even step foot on the field. I got taped, stretched, warmed up, and watched two freshman running backs put forth rookie performances from the sideline. We squeaked out a lackluster win lead by a solid defensive effort. The offense never got going but pulled together enough points for the W. Despite the team's win, the personal loss I experienced that night will stick with me forever.

After riding the bench for the second straight week, I put my tail between my legs and met with the head coach again. I pleaded with him to put me at any position he desired and he promptly put me back on defense. At this point though, it was too little too late. The defense was playing well, and my assumption about the linebacker who was behind me on the depth chart the year before was correct. He was a star player. I was positioned at the bottom of the depth chart again and was expected to work my way up. I had lost my passion to be great, and at this point, I was just going through the motions. The coach, on the other hand, wasn't done asserting his authority quite yet. He decided to continue to punish me by making me run with the delinquents. I was walking a fine line, making sure I did everything I was asked to avoid this. When I ended up on his shit list again, I was shocked. When he told me to line up for extra conditioning after practice, I ensured him that I had done nothing to deserve this. He said, "Get your ass on that line, and do what your told, or turn in your pads after practice."

I turned around and walked off the football field for the last time. I couldn't believe it had come to this. I loved football, but this wasn't the game I had grown up playing. I was out of my element when I offered myself to a political system that had so much disorder in its regime. Had I analyzed the playing field with sharper senses and taken a centered approach, I would have gained insight to where I stood, and my rank would never be in question. My passion to push beyond what I could reach turned an honest effort into a desperate plea. When the rules of engagement are altered in any game where politics are involved, a cloudy mess of a storm can extinguish even the brightest flame.

Living with two football players didn't make my decision any easier. There were times when I regretted leaving the game because I felt like I didn't finish what I started. But it just wasn't fun anymore, and when the NFL was out of the picture, fun was all I had left to hold on to. When Bano and Lamb came home from practice or a game, the empty feeling I experienced took me to a *Dark Place*. I put so much time and effort into the game that I felt robbed of closure. It just became something I learned to live with. There are no guarantees in life, and when something is over, it's just over. The irony in it all was that my master plan went against a promise I made to myself about throwing in the towel when my body told me to. Maybe this was a *Sign*. Maybe I created this pain as some type of reminder.

I navigated my life in the direction of a higher education for a reason. The next challenge on the horizon was to push myself in an area where I traditionally struggled. I knew that educating myself for the future was a top priority, but balance was crucial moving forward if I wanted to succeed with my studies. I needed to find a place to channel my energy where I could get a good return on my efforts. Since school remained a challenge for me, I needed something positive beyond the classroom to balance everything out.

There were a few guys on the team that had a more laidback approach toward football. They saw it for what it was and found balance with life outside the game. Over the summer, I developed a *Friendship* with these dudes, and we spent a good deal of time surfing and partying together. They were creative people who enjoyed music, art, surfing, and skateboarding. I was always intrigued by this lifestyle but never really slowed down enough to consider it. Rondingo, Scrappy, and Combs were three new cartoon personalities that brought an artistic and refreshing perspective to my life after football.

Dingo and Scrappy created a television show where they were getting elective credit for the media portion of their communication degree. It was a garage-based local show about the college beach culture. They used their unique personalities to interview people and create buzz-worthy sketch comedy. I saw brilliance in their efforts and wanted to help in any way that I could. Every idea was a good idea as long as we had fun shooting it. The world of film production was an exciting new experience that offered a seemingly limitless platform for creative expression. It was exactly what I needed at just the right time.

In a world of synchronicity, a few more chance encounters presented themselves disguised as dumb luck. My college counselor was the director of the television network at the university and was looking for ideas to expand the program. I was able to see where my skill set fit into the TV show that my buddies came up with. The creative aspect to their efforts lacked structure and direction. Their idea was solid but needed a bit of strategic thinking to turn a great concept into a polished product. I approached my counselor with the idea of giving us a fully credited opportunity to pull together a legit production staff. The distinction was different than an elective course because it was now a class that fulfilled requirements toward our communication major. He let us draw up applications for the show and hand them out to anyone interested. The school-syndicated cable network only had a few programs consisting of news and freelance projects. There was an entire class filled with eager students looking to get involved in television production, and we got to choose who we wanted to work with us. Once we submitted a list of our desired candidates, my counselor made the TV show a fully accredited class, applicable to our major.

I started to notice that everything around me was strangely falling into place. Being caught up in a world that facilitated expectation and illusion made some of these *Signs* hard to interpret. The flow of things often presented many options to choose from, and making the right choices was sometimes difficult. I always assumed that my future would play out the way I saw it in my head, but for some reason, *Life* had a way of taking its own course.

Subtle cues were always present guiding my decisions, but I previously just dismissed them as fleeting thoughts. I never doubted that destiny had a plan for me. I just had no idea what the plan was anymore. I always had a firm grasp on what I wanted, and I was good at finding a way to get it. As much as I wanted to believe that the flow of life would just bring me to where I was supposed to go, I wasn't about to throw caution to the wind. I set goals, and I accomplished them. I was good at creating, and I enjoyed being an overachiever.

The TV show was a hit, and it offered opportunities beyond my wildest dreams. We got to meet movie stars, popular musicians, television personalities, local business owners, and urban legends that had been part of the beach culture for decades. We even got to meet the university president. She agreed to let us bring cameras in her house to shoot a segment similar to MTV cribs but, instead, a campus version highlighting a day in the life of the president.

All the *Friends* I made that were my age began to graduate and transition into adult life. Some got entry-level corporate jobs, and others went off to grad school. Bano and Lamb completed their degrees and moved on to the next stage of their lives. When they left, it ended a certain phase of my college experience that facilitated brotherly comfort that I'd grown used too. I needed to find new roommates, and *Chance*, once again, brought me to my next learning opportunity.

I grew up in a house full of boys where jock straps and rough housing dominated our daily activities. Even though *Dad* brought home the bacon, *Mom* ruled the roost and fulfilled the warden role. She did so with an element of *Grace* that taught my *Brothers* and me the incredible complexity that an amazing woman can bring to a household. If we scraped our knee or fell off our bikes, *Mom* was always there to make it better. If we failed a test or got in a fight at school, *Mom* played the mediator as to whether or not *Dad* needed to get involved. In one way or another, *Mom* was always there to make sure that we developed into respectable young men. In turn, we learned the importance of having a good *Mother*. *Respect* was a lesson that radiated through every action that took place in our home. My *Dad* dedicated his *Life* to my *Mom* and showed us how to *Respect* the presence of quality feminine energy.

My goal in *Life* is to duplicate the *Unconditional Love* that I experienced growing up. The reason I was in college was to put myself in the best position to be able to do just that. Girls always played a pretty vital role in my existence. At this point, I realized that I didn't want to marry some silly girl; I was interested in finding a woman to make my *Dreams* come true. There was one small problem the way I saw it; I was ill equipped. I had only lived with sweaty, stinky boys my whole life, and I didn't know the first thing about what it was like to coexist living with women.

I enjoyed females in a much deeper way than most of the guys my age. I had a *Respect* for their internal beauty because they brought something to life that made it special and fun. Growing up in a home that taught me to *Respect* feminine energy helped me understand what a healthy relationship between members of the opposite sex can bring. I learned to listen and be *Compassionate* toward the differences I didn't understand. I realized that being genuine with my thoughts and emotions was the doorway to a woman's heart. Once you walked through that doorway, it was important to tread lightly. I learned that every girl who was willing to let me into her heart was a *Friend* that could offer insight to the magical world of females. Getting a girl to take off her clothes would only bare her skin. I was much more interested in getting them to bare their *Souls* so I could figure out who they were and what made them tick. Creating genuine *Friendships* with women opened up a world of possibility that hardly any sex-crazed, testosterone-driven college student understood. I took this experiment to the next level when I invited two girls to share the master bedroom that had just been vacated by one of my smelly boy counterparts.

My favorite place to meet girls in college was at the campus general store and the dining hall. Anytime I'd meet someone at a bar or party, they were all dressed up in fancy clothes with their faces painted, usually half-drunk with a bunch of their friends. The group mentality brought out a superficial nature that drove a false sense of expectation into most girls' efforts. Singles in packs often turned into a ridiculous competition. In this light, society's standards really screwed up people's ability to share their true colors. The funny part is that everyone was under the impression that a little alcohol did just the opposite. I saw through this game and was more interested in catching girls off guard.

One day, I was sitting in the dining hall with a buddy when his chemistry lab partner plopped herself in the seat next to me. She had on a pair of rubber gloves, a surgical mask around her neck, and a funny blue operating hat still fashioned atop of her long blond hair. She then proceeded to attack her lunch with surgical precision. She rifled off exploits of the previous weekend in an attempt to recall a night that she had mostly forgotten due to chemicals and alcohol. I was so wildly entertained by this specimen of human being that I stopped what I was doing and listened to every word of her crazy rambling. When she dove back into her vegetarian assembled cafeteria meal, I took the opportunity to ask her name. She swallowed her broccoli, tossed aside her fork, and extended her rubber-glove-covered hand and said, "I'm Dr. Livingston. It's a pleasure to meet you."

Before the meal came to an end, I made sure to arrange another meeting with this Dr. Livingston person. She was an attractive girl with long blond hair and light blue eyes, but living in a Southern California beach community there were many girls that fit this physical profile. There was something special about her, and I needed to know more. She insisted that she wasn't in college to score the cliché boyfriend to run off and marry in order to live happily ever after. Once I convinced her that I wasn't about to get bamboozled by some spoiled little Goldilocks looking to resolve a daddy complex, she agreed to have lunch with me. I came to learn that this girl was an extremely motivated young woman that learned some tough lessons at *Life's* school of hard knocks. She busted ass to earn her ticket and planned to be a brain surgeon that drove a Hummer. Every man that had ever been in her life always needed or wanted something from her. I wanted to be the first man she ever met to accept her as is with no questions asked. The road chewed her up and spit her out, but she just kept fighting. This was someone who I wanted to know forever, and I knew that honoring the person she was would be my ticket to doing so.

Dr. Livingston and I became close *Friends*, and when the year ended, she moved out of the dorms and spent the summer at home in Lake Tahoe. About two weeks before the summer came to a close, I was scrambling to find new tenants to occupy my empty rooms. I got a call from Dr. Livingston, asking if I knew anyone looking for a roommate. She was short on money, so she proposed sharing the master bedroom with her best friend from childhood. Her friend wanted to go to junior college by the beach, and rent wouldn't be an issue if the two of them split the bills. I had never lived with girls before, and I thought it would be a good experience having a few around to initiate me into the world of living with women. I stacked the deck by renting the other room to a guy on the football team to add a dimension of familiarity and comfort.

Two weeks later, the tidal wave of new roommates hit my little beach apartment oasis with full force. Dr. Livingston's friend was a tall good-looking brunette that was ready to set the beach scene on fire. She had dark-brown eyes with the mystic gaze of an alley cat. She was sweet yet stealthy and had a gypsy-like draw to her. These girls were not rookies when it came to glamming men with their girly curves and pretty faces. They were both hustlers far beyond the skills of preppy college kids, and together, they acted as a cyclone devouring any weak game that amateur boys threw their way. Sometimes our other roommate would bring football players around, and they would get shot down in flames when trying to court either of the two alley cats. I was in a whole new world, watching these girls prey on their victims from inside the lion's den. Both of these sweet little kitties had sharp claws that you didn't want to mess with. They were so good at running their game that most of the guys they hypnotized wouldn't know what was going on until it was too late. The insight I got into the world of women was invaluable. I got a behind-the-curtain look at how girls used their seductive tactics to work the dating and intimacy scene.

Outside my new life of hair dryers and curling irons, I had one final year of school to complete. The previous year when football ended, I came up with a pretty fancy strategy to offset the shackles that confined me within the structured learning system. I devised a plan to level the playing field with my unique style of learning. When I walked away from the gridiron, I did so with an emotional burden that weighed heavy on my heart. I never stopped to realize that the football program had a good deal of influence on the amount of financial aid I received. When I turned in my pads, I also forfeited the opportunity to benefit from the luxury of being a privileged athlete. This meant I had to take out monster loans that would take years to pay off just to finish what I started in the classroom. Scorned and overly emotional, I leaned on the crutch of a "destroy and conquer" mentality.

Instead of registering the right way like a normal college zombie, I developed a system to "crash" classes to complete my entire academic curriculum. I formulated my strategy in junior college when most of the important classes were full. It was a hassle to register for a semester worth of courses just to show up and find out there wasn't a seat for me. Second- and third-option classes filled up so fast that if I wasn't preregistered, there was no chance of getting in. By the end of the second week, the only choices left were the crap nobody wanted to take. The old-school method suggests that I struggle through a course for elective credit that I cared nothing about. I didn't want to do that because I wanted to use my elective opportunities to expand my knowledge in a subject matter that interested me.

Being at a private university was different in my mind. I knew which requirements I needed to fulfill in order to graduate, and I was going thousands of dollars in debt for this degree. It was **my** education, and I was already displeased with the idea that I had to waste time and money retaking classes I passed at previous schools. When it came to courses related to my major, I found the *Teacher* I wanted to *Learn* from showed up at the class and never left.

The system worked like this; if a student wasn't preregistered in a class, an add/drop paper needed to be signed by the professor for the student to become permanently added to the official class roster. If the class had room, there was no drama. I would get the signature and bring the paper to the registrar's office, and I was in. If the class was full, I had a bag of tricks to get the professor to sign my paper that never failed me.

Of all the courses I took in college, there was never the same number of students on day one as there were during the final exam. College was a dramatic place and the mentors passing on knowledge had heard every story in the book. I flipped the script and turned this soap opera into an opportunity for success. When the professor said the roster was full, I went into my bag of tricks and told them I would continue coming to class, buy the books, and be an active participant in lectures. I was always told I was free to give it a shot, but there was no guarantee I would be added. In exchange for taking the risk, I asked them to promise I would be the first one added when someone fell off.

There was a method to my madness. I separated myself from the other students by adding a face to my name. By putting myself on the hot seat, I could prove my worth to the professor. This not only got me a signature for my add slip, it also showed the professor I wanted to be there and established a personal relationship that I could cultivate throughout the semester. I was really interested in the potential knowledge these seasoned professionals had in store for me. The way I saw it, there were only a handful of highly prestigious schools in the nation. Being educated at a school of this caliber meant I had the opportunity to learn from some of the greatest minds of our time.

When it came to "must take" perquisite courses, there were always multiple options at different times on different days. The *Lecturers* and *Instructors* were like wind blowing the sails of medieval cargo ships through crowded merchant corrals. They came and went as they were usually part-time contractors that worked multiple jobs. There were a few gems scattered among the lot, but they needed to be ferreted out with a sharp eye and a bit of moxie.

Once I landed a few *Teachers* bettering the world with their brilliance in major related classes, I spiced up the game with a bit Russian roulette. I'd randomly choose a mixed bag of courses with the potential of fulfilling prerequisite requirements. I would attend the first lecture of as many classes as I could in search of a handful of desired inception points. If I had to pay for monotonous regurgitation of meaningless facts for a second time in my college career, I was going to make it worth my effort.

The first two things I would study were the course syllabus and the overall approach of the lecture style. When I could run a straight hustle and make off like a bandit, it was money in the bank. Two major scenarios existed, and I had a different story for both. The first scenario was easy—if the professor didn't care, neither did I. The second variable I searched for was the *Instructor* who was a diamond in the rough. A few special *Souls* filled their positions out of sheer love for the art. I appreciated these people and their zest to fight the good fight. When they showed genuine *Compassion* toward each student's future, I in turn gave them my full *Respect* and put forth an honest effort regardless of the material. It was the least I could do to honor their effort and dedication. If neither of these scenarios existed, I settled for the class with the cutest girls or the most favorable time that fit my desired schedule.

Companionship was another deep-seated goal in my quest to attain future happiness. I desperately wanted to find someone that could be the milk for my cookies. I took a stab at young love that crashed and burned pretty hard at the tail end of my teens. My heart was broken into a thousand pieces. Unconditional love is a rare find, especially when two teenagers are blossoming into young adults. It left me pretty guarded when it came to matters of the heart. I was cut so deeply that I swore I would not enter any type of committed relationship until I was absolutely certain I found "the one." Until then, I vowed to have as much fun as possible. I also promised myself that I would do so in an honest, respectful manner, paying close attention to the frailty of others' feelings. Being an emotional guy had its advantages, but it came complete with a black hole of self-destruction. Heartbreak was something I never wanted to deal with ever again.

The college party scene began to lose its sparkle for me. I had been at the heart of many successful non-sober get-togethers, and the bar scene was never really my thing. Themed gatherings like pajama parties and Valentine's Day red-and-white soirées always brought prospective suitors directly to my front door. Having two smokin' hot roommates and a TV show that broadcast in every college dorm room also worked in my favor. I enjoyed the company of women and had developed a pretty healthy collection of phone numbers. My secret was being *Respectful* and mysterious, which added an element of fun to the chase. If I ever brought around anyone that was slightly unworthy, they were torn to shreds by the two alley cats. The game was fun, and I played by the rules. But for some odd reason, I always found a way to make things complicated.

On a random afternoon in the dining hall, one of the party-hoppin' cafeteria girls caught my attention. A buddy I was eating with told me that she was the roommate of his longtime girlfriend. He knew my personality and immediately said, "She's not for you, dude. She's different." At this point in my life, those were the exact words to get me to do just the opposite. I loved a challenge, and I got a kick out of the chase. Besides, I liked *Different*. I was unamused by the typical run-of-the-mill college girl.

A few weeks later, I shared a long stare with this lady from across the room at a crowded party. Before I could wade through the inebriated mass of dancing partygoers, she slipped out the backdoor. I recognized one of her friends and told her that I needed to meet the girl she came with. About ten minutes later, they returned, and there we were standing in front each other. After she laughed at one of my lame jokes I said, she couldn't leave until she promised to go out with me sometime. I made a favorable-enough impression to get her number, and that evening the great chase began.

I was seeing a number of girls at the time. I wasn't sexually burning through them like a box of matches, I was actively interviewing a number of ladies I might be interested in settling down with. I was turned off by girls that used the commanding presence of sexuality to entice guys with potential erotic encounters. I enjoyed the celebrity status of being a star athlete for many years, so I was immune to plastic smiles and false confidence. I wanted elegance and grace. Style with class and just enough sassiness to keep life interesting. The women I chose to spend my personal time with had been carefully chosen and needed to stimulate my intellect before they got a chance to stimulate anything else. I wasn't looking for a wife quite yet, but I was looking for someone that embodied the qualities to one day fill the position.

This new girl was like a beautiful butterfly floating around an elegant garden of exotic flowers. She had a rare combination of mystery and grace that snared my attention. It wasn't long before I completely lost interest in the entire garden altogether. I had always been the type of person to stop and smell the roses, but the Butterfly hypnotized me in such an enchanting way that I no longer cared about any of the flowers at all. I shifted my focus from the ground of growing things to the sky filled with flying things. With my head in the clouds, I traded in my work gloves for a net attached to a long stick. Off I was to chase the Butterfly.

Life started moving extremely fast at this point. I was producing a TV show that required full-time-job type of hours. It went from having fun and filming nonsense to managing an entire production crew pumping out weekly episodes. I also miscalculated my course load and had to take six classes in my final semester. If I wanted to graduate on time, I had to find a way to balance all this while wrapping up my final major-related courses. I had thirty-page thesis papers to write, group projects that required forty-five-minute lecture presentations, short-film teach-tape assignments, midterms, and finals. On top of it all, I continued to chase the love and affection of the elusive Butterfly.

Every once in a while, Dr. Livingston and I would catch a sunset or get ice cream to cut away from the drama. She, too, had a mountain of weight on her shoulders. Balancing a premed courseload and a long-distance relationship dangled love just beyond her fingertips. We found ways to laugh at each other's ridiculousness that kept us both strangely grounded. The fact that we were both crazy and stubborn worked for our *Friendship* but not always so good for our dispositions. If we would have listened to half of each other's heartfelt advice, our lives could have run so much smoother. It was nice having a *Friend* to lean on in a pinch, but looking back, I wish I had the emotional intelligence to really understand what she was saying.

If Dr. Livingston and I didn't have each other during these challenging times, we might have both lost it. Finding balance in our tangled maze of emotions wasn't easy, especially while trying to entertain loving another person. I never had a sister, so being able to get a female perspective from a genuinely loving place truly added *Value* to my *Life*. I really liked her boyfriend, and from the moment we met, it was as if we were long-lost brothers. They seemed to be perfectly imperfect for one another. Most importantly though, I had never seen anyone make her so happy. And sad. And angry. And frustrated. We both thought that's what love was all about. You take the good with the bad when you unconditionally love someone.

Sometimes the Butterfly flew to *Dark Places*, and I didn't really know how to deal with it. I was a spaz, but overall, I was a pretty happy person. Whenever I found myself in a *Dark Place*, I would always find my way back to the *Light*. I didn't like being unhappy. It made me feel uncomfortable. I grew up playing the role of Peter Pan, and there was always something fun to do in Never Never Land. You just had to want to see the brighter side of things.

The Butterfly liked to play hide-and-seek in the *Shadows*. It was fun showing her the *Light*. Each time I would pull her back into the sun, she acted like she forgot how good it felt to be happy, and that was quite rewarding for me. But somehow, she always found her way back to the *Shadows*. It was like the chase was never-ending. All I wanted to do was be the boy who rescued her from the *Darkness* so that we could be happy forever in the sunshine. But she seemed to be eternally drawn to being uncomfortable, and I was addicted to the chase.

Scholastically, my fancy strategy for dealing with the education system started to unravel at the seams. Upper division communication professors were sharper than a razor. They caught on to my slippery approach and pinned me in a corner. They understood that letter grades meant little to me, so they found ways to get the most out of my efforts. They made me work for the knowledge much like others earned grades. If I really wanted to learn, I was expected to prove it. I was impressed that they were calling me out on my nonsense and making me earn my higher education. I brought a hard lesson upon myself though, and it exposed my compensation strategy that I had been using to manipulate the system. In turn, I received a fairly significant slap on the wrist for not doing things the right way.

By miscalculating my required units for graduation, I ended up taking logic and accounting in my final semester. I had been dreading these classes since finding out I needed to retake them. They were both repeat courses that I passed at another university. It wasn't that they were hard, just time-consuming and meticulous. I struggled with these disciplines the first go around because of the memorization and categorical structure of the subject matter.

My personality meshed well with interpersonal material. When structure and formality dominated the picture, I felt boxed in. I had no interest in credits and debits. Logic was interesting, but it's a mountain of math governed by words and definitions. They were both mind-numbing to me, and I lost my attention quite easily. Because of this, I had trouble plugging into the material and became aloof to its discipline. These two classes were used early in most college curriculums to make sure students were serious about being educated. The prerequisite staples earned the allegiance of a small percentage of scholars but, for the most part, just weeded out people that shouldn't be studying at a university.

The trouble with Russian roulette is that sometimes you have to deal with the bullet. There just weren't enough hours in the day to excel at all the work I had in front of me. I was committed to an entire production staff that counted on me to deliver solid content each week for the TV show. I also had six courses I needed to pass in order to participate in the graduation ceremony, and my head was in the clouds, trying to make a relationship work. I was out of cheap tricks, and there was no room left to run a hustle. Reality set in, and it was time to pay the piper. I had been operating way out of my league for some time, and coming back down to earth wasn't a pleasant descent. A rare few have what it takes to gracefully breeze through their tumultuous twenties. I was not one of these people. Something had to give in this situation. Being stubborn and overly emotional definitely did not work in my favor.

With time running out, I needed to make some razor-sharp decisions if I wanted to deliver on all my priorities. It was crunch time, and every moment of the home stretch needed to be executed perfectly if I wanted to graduate. Unfortunately, my game was flawed, and I pulled up lame right before the finish line. When I needed to be ultra-disciplined, I fell short because I spent so much time doing things my own way. I hadn't yet developed the skill set to multitask at the level I needed to. Instead of buckling down to clean up the mess I made, I leaned on the *Illusion* of comfort that I tried so hard to avoid. I knew there was a correct way to do things; I just chose to see the world the way I wanted to. I had fallen victim to the college theme park that swallowed thousands before me. Pretending I had my adult life all figured out had caught up to me, and the reality of failure was on the horizon.

An incredible act of God somehow poked a ray of hope through the clouds of yet another storm that I created. My effort in the logic and accounting classes was deserving of failing marks. For some reason, my logic *Instructor* took pity on my situation. At some point during the semester, I let her in on the insanity I chose to take on in my final semester. She had an appreciation for the bold move I made by taking on such an incredible workload and was actually a fan of our TV show. I was just short of passing the class, and she gave me the benefit of the doubt. It wasn't glamorous, but in this situation, the D I received meant I earned a degree. Well, sort of.

There was a loophole in the system that let students graduate with their peers even if they had a few more classes to complete. I was aware of this loophole and planned on completing my final two classes in Mexico while participating in the school's study abroad program. It was significantly cheaper to study in Mexico than to take summer school classes at the university. It was a no-brainer to me. It seemed to be an outstanding way to polish off a lengthy college career. Finishing my final two elective classes in the tropical paradise of Mexico seemed like a pretty sweet deal.

I thought I was pretty slick traveling deep down the rabbit hole to pull this final ace out of my sleeve. The plan that seemed too good to be true ended up being just that. In the real world of credits and debits, I had fallen just short. In the eyes of the business world, I put forth a failing effort in my accounting class. Business is cutthroat, and at the end of the day, if the numbers don't add up, harsh reality sets in. My accounting *Lecturer* was also amused with my extreme efforts to finish, but the bottom line was I just didn't make the cut. I failed the class, which meant I had three more courses to complete in order to receive my degree.

If I only needed to finish two classes during summer school, I would have received my diploma on graduation day. I was permitted to walk with my class at the graduation ceremony, but I still needed to retake accounting in the fall. Because of this, the fancy leather sheath with the golden university insignia that I was given when I walked across the stage was empty. My entire *Family* was in the stands, cheering when my name was called. My *Mom*, *Dad*, *Brothers*, and *Grandparents* had all made the trip to see me close out the final chapter of this incredible journey. I was the only one who knew the receptacle was empty. After all the years of hard work and struggle, in the end, I had only hustled myself. The "my way" mentality fooled everyone but me.

Things had become pretty serious with the Butterfly. I was infatuated with what we were working on and began believing she might be the one. Being burned by a long-distance relationship in the past heavily influenced my decision to put our romance on the shelf for the summer. It wasn't the freedom of being single that motivated my decision. I wanted to figure out what my heart desired without the presence of outside influences. Any temptation I might experience was a good indicator as to whether or not I was ready to settle down.

Mexico had many gifts for my thirsty *Soul*. Being in a foreign country offered an opportunity to explore the depths and corners of who I was *Becoming*. The language barrier turned my thoughts inward, and I used the silence to unravel my thoughts. I studied the process of loss and was able to breathe in the true exploration of what it means to *Be*. I was free to experience the longing for something greater with my whole life still in front of me. In many ways, time stood still. I enjoyed the process of learning myself, and before I knew it, three months had passed. I missed the Butterfly and my desire to paint the canvas of my dreams had fallen upon me. I believed I knew what I wanted. When I got home, I planned to go get it.

Upon returning to the States, I expressed my clarity to the Butterfly in the form of an ultimatum. I said if what we shared meant anything, we should commit to each other as though we were *One* or stop wasting time and go our separate ways. Life was too short to screw around, and we should make the most of the time we have on this earth. Thrown off by the sudden fork in the road, she hesitantly agreed, and we moved in together. I had so much confidence in the future that I desired, I figured if I paved the way she would surely follow.

Classes began about a week after we moved into a small apartment two blocks from the beach. I only had one class to finish, but the Butterfly had two full years before she would receive her degree. When I completed accounting, the party was over, and it was time to wrestle the real world. School loans no longer paid the bills, and the time had come to get a job.

My *Friends* informed me that the transition to the daily grind was raw, and being a rookie in life wasn't easy. I heard the words coming out of their mouths, but living this uncomfortable reality was much more of a challenge than I expected. Living at the beach was something worth holding on to, but doing so on an entry-level salary was stressful. There were five colleges in the area, and as it turns out, I wasn't the only graduating scholar to have the bright idea of sticking around the beach once school was over.

I searched for months to try to find a career-worthy job. I went from being intent on finding something that was stimulating and interesting to taking anything that paid the bills. I settled on a sales position at a discount furniture warehouse that was right next to one of the largest television studios in the area. Another grand hustle had entered my mind and also offered a temporary solution to getting the bills paid. The plan was to exercise a persistent yet humbling effort to make money while I schemed a way to get on set at the production studio. My priorities still mirrored my college efforts, and finding balance was again my Achilles' heel.

Things were good with the Butterfly, but never great. The relationship took constant effort, and no matter how hard I tried, there was no permanency that offered stability for either one of us. The commonality we shared with a college lifestyle had changed, and we were now on different pages of two completely different books. The nature of the stress we were experiencing had driven a wedge between us, and we began to grow in different directions. Waking up next to her every morning was still enough to keep me motivated to continue pushing forward though. I let too many things come between me and my goals in the past, and I was intent on making this work.

One day the Butterfly's dad had come in town to visit bearing gifts. He brought a DVD of the movie *The Messenger*. As it sat there on our coffee table, I thought to myself, *Maybe this is another sign.* Maybe this relationship was meant to show me something about myself that I was unable to see on my own. Maybe she wasn't the *One* but instead an important messenger to guide me along in my travels. I wasn't ready to accept this as a possibility, so instead, I chose to ignore the crazy idea that this was another *Sign*.

The effort it took to keep this uphill battle going left little room for much else. I didn't dedicate adequate time to cultivate my relationships with *Friends* and *Family*, which narrowed my opportunities to find balance. I drew strength from these relationships, and their absence put all my eggs in one basket. I was so focused on trying to make things work with the Butterfly that I never made my way over to the production studio. The grand hustle to work my magic never got off the ground. Instead, I took on more work doing deliveries at the warehouse to make a little extra coin.

At some point, the Butterfly and I came to an agreement that this wasn't what either of us wanted for our future. If we were going to work out, we both agreed that something had to give. I took a job at an annuities brokerage back home and planned on moving in with my *Parents* to stockpile money while she finished school. The time away from each other was meant to give us space to focus on our priorities. When she finished school, we would have the resources to reevaluate our options. Since we were only an hour's driving distance from one another, it meant we didn't need to totally break things off. This plan would give us time and space to get our ducks in a row, and we could still maintain some type of relationship. It felt like a huge weight had been lifted off our shoulders, and we were happier than we had been in quite a while. It was summer, and our lease was a week away from being up, so the timing was perfect. I just completed the final phase of the interview process at the annuities brokerage, and I was to begin the training program the weekend after an annual *Family* vacation.

Fear

E very summer, my *Family* packed up our belongings and headed
to the desert for an end-of-summer getaway. We paired up with
Family and *Friends* in a group effort to enjoy some fun at Lake Mead
in Nevada. It was a secluded desert experience where we would rally
together boats and jet skis at our favorite beach. We would pack all
our favorite picnic foods and camp out during the day at our secret
little cove.

Early one afternoon on the second day of the trip, we were
lounging on the sand, enjoying some good music. Half the group
was frolicking around the cove on jet skis, while others were water-
skiing behind a boat. Everyone else was soaking up some sun on the
beach. It seemed like a normal summer day, but little did I know my
life was about to change drastically.

I was on a pontoon boat that was docked on the shore. The
front end was on the sand, and the back half extended out into the
water. I just finished my first margarita of the afternoon when the
blazing desert heat had become too much to bear. I headed to the
back of the boat and prepared myself for a soothing dip in the lake
water to cool off. I steadied my feet on the back edge of the boat, put
my arms out in front of me, and dove into the lake water.

The second I hit the water, I knew something was wrong. Upon
entering the lake, I heard a sound that signified a departure from the
life I had grown to love. My own personal version of the Big Bang
sounded like two bowling balls colliding. The collision thrust me
into a world that would change everything I had ever known. My

body lay lifeless in the water facedown, looking at the bottom of Lake Mead. I was confused because I didn't see anything around me that I could have hit, yet I was floating motionless on the surface of the lake unable to move.

When my *Family* realized I wasn't playing some sick joke, they frantically jumped into the water. When they turned me over, I tried to scream, but a muted moan was all I could belt out. My *Dad* asked me what was wrong, and I told him I couldn't feel my body and I couldn't move anything. As they dragged me up to the sand, I kept repeating, "This isn't mellow. Something is very wrong." They laid my limp body on the shore with my legs dangling in the water. Somebody stabilized my head with sandbags, and the last thing I remember was the feeling of my numb appendages swaying back and forth with the rhythm of the lake and my brother wailing in the background.

When I woke up from a ten-day coma, there were two strange people sitting in front of me. The one flashing light in my eyes appeared to be a doctor, and the other must have been a nurse. I was severely disoriented and had no idea where I was. When the doctor asked me if I knew why I was in the hospital, it took me a second to come up with a possible answer. I ran my tongue across my teeth and realized a few of them were badly broken. I thought to myself, *My teeth are jacked. I must be here to see a dentist.*

The doctor then told me to try to touch my nose. I couldn't! I was unable to move or feel anything below my chin. The doctor then went on to tell me that I had been in a terrible accident. He told me that I dove into a lake and suffered a spinal cord injury rendering me paralyzed from the neck down. I dislocated my fourth and fifth cervical vertebrae, which pinched my spinal cord. This created a spinal lesion that was blocking signals from my brain to the rest of my body. He said, "You're going to be paralyzed from the chin down for the rest of your life."

This story began with an out-of-body experience that changed the way I understand my existence. Everything that happened before this moment seemed like a fairy tale, and when I woke up to a pirate doctor shattering my *Illusion*, only ashes were left from my previous life that had burned to the ground. *What the hell? Who is this guy?* I thought to myself. I immediately flashed back to the surreal experience I had with the *Light*. It seemed to have only been minutes before Dr. Wingnut came in with all his doomsday crap. "Has anyone ever recovered from an injury of this magnitude?" I asked with a scowl on my unparalyzed brow.

"Well, yes," he explained. "But the odds are not in your favor. There's a 10 percent chance you will recover some function. And a 1 to 3 percent chance you'll make a full recovery."

As politely as I could muster, I said, "Please go out in the hallway and explain those odds to my *Family* because they might be interested in your medical percentages, but I am not. You don't know me, and if there's a way, I will find it. You have no business taking *Hope* away from me."

Later they sent in a psychologist to try to talk some sense into me. The doctor feared I was suffering from shock and that my attitude was some sort of coping mechanism. When the therapist was unsuccessful at trying to shrink my *Will*, he reported his findings to my *Dad*. His diagnosis was that I was "too happy" and that I must not understand the gravity of the situation.

When my *Dad* came into the room, he said he tried to tell the psychiatrist that I was crazy, but he just wouldn't listen. Pops was always so good at creating comfort in tight situations. This time was different though. He sat down next to my bed with sense of defeat in his demeanor. His eyes were swollen with tears. I had only seen my *Dad* cry a few times before this, so the moment weighed heavy on my heart.

I thought back to the conversation with the *Abundant Being of Light*. The present moment was my first significant opportunity to begin working on my *Purpose*. My *Dad* dedicated his life to being the best *Father* he knew how to be. Now it was my turn to reflect *Grace* back to him. I told him the counselor had to be a quack because if there was anybody in the room that understood the drastic effects of gravity, it was me. Then I told him, "I have two choices. I can either be angry and sad that I'm paralyzed, or I can just be paralyzed. We can get through this together, *Dad*."

In the midst of one of the more chaotic experiences a *Family* could go through, somehow I got to my *Dad*. I expressed to him from somewhere deep within me that I was going to be okay. The wounds would take some time to heal, but he knew that I would somehow find a way to make the best of the situation. The process of finding *Oneness* began right there in that hospital room.

The situation was definitely not all peaches and cream. Part of me died on the beach when I dove into reality that sunny afternoon. The event changed my life forever, and the road to rebirth was a long, dark road. I was an extremely independent, athletic, outdoorsy, person; and that all changed in the blink of an eye. I had previously taught myself to eliminate the idea of fear and pain. I challenged my limits by playing contact sports, jumping off cliffs, and dropping into waves much larger than my skill level could handle. Fear and the possibility of pain was always a rush before as I lived to push the limits.

This new type of *Fear* sucked, and the *Pain* was so extreme I had no idea how to process it. I was devastated in a way I'm not sure words can adequately explain. In the first month of my injury, I was transferred to three different hospitals in three different states. I spent an entire month in intensive care with fluid in my lungs, two bouts with pneumonia, a staph infection that required quarantine, and a hole in my throat from an emergency tracheotomy. This wonderful contraption required constant suctioning to remove phlegm from my throat due to my inability to swallow. Each time the nurse would perform the procedure, it felt like someone was jamming sandpaper doused in sulfuric acid down my windpipe. Just watching me bear the pain was so intense on my *Family* I eventually asked them to leave the room until it was over.

Another exquisite device I had the pleasure of enjoying was a feeding tube that was stuffed up my nose, down my throat, and into my stomach. The tube was eventually replaced with a different feeding apparatus that was punctured directly into my solar plexus. I had so many botched IVs stabbed into my veins that I elected to surgically implant a PIC line in my shoulder so that a surplus of pharmaceuticals could get directly uploaded into my bloodstream.

I had a catheter jammed in my wiener and needed a suppository accompanied by digital stimulation every time I needed to poop. They figured this out ten days after I had not taken a crap, when my stomach was so distended it was as firm as a watermelon. Then they stuck an NG tube up my nostril and sucked all the contents out of my stomach for three days. It was a sweet party favor for all my *Friends* and *Family* to gaze upon when they came to visit.

I was optimistic about my recovery, but in that moment, I was drastically paralyzed. To say I was scared would be an understatement. In the first month or so, it was a daily chore to find the will to stay alive. Every few hours, doctors or nurses would come in to check my vitals, do blood draws, or stuff me full of medication. This meant sleeping was pretty much out of the question. Even if there were a nice five-hour chunk of time to rest, it's not like I could toss and turn to get comfortable.

I was on so many heavy drugs in the first month that I had horrific hallucinations and thought people were trying to kill me. At one point, my *Dad* had to talk me down from a panic attack because I swore there were drug dealers in the hall blasting reggae music. Trying to grasp ahold of this new reality proved to be extremely challenging. I used to tell everyone that being paralyzed was the easy part; it was all the other drama associated with the condition that made things so difficult.

The only thing that kept me sane was an overwhelming support system that came from every direction imaginable. My *Faith* grew in ways I never even knew was possible. I always had a strong connection to our Creator, but during this time God was shown to me in *True Abundance*. At times, when I doubted my own personal strength, there was always something to remind me of how much of a gift it was to still be alive. As isolating as it was to be locked in my body, I was never alone.

Knowledge of my injury traveled all across the US. I got e-mails, cards, and gifts from dozens of places in California and at least ten other states that I can remember. There was one family that apologized for not being able to send weekly gifts because they had to relocate after hurricane Katrina completely destroyed their home.

The outpour of *Love* and *Affection* that consumed me left no room to wonder if my life was worth living. The generosity behind each person's effort offered daily encouragement to never give up.

Multiple fundraisers were thrown to help with my medical bills, which included a local fire station, the annuities brokerage I was just hired at, and my high school alma mater. During one of the fundraisers, a volunteer was approached by an eight-year-old boy with a bag of change. The youngster insisted that they take his money and said if it wasn't enough for my surgeries that he had more in his mother's car.

My *Family* had a very difficult time dealing with the injury at first. There is no instruction manual detailing how to respond to a catastrophic spinal cord injury. Nobody had backup plans for what to do if Peter Pan lost his ability to fly. Never Never Land was a *Dark Place* and all the Lost Boys were stunned like deer in headlights. Everyone put on their game face, but there was no way of avoiding the heavy weight that accompanied crisis mode. Emotions were at an all-time high, and navigating through the fog came with a considerable amount of collateral damage.

The Butterfly offered her best effort at trying to fly through the storm. When she first got the diagnosis of the severity of my injury, she told me that she wasn't sure if she had it in her to be what I needed. That didn't stop her from giving her best effort. She was by my side in every way she knew how to be. The *Shadows* constantly wore her thin, but she warded them off and took on more weight than I had ever seen her handle. Her efforts complicated *Family* dynamics though. The toxic emotional complexity of the situation created an ambiguity in everyone's ability to do the right thing. In reality, it was a combination of everyone's best efforts that got me through the toughest months of my life.

After a month in intensive care, I was airlifted to a spinal cord specialty center in Colorado. After another month in acute care, I transferred to the extended living wing to complete the final two months of my hospital stay. I spent many long nights crying myself to sleep as the reality of my new life began to sink in. I did my best to feel bad for myself in private because my *Family* was extremely overwhelmed. Losing complete control of everything demanded attention in an area where I had always had trouble. Being able to control the emotional aspect of my situation was the most significant opportunity in front of me.

Even though this was the most difficult challenge I had ever experienced, a gimpy birthday suit did not limit my ability to grow my support system. As chance would have it, I was in a hospital with thirty other spinal cord injury patients that were also adapting to their new way of life. "Why me?" seemed to be a pretty lame question as just another face in the crowd. My first roommate in Colorado was a middle-aged gentleman that was depressed beyond repair. He would wail day and night, "I wanna die! God, please stop punishing me and take my life. I wanna die. I wanna die."

I immediately requested a room change. No offense to the guy that wanted to kick the bucket, I was just on a different trip. Too much drama was coming from every angle, and I just didn't have time for that. I was wheeled into a new room where I had multiple roommates in the first few days. After a week or so, I got set up with a permanent bunkmate that was a full on character.

The first few days I spent with him were outrageous. He was on enough meds to sedate a silverback gorilla, and I think he was a bit concussed from the car accident that broke his back. He would go into detail for hours on end declaring to his friends and *Family* that he was a kung fu "warriya" and a Black Ops "'Soldja" in a heavy Jewish New York accent. Drugs and head injury aside, he was the perfect medicine for me. The "'Soldja" made me laugh so hard it hurt at times.

The nights were much different though. I connected with another *Soul* that understood the *Fears* that go on behind closed doors. Neither one of us could sleep, so we stayed awake, talking each other's ears off. The tracheotomy procedure I had during one of my surgeries left a hole in my throat that made it difficult to speak. He was all the way across the room, and my voice wasn't always strong enough for him to hear me. When my voice was too weak, I used my tongue to make clicking sounds. Since we were both determined to find comfort in the *Dark Hours*, finding new ways to make things work was a task we got better at together.

I started to *Learn* that this injury was an *Opportunity* to find new ways to make my *Life* work. Everyone has problems, but most people avoid dealing with them because they bring to mind a great bit of discomfort. The longer we put them off, the stronger the *Signs* become that we need to *Change*. At some point, we all know we are going to need to deal with our problems. We see and feel the *Signs*; we just find ways to ignore them. Oftentimes the go-to strategy is to numb our senses so that we don't feel bad about ourselves all the time. Then *Life* responds with a dramatic scenario that demands action.

My new *Friend* and I kept each other in check. Even though there was no denying the *Opportunity* in front of us, we still tried to cut corners. We were both pretty good hustlers at denying the *Truth* before our little spinal intervention, so reprogramming our approach was no easy task.

The Soldja was Mr. Independent before his accident. He had a *Family* that smothered him with affection, and it suffocated his will. He was a bird meant to soar at great heights. But just like Icarus, the legend from Greek mythology, he flew too close to the sun, and it melted his wings. His accident thrust him into a perspective that he might not have entertained without some type of call to action.

When he would come off painkillers, his demons overwhelmed his goodwill, and homeboy got a bit nasty. The emotions of dealing with the injury coupled with his deeply rooted denial proved a wicked combination. He would lash out at the people that *Loved* him, and he did so with the ferocity of proper New York slang. From an outsider's perspective, I had an easier time wrapping my head around his situation. One day after a total blowout with his *Family*, I called the nurse in and had her roll my bed next to his. I wanted him to be able to look me in the eyes and clearly understand what I had to say. In short, I told him to pull his shit together or I would find a new room that didn't have someone disrespecting their *Family* in it.

A few days later, he overheard my *Family* speaking about how I wouldn't let them push me into the elevator facing the mirrors. My vice was pride, and I was unwilling to look at myself in this situation.

My *Life* also needed a call to action. Previous hardships had nudged me to be a good person, but I hadn't yet fully embraced the path to *Oneness*.

I also resisted using a power wheelchair that was operated by blowing into a straw. After months in the hospital, I still had no movement below my chin. I was so sure that I would recover that I was unwilling to accept the fact that this technology would bridge a gap until I was more functional. I had the nurse disengage the brakes and manually push me up and down the halls. Including my body weight, the chair weighed over three hundred pounds.

One morning, the nurse on call came in wearing a walking boot due to an accident she had over the weekend. My thoughts were, *The chair glides on the tile floors. It won't be any trouble for her to push me fifty yards down the hall.* The Soldja took one look at my scheming eyes and asked the nurse to step out for a moment.

He said, "Look, man, when you gonna stop actin' like such a bitch? First, I hear you don't think you're pretty enough to look yourself in the mirror. Now you're gonna make this hobbled-ass nurse push you in that tank down the hall. That's bullshit, yo."

His response was brilliant. I laughed so hard I cried. The tears were an important step toward being able to laugh at things I would normally cry about. I cried so many sad tears that I was just over it. I was done feeling devastated. The relationship I created with the Soldja reminded me of how much I loved life and the *Opportunity* to be myself. That was the last day I let someone push the heavy sip-and-puff wheelchair up and down the halls.

I realized that once I could find the *Will* to make it out of bed and past the door frame, everything would work itself out. When I became a master at sippin' and puffin' to make the wheelchair go, it was like being sixteen when *Mom* and *Dad* handed me the keys to their car. I started going from room to room, meeting people. I made all kinds of new friends.

I met a man who fell rock climbing, a drug dealer that got thrown off a five-story building in a gang conflict, and a tattooed heavy metal enthusiast that owned over thirty semiautomatic firearms. I met a super cool OG in a hard-core biker gang, a mother of four from the deep south, a young girl who accidentally got shot by her brother, a guy who broke his back in a water skiing accident, and a lady that got clotheslined by a Mack truck.

In this setting, we were all the same. We were brought together to share an *Opportunity* where the qualifying experience was *True Suffering*. All barriers were broken down, and each person was available at their core essence. It made me realize that in some shape or form, we are all suffering in this life. It definitely wasn't the easiest way to learn this lesson, but my eyes were open to a *Different* world.

My eyes were also opened to what *True Compassion* is. Outside of my personal support system was a group of people that checked into work every day to offer themselves unconditionally. Therapists, nurses, technicians, and a few of the doctors truly saved my life. Sure, I needed surgeries to keep my body working, but this special group of people dedicated themselves to a *Life of Purpose*. When they clocked in every day, their efforts went far beyond the paychecks they earned. They worked grueling hours in extreme conditions with *Hope* that they could make a *Difference* in someone's life that really needed it. These people saved my *Soul*. They taught me how precious life truly is and no matter how hard things may seem, there is always a guiding *Light* in the darkness. I just had to be willing to accept the challenge.

Chess

B eing in the hospital was like being in a bubble. I was a push of
a button away from immediate medical assistance. It gave me a
sense of security knowing that all I had to do was ring and a nurse
would be there to help. I was taught many things about my new body
and life while in the hospital. Since I had no reference for to what to
expect, this freshly obtained knowledge was like the newly disabled's
guide to the galaxy.

The theories that defined living in a wheelchair were tough for
me to swallow. Scare tactics of the worst case scenarios were used to
outline potential dangers associated with the condition. I was shown
how pressure sores could develop, leaving holes the size of baseballs
in my skin. I was exposed to pictures of black urine which developed
from an unattended kidney infection that eventually lead to death.
The damage to my central nervous system was so severe I was no longer able to sweat. This meant if I was in the heat for too long, there
was a possibility that I could have a stroke and die. I was also now
dependent on a caregiver to tend to my every waking need.

When I was finally discharged from the hospital, I had another
milestone to overcome. What it meant to live full-time as a quadriplegic hit me like a ton of bricks. After four months of the best
Western medicine I could find, I was still paralyzed from the neck
down. The doctors didn't have any definitive answers regarding my
long-term prognosis. I had a few promising signs, but that's all they
were. Promising. I was given a handful of devices to make living

without movement possible, but there was a whole new learning curve I needed to adapt to.

For every rain cloud, there is always a silver lining. The hospital tried to say it was great parking and stellar seats at rock concerts, but I knew it was always the people I had around me. From the moment I opened my eyes, I was shown a version of *Unconditional Love* that *Changed* the way I saw the world. When I got off the plane in California, I was met by an entourage that made me feel like a movie star. Seeing how many people had *Compassion* for my situation truly blew my mind.

My *Grandpa* had a one-story home that he said I could live in for as long as I needed to. Contractors donated time and materials to build ramps and an accessible shower for me to use while I recovered. My whole *Family* developed a strong bond with one of the technicians that helped me in Colorado. He knew how tough it was re-acclimating to life outside the hospital, so he flew home with us to help find a permanent caregiver.

Even with an *Abundance of Love* coming from every direction, I struggled with a broken heart. I had no way to prepare for how being home would remind me of all the things I was unable to do. My dreams of achieving success and creating a family of my own seemed impossible. Before my botched diving performance, I had plans for how I would create the things I wanted in my life. But now I was blank. I had *Faith* that God would show me a *Way*, but at times, I had trouble finding faith in myself.

The people supporting me did not share the same wavering faith. When I was in a coma, my *Mom* and youngest *Brother* somehow knew before I woke up that everything would work out. The rest of my support system exercised their deepest understanding of what it meant to have *Hope*. The theme was, "If anyone can do it, he can do it." The fundraisers that went on while I was in the hospital raised a considerable amount of money to cover the costs of rehabilitation. One of my *Dad's* old business partners also offered to cover the cost of my first year of therapy at a clinic of my choice. To sweeten the deal, one of my old high school teammates donated a fully accessible minivan that I could drive my power wheelchair directly into. In my mind, it left me with one significantly purposeful option. Stand up out of the chair and prove to the whole world that anything is possible.

At this time, I couldn't see very far past my nose. All I could really feel was the pain I had on the inside of loss and despair. My *Family* was supportive, but the crystal ball of expectation that previously showed a fairy-tale life was now nothing more than shattered glass. Nobody knew how to move forward, and I was such a mess I had no idea how to lead. Since there was nothing anyone could do to make the elephant in the room go away, it was often easiest for those closest to adopt an "out of sight, out of mind" mentality. This made my understanding of how things work extremely complicated.

In school, I found ways to manipulate the system so that it worked for me. Cutting corners never seemed to hurt anyone in an already flawed system. In the end, I only hurt myself. I was in a tight spot that I couldn't use charm or moxie to wriggle out of. This forced me to look at my *Life* for what it was. The life I was living before was merely an *Illusion*. I chose to believe it because that's what I was comfortable seeing. I handpicked the elements that seemed to satisfy the curriculum for being a good person and bypassed the rest. Instead of focusing on my own flaws, I chose to help others around me that had similar problems. This way, I could make the world a better place without ever looking in the mirror.

Weeks raced by, and the gray fog around me only appeared to thicken. All the statics supported theories of the first two years being the most significant window for neurological healing to take place. My salvation was clinging to hope that the first twenty-four months would offer something miraculous. There was a spinal cord rehabilitation center about an hour and a half from where I lived. It wasn't covered by insurance, but thousands of people donated time and money to make sure I was able to attend.

Every Monday, Wednesday, and Friday, I'd make a three-hour round-trip drive to try to jumpstart my body. I spent another three hours in therapy each day, trying every experimental technique this rogue rehabilitation outfit had to offer. I was tied up, strapped down, and twisted like a pretzel to stimulate my nervous system in any way that seemed like it might work. This establishment worked for me because it was set up like an adapted sports gym. Every client had some type of spinal injury, and people traveled from all over the world to be in an environment that offered *Hope*. The trainers were extremely positive, and even though everyone's body was compromised, each patient was treated with *Dignity* and *Compassion*. They taught us not to fear our bodies but to push their limits.

I created lifelong *Friendships* with a few of the trainers at this facility. Their dedication and drive to be there for people who truly needed them is the kind of effort that makes the world a better place. The one-on-one contact in some of the toughest hours inspired me in ways that I couldn't even comprehend at the time. It wasn't always smooth sailing though.

There was one trainer that stood out among the others, and everyone wanted a piece of his time. He was a cocky alpha male with a pretty impressive swagger. He had a holistic organic approach that really tuned into each client's energy system. He understood that even though the physical body was compromised, elements that lead to overall *Wellness* should also be taken into account. He lived a healthy, active lifestyle that involved balanced nutrition and daily exercise. He was known for being the resident Hippy among his coworkers, and whether others loved or hated him, everyone respected him.

I was always a very particular person. The details that surrounded my discomfort were tough to handle if someone lacked a strong personality to counter my own. Some trainers targeted me as a client that was tough to deal with. The way that I struggled with my injury sometimes made their jobs more difficult than it needed to be. The resident Hippy didn't seem to mind that I was a bit wily. We actually had fun going back and forth as he taught me how to laugh at life's ongoing blunders.

One day, I came to therapy on a good one and was a complete downer. I was rather grumpy, and the Hippy cracked a joke that I took personally, so I threw fire back in his face. He stayed professional, finished our session, and sent me on my way. The next time I came to therapy, he had been taken off my schedule for the rest of the month. I decided to be stubborn and proceeded on like it didn't bother me.

My unwillingness to compromise a jaded perspective continued to make my *Learning Process* difficult. About a month after my flare-up, I caught wind that the Hippy had given his two weeks' notice because he was moving out of the country with his family. The blunt impermanence of the situation knocked some sense into me. That afternoon following therapy, I approached him and apologized. I asked if he would train me a few more times before leaving, and he agreed.

During one of our last sessions, I questioned him about why he chose to stop training me. He had broad shoulders, so it didn't make sense that one little tantrum would end what seemed to be a genuine *Friendship*. He said, "Because you're not ready to hear what I need you to understand. Since you asked I'm going to tell you anyway. I *Believe* that you have the ability to accomplish incredible things, maybe even walk one day. But if you don't *Learn* the *Lessons* behind why you're in this situation, you will be paralyzed for the rest of your life."

He was right. Being crippled is a state of mind that has nothing to do with a person's abilities. Choosing to accept that there's no meaning behind what we don't understand is a dark, self-defeating mind-set. *Greatness* resides in everyone. The question was whether I was willing to go the distance to unlock my *Potential*. I knew what I needed to do, but he was right about me not being ready to accept it.

On Tuesdays and Thursdays, I tried my luck with a bit of occupational therapy. It made sense to also establish some functional life skills since my days were spent living from a seated perspective. The insurance-driven atmosphere offered a completely different setting. The clientele consisted mostly of senior citizens with declining health, broken hips, strokes, Dementia, and Alzheimer's. There were definitely skills and appliances that could have been beneficial, but the walls smelled funny, and everything was just way too sterile. Their intention wasn't to empower people that needed help; it was all about logging disabled folks into the system. I was twenty-five years old at the time, and this was the last place I wanted to be. Insurance only covered a few sessions, so I did my time and busted free of that joint.

Beyond therapy, I didn't have much going on. I didn't even know where to start. One evening, I met an incredible guy outside a movie theater that was getting out of his accessible van, and it offered a refreshing perspective. My *Dad* cruised by to check out his setup and was floored when he saw another quadriplegic all by himself doing everything on his own. We got to chatting, exchanged numbers, and made plans to get lunch about a week later.

We met at a restaurant, and he brought a *Friend* that was also in a wheelchair. These two guys were truly incredible. They were both married to women they met after their accident and were living fully functional *Happy* lives. His *Friend* was a full-on commando warrior that lost a finger playing wheelchair rugby. He did marathons and Ironman competitions in his chair. They both carried on like it was no big deal. I just couldn't wrap my head around this. I didn't even like the idea of being at a table with two other guys in wheelchairs. Everybody would stare at us, and I felt like we were a rolling circus. My stubborn ass wouldn't let go of the *Illusion* even after I gained insight from this life-changing experience.

The first two years after my injury are difficult for me to reflect upon because everything seemed overwhelmingly gray. I don't recall if the summers were hot or if it rained in the winter. I don't remember listening to music or reading any books. I think I watched a bunch of football, but I couldn't recite a single score or who won the Super Bowls. I tried to be positive, and people told me that I was, but all I really remember was the gut-wrenching pain I felt on the inside. I was a fighter, so letting go never came easy for me. This situation tested my *Will* in every imaginable way.

Life with the Butterfly became as turbulent as a cargo plane with one-engine flying through a hurricane. She wasn't built for this kind of weather, and she knew it when she told me so in the hospital. The relationship was part of my *Illusion*, and even though everything else seemed to crumble, I had hope that maybe there was a chance. It wasn't exactly working before the accident, but I lost sight of that among the wreckage. Her efforts got me through some really tough times, and there was never any doubt that she cared for me.

When I was first injured, she dropped out of school to be by my side full-time. She was there every day and flew out to Colorado with my *Family* to live in the dorms next door to the hospital. When we came back to California, she lived with me on the weekends and finished her last semester of school during the week. After graduating, she moved in with me full-time and got accepted to a grad school thirty minutes away.

The weight of being around such a heavy situation put distance between us. After living under the same roof for a while, she yearned to grow under a different patch of sky. When she finally moved out, the hustle was that we would stay together, but the writing was on the wall. I was too damaged to accept letting go of what I thought I once had. One weekend, she told me of a trip she planned to Mexico with her sister and a bunch of girlfriends. The trip ended up being the weekend the Butterfly flew away and never came back.

Since she stuck around for two years after the accident, her dissent was incredibly hard to deal with. Her best effort came across as true love, and maybe it was. It just wasn't the kind that lasts forever. I learned an extremely important lesson from this, but it took years to fully comprehend. When someone gives their best effort, there is nothing left to give. You can't really ask for more. You can take it for the gift it is or get disappointed in the hollowness of your own expectation.

Seeing life for what it is was hard-core. The rose-colored glasses through which I chose to view the world completely distorted reality. I always maintained my childlike essence by turning things into a big game. The way I saw things, instead of aging to perfection, people tended to grow old and it rotted their core. Before the spinal tweak, I swore to myself that this would never happen to me. But how was I supposed to stay true to my promise when the game seemed to take such a cruel and unexpected turn?

Friends seemed to come and go, but the landscape was also a rude awakening for me. Those that I figured would surely be around during critical times were off doing their own things. When stuck in the middle of a crisis situation, it's very hard to see things from other people's perspectives. People had a tough time seeing me go through this, and there was no perfect thing to say or do. The ambiguity made it hard for anyone to get close, especially when the mere sight of what I was going through evoked *Fears* that most would rather never even think of.

When my ability to move through space and time became compromised; my other senses sharpened dramatically. There was a certain suspended animation that accompanied this new perspective, and the ability to read people heightened my *Awareness*. It was a skill set that took some getting used to. I was always pretty dialed in with people's energies and body language before, but my new way of *Being* became hyper-focused on these traits. At first, it was overwhelming because it really bothered me how everyone reacted to a young guy in a wheelchair.

When I was in junior college, there was a sandwich shop across the street from the university. One day after class, I went in to grab lunch, and there were two pretty girls at the first table on the left as I walked in the door. I pretended not to notice as I walked past them on my way to the counter to order my hoagie. Out of the corner of my eye, I saw them whispering to each other as they flipped their hair and shifted nervously in their chairs. The cashier rang me up, and I casually put on my sunglasses as I smirked at the girlies on my way out the door.

A few years later, I stopped by the same sandwich place to grab lunch, but this time, I was in a large power wheelchair that was operated by blowing into a straw. At the very same table, there were two young girls that noticed me right when I rolled through the door. Instead of nervously flipping their hair, they couldn't stop staring and whispering back and forth to each other. When I was leaving, instead of flashing aroused smiles, they turned away to avoid making eye contact.

What a difference a few years and a drastically broken neck seemed to make. My sensitivity to this perspective was off the charts. When a person becomes blind, they must focus on their ability to hear, smell, and feel much more. For me, it wasn't that obvious, and the adjustment period was intense. There was no how-to manual that made getting used to this any easier. It was extremely isolating, and as much as people tried to understand, there was no way that anyone ever could. It's exhausting putting on a happy face when I am constantly dealing with neck and back aches, nerve pain, throbbing ankles, muscle spasms, and all the drama that goes into using the bathroom. People thought paralyzed meant I didn't feel anything. The reality was it took everything I had to pretend like everything was okay. The physical pain and paralysis was tough, but the social gap between myself and the rest of the world made me feel like a creature from a Steven Spielberg movie.

This *Humbling* perspective had me truly stumped. Having a positive attitude was one thing, but dealing with the pain I felt on the inside was like trying to slay a dragon with my hands tied behind my back. I was raised to be a fighter. I took pride in rising to a challenge, but for the first time in my life, I felt like giving up. This was a *Problem* because I just wasn't wired that way. I honestly didn't know how to quit. Without the use of any of my limbs, I would need to be creative if I was going to consider quitting as an option. So I put some thought into it and came up with a plan.

I would have my caregiver take me to the lake a few miles away from where I grew up. Then I would carefully drive my wheelchair out onto one of the boat docks using caution to not stir up any suspicion. After a few minutes, I would tell him I needed some time alone and to go wait for me on the shore. If I drove my electric-powered tank directly off the dock, the weight of the chair would push me to the bottom. I would run out of air before anyone could come to my rescue. I thought about it for a few days and planned a day to do it.

I pray about most major decisions in my life, but I didn't about this one. I was so ashamed for even entertaining the possibility that I couldn't bring the idea of God into it. This was a truly selfish act that I would be doing to satisfy my own desires. Praying was an opportunity to thank my Creator for *Blessing* me with all the things that made *Life* worth living. Since this decision would end my physical existence, I didn't see the point. The night before I planned on doing it, I went to sleep without praying, thinking, or appreciating anything. It was the only time in my life I can ever remember being *Totally Alone*.

When I woke up the next morning, I laid in bed, staring at the ceiling for almost an hour. Thousands of thoughts raced through my troubled mind. The progression went something like this: "What would my *Parents'* faces look like at my funeral? What would my *Brothers* think of me? How much pain would I cause in the hearts of everyone that *Loves* me? I would be letting down all the people who *Believe* in me. What would my Creator have to say about this? This decision means I would be giving up on *Myself*. I just can't do it."

These thoughts conjured up a surprising moment of clarity. A certain amount of sorrow died that morning, and in its place grew an *Opportunity* that was totally unfamiliar to me. The catch was that it was always present. It was buried in a place that I chose never to go because I was afraid of totally losing myself. The *Opportunity* challenged me to find *Value* in everything that happens, including the things that I didn't agree with or understand. If I chose to get out of bed each morning, it meant I wanted to. I had to be ready for whatever came to me with no judgment. I was the master of my decisions, and if I wanted to attract *Good* things toward me, then *Good* things is what I needed to focus on.

My *Life* was mine to *Live*, and what I made of it each day was completely up to me. I *Promised Myself* in that moment that it was the last time I would ever consider ending my life. I was either going to do it that day or never think about it again. Being dependent on another person to shower and stretch me, empty pee bags, help me poop, brush my teeth, put on my clothes, and hoist me into a chair was pretty stressful. If I could make it out of my room each morning, then I could accomplish pretty much anything.

The problem with a moment of clarity is it comes just as quick as it goes. Having a revelation is great, but acting on it day in and day out takes serious *Effort* and *Discipline*. One day, I was sitting in the living room, watching court television on a Tuesday afternoon. I was in a gated retirement community with a strange caregiver that hardy spoke English. I thought to myself, *There has to be more to Life than this*. I still felt stuck, and being paralyzed was no longer my biggest problem. Coming to terms with the *Illusion* I was living was just as hard as not being able to move. According to mainstream society, I was young and well educated, so I had all the means necessary to succeed. The trouble with this "accident" is it seemed to have opened my eyes to a world that I was previously unaware of. There was so much more going on around me that I never seemed to question. With a bit of perspective, it was now time to search for *Purpose* behind it all.

After months of rehabilitation, I recovered decent function in my left arm, and my right side began to flicker. When I was discharged from the hospital, a bag of tools were sent home with me for when I was ready to accept the *Challenge*. In the bag were Velcro cuffs that wrapped around my hand with small pockets for silverware. I had my caregiver break a pencil and shove the broken end into the cuff with the eraser poking out. I took another leap forward in my search for *Purpose* when I strapped that pencil to my hand. My fingers might not be working, but I was determined to find a way to make a *Difference* with my *Life*.

About a year before I rearranged my vertebrae, I came across a book about how to pursue a passion. I opened it to a short story about an amateur writer that was detailing her process of becoming a published author. She said there is one major step that needs to be taken in order to be a writer. YOU HAVE TO WRITE! Write about anything, she said. In a journal, on a napkin, toilet paper, a moving box, it doesn't matter. The act of putting words on paper creates the spark that can one day become a forest fire.

I thought back to the encounter with the *Abundant Being of Light*. According to the agreement I made to return to my *Life*, the first order of business was to fix myself. The problem with this is I had no idea where to begin. Everything I valued about myself felt like it was burned to the ground. In order to be the phoenix that would rise from the ashes, I needed to pull my shit together. So I started to write.

Since I was unable to put a pen to paper, I used the pencil strapped to my hand to poke the keys of a computer one at a time. I was naturally right-handed, but since my left arm was functional enough to jab the keyboard, it would have to do. When the *Light* mentioned that my return to *Life* would be *Different* than anything I had ever known, I didn't think it involved being ambidextrous. The fact that I needed to learn how to write in a *Different Way* was a good lesson for what it would take to accomplish *Purpose* in my *Life*. I needed to look at everything completely *Different*, and the process wasn't going to be easy.

I didn't necessarily begin writing with the intention of becoming an author. I started with a journal to try to wrap my head around what I was feeling. I didn't exactly want to write. It was hard work, and it took way more effort than it used to. At first, every time I strapped the pencil to my hand, it was a reminder of how bad the situation sucked. I barfed up my feelings one agonizing letter at a time and forced myself to do it every day. Each day I would read what I wrote the day before and attempt to makes sense of myself. Once I began to see everything in front of me, I started to *Understand* why the process of finding *Purpose* began by turning inward.

My psyche was mangled, so I turned to a professional for help. I was a good problem solver, and I enjoyed being the fixer, so reaching out for help wasn't something that came naturally to me. When my buddies had discipline problems in high school, there was a counselor on campus that helped them through difficult times. They always came out of sessions with him raving about how cool it was, and everyone liked how he listened instead of telling them what to do. Even though every teenage kid could use a bit of good advice, pride kept me away from his office. When I was young and dumb, I figured I could manage my crooked melon on my own. Since I was desperately in search for answers, I figured it was time for a piece of humble pie. Shortly after I graduated high school, the counselor began a private practice just miles from where I grew up. I did some research, tracked down his number, and made an appointment.

There was nobody in his office when the secretary escorted me into the room. Since there was no desk, books, or file cabinets, I wondered if I was in some type of waiting room. There were a couple of couches, a few plants, and paintings on the wall. One particular painting caught my attention. It was of an old man sitting in front of a chessboard, seemingly pondering his next move. I enjoyed a good game of chess and took a liking to the way the game was a good metaphor for life. The one thing I found odd about the painting is that there was only one person playing the game. Before I could put much thought into it, in walked the master inquisitor.

He was wearing a button-up polo with khaki pants and loafers with no socks. He sat down on the couch and kicked his feet up like he just got finished golfing the back nine at the local country club. He reminded me of a business professional that came in for a half day of work on casual Friday. He looked me squarely in the eyes and said, "So, why are you here?"

In the spirit of what I thought was about to be a zestful debate about shrinking my drama, I said, "I'm here to sell you a boat. But by the looks of things, you probably already have one."

He said, "Well, I'm always in the market for a good investment. But based on your obvious inability to sail, I'm not sure you're the type of guy I would buy a boat from."

I immediately loved his style. He asked all the right questions, and it was okay to ramble on when I needed to vent. Dodgy nonsense was off the table though. He didn't put up with any of my bullshit, and whenever I got offtrack, there was always a witty comment reminding me that he wasn't there to babysit. It wasn't a medical ambush with heroic intentions to "fix me." He was there to try to *Understand*. Conventional protocols were thrown out the window, and he didn't use fluff to try to get me to spill my beans. What I was going through was outrageous, and he acknowledged it by pointing out pieces to a puzzle that I needed to solve on my own.

Nobody could relate to the unique circumstances that I was experiencing, so he didn't try. What he did do was put himself in my shoes to generate questions that might offer solutions. We only met a handful of times, but I always left with another piece to the puzzle. Sometimes it was a book; other times it was an idea. The last time we met, he asked a question that gave me a clue to *Life's* grand riddle. The clue helped me *Understand* the painting of the old man playing chess.

We spend our *Lives* trying to figure out which move to make. Every game is different and each move affects the entire board. No matter how hard we try or how skilled we become at playing the game, every move matters. For every action, there is a reaction, and each move has its own set of consequences. *Purpose* can lead to *Happiness* only when the player takes *Responsibility* for every move that is made. What we *Learn* we can take with *Us*, but in the end, the game we are playing is against *Ourselves*.

Change

Taking care of myself was no easy task. It was hard enough to do when I had full control of my body. Now that I had to rely on other people to do everything for me, a huge amount of strategy went into every maneuver. The first few years were intense as I needed people to feed me, style my hair, turn pages, scratch my nose, and pretty much everything else that goes with no coordinated movement. As I started to get function back in my arms, there was more opportunity, but the frustration seemed endless.

Finding new ways to do everything was exhausting both physically and mentally. I was a do-it-myself type of guy before I got hurt, and asking for help was a constant struggle. I wasn't a patient person. I liked doing everything as quickly and efficiently as possible. The more people and steps that were involved, the more complicated things became. If I saw a better way of doing something, my first instinct was to do it myself. My hardheaded demeanor was a hurdle I'd been working to overcome for years. Right when I started to wrap my head around letting others help me, I almost snapped it right off my shoulders.

I was a prideful person when it came to how I looked. I used to enjoy doing the little things that went into looking nice. My clothes always matched. I always wore cologne. I made sure to clip my nails, line up my hair, clean my ears, and have a close shave. I even matched my boxer shorts to my pajamas when I went to sleep. I didn't do it for the approval of others; it was fun, and I liked how it made me feel. It helped me enjoy being who I was.

After the injury, fine details complicated everyday life. Since I was unable to do things on my own, and I lacked that patience to go through each meticulous step, it wasn't fun anymore. I tried to instruct whoever was helping me, but it just wasn't the same. It's like the barber styling your hair after a fresh cut. Even though he's a professional, you're the only one that can make it look perfect to your own standards. Getting frustrated only made matters worse. Each person helping me tried their hardest to get everything right. When I wasn't satisfied with their best effort, it was a bummer for both parties.

Securing a stable caregiver was like finding a piece of hay in a stack of needles. It's not exactly the type of job that people aspire to grow up and be. Most people in the industry are looking to land a gig with an ocean view guesthouse, where they make top dollar handing elderly people a handful of pills and the morning paper. Those positions do exist, but they are filled by the best caregivers in the industry. Everything else is a crap shoot. The diamonds in the rough are scattered among the classifieds, Craigslist, and sketchy caregiving agencies.

I began my trip down the rabbit hole with the agencies. It seemed the most logical route, and it was the most commonly suggested option by hospitals and mentors. They seemed to have a screening process that offered a variety of options tailored to the needs of their clients. At this time in my recovery, I had government funding that covered half the cost of twenty-four-hour care and fundraiser dollars that paid for the rest.

Once I submitted my application and the agencies found out that a young two-hundred-pound male needed twenty-four-hour care which included transfers and personal hygiene duties, there were only a few candidates willing to take the job. Then the interview process began. At first, I had no idea what I needed or what to look for. My *Family* tried to help, but they were as scared and skeptical as I was. This type of energy attracts a certain type of person, and it complicated the selection process. It was an intense situation inviting a perfect stranger into my home to care for every possible need. They had access to my house, my bank card, my car, and all my medication.

I had every type of person imaginable work with me. I've hired men and women from all different races with ghetto, farm, suburban, and Third World upbringings. I employed those with brightly colored religious and criminal backgrounds from the highly privileged to drug-addicted, under-the-bridge type of characters. There were those with mixed sexual orientations and political views, to ex-convict orphans that never made a taxable paycheck. I also worked with soldiers, baby boomers, grad students, and high school dropouts.

I've been lied to, stolen from, hustled, cheated, empty promised, and sexually advanced. One time, I was being helped into the shower, and I was dropped on the floor during a person's first day. Mangled and naked on the bathroom tile, this individual made me promise not to fire him before he put me back in the chair. Numerous people pulled "the ole" and just didn't show up to work, leaving me stranded with no help. One time, a guy took a personal phone call while he was helping me shower. He got into a heated argument with whoever was on the line and began yelling and screaming like a total nutjob. He left me soaking wet in the bathroom for two hours while he went to the back porch to smoke joints and contemplate life. Then there was the guy that decided to quit on Thanksgiving. He found out that we had proof of him stealing money and medication, so he left me alone in bed on Thanksgiving morning. When I was three hours late to the *Family* picnic, my *Brother* swung by to find me staring at the ceiling, still in bed.

The physicality of being paralyzed was easy compared to what came with it emotionally. It was like I'd been shipped off to a different planet where all sensible logic got thrown out the window. These people worked for agencies that supposedly had a screening process and background checks. I'd come to find out that the few hard-working, semi-normal candidates had to work multiple jobs because the agencies were taking such a large chunk from their paychecks. I was a fairly sheltered college boy, so this harsh reality showed me a dark, cold side of life.

While the circus carousel of caregivers continued to rotate, my *Family* took shifts tending to my needs. The dynamic of how to properly play their roles in this chaotic mess was like an afterschool special that had been dosed with hallucinogenic mushrooms. Dysfunction was at an all-time high, and the mirage that this would neatly come to an end in a timely manner was beginning to fade. My youngest *Brother* and his best *Friend* took on the primary caregiving duties, and everyone else offered what they could to keep the *Family* afloat.

Weeks turned into months, and months turned into years. Before I knew it, I was well beyond the two-year mark that medical science said was the most significant window for recovery. I told myself in the hospital that I would use the first twenty-four months to evaluate where I was at. Since I was still showing signs of recovery, I didn't see any reason why I should give up trying to walk away from the injury. I had such a hard time focusing during the first few years of dealing with life in a chair that it was nearly impossible to strategize an effective rehabilitation approach. There was so much going on around me that I had trouble seeing what was right in front of me.

My *Brothers* did what they could to help, but the emotional damage that set in after years of trauma had them completely overwhelmed. The term thrown around in the medical world is *Post-Traumatic Stress Disorder*. It's science's way of trying to categorize people's reactions to life-altering stimuli. The way I see it, everybody responds differently in situations that *Challenge* the way we view the world. PTSD is a nice way to dress up a general name for the phenomenon, but the bottom line is that people's emotional states are extremely fragile. Each person's response to high-impact drama needs to be dealt with on a case-by-case basis. Having a spinal cord injury and trying to understand why people act the way they do was astoundingly difficult.

While my fifteen-year-old *Brother* called meetings to iron out the wrinkles in the *Family* fabric, I turned to Craigslist to recruit new monkeys for the caregiver carousel. Strange got downright creepy as interviews for the position started to resemble comedy sketches that could have ended up on Saturday Night Live. I began to notice a trend with the types of people that were attracted to this type of job. There were a lot of *Unhappy* people in the world trying to make a *Difference* with their *Lives*. Being broken wasn't what made us different; it's what was bringing us together.

Since anyone could respond to an ad in the newspaper or on Craigslist, the only real qualification to apply was a willingness to do the job. I noticed that a majority of the people that interviewed for the position were deeply bothered by one thing or another. I might have been the one in the chair that needed assistance, but most of the applicants were searching for more than just a job. There was a common underlining theme for almost every person interviewing for the position. It wasn't about money as much as it was about doing something *Good* for another person. These people were searching for *Purpose* beyond themselves, and most of them didn't even realize it.

With this *Knowledge* came a certain *Responsibility*. If I wanted to make something *Good* out of what happened to me, I had to find *Compassion* in my search for meaning. I wasn't just looking for someone to take care of me. I was trying to figure out a way to find *Value* in taking care of myself. Letting go of the gut-wrenching anger of how unfair this disposition was gave me the freedom to look at life *Differently*. My frustration was only complicating things. I didn't want people's pity as they fell victim to my struggle. I wanted to *Inspire* people with my *Life* by creating something brilliant out of a tough situation. The place to start was finding *Compassion* for myself.

Before I got hurt, I was fearless. Now I was so riddled with *Fear* that I had trouble making the simplest decisions. Since I was so unfamiliar with how to move forward feeling this way, there was a lot of stagnation, and it drove me crazy. Before I could begin to have patience with *Accepting* other's help, I had to find *Patience* with my own *Process*. I began to take everything one step at a time. When I started to do this, it opened my eyes to how the *Fear* I had was pushing people and opportunities away from me. This was another realization that truly sucked.

Everything seemed to be an uphill battle, and I felt so out of control. Every time I would move a few feet forward, I would roll ten feet back. Walking uphill seemed so much easier than rolling a chair up one. This mind-set was on loop in my approach, and in order to move past it, something needed to *Change*. I prayed about it and came to the conclusion that maybe instead of trying so hard,

I needed to back off being so intense about everything. Since I was a fighter, I had no idea where to begin, so I started simply.

Each morning when I got out of the shower, I had whoever was helping me leave for a few minutes so I could focus on my breathing. It amazed me how much trouble I had doing something so simple. My mind was like a prison riot, and all the darkest, meanest thoughts were holding my *Happy* feelings hostage. There was no order or discipline, only chaos. I took some yoga classes at the tail end of my football career, and I remembered a few of the breathing techniques, so that's where I began.

In the beginning, I did the exercises thirty seconds at a time, and each day, I would try to increase my level of focus. I concentrated on my breathing to clear my mind as I went deeper and deeper into stillness. I treated it like a gym workout using each second the same way I used to complete repetitions lifting weights. I would set a goal, and then I would close my eyes and go into myself. I would rhythmically breathe until I reached the desired amount of time I agreed upon in my head before starting. Each day, it became a little easier. After a few weeks, I looked forward to quieting my monkey mind each morning.

When the time came for me to cross the threshold between the door frame of my room to the rest of the world, I found myself more prepared. I was still hurt and broken, but my mind had begun to *Change*. I had a sense of mental clarity that inspired a curiosity inside of me. It demanded more out of my everyday experiences. The mundane details that cluttered my understanding of life began to dissolve. Surface level desire of what seemed to matter was no longer enough. The *Illusion* started to crumble, and the chess game I was playing against *Myself* had begun to take shape.

As the fog cleared, I realized that my strategy was bogus. If I wanted to win in this *Game of Life*, I needed to stop acting like such a zombie. So I started reading. My *Belief* system had holes in it, and I had questions that needed to be answered. If I had a flawed approach, where were my thoughts and actions failing me? Why did I choose to come back to this life? If all the stuff I was conditioned to believe is not important, then what is the *Purpose of Being* here?

There were a few undeniable solids that I knew for certain were genuine to my existence. My *Faith*, *Family*, and *Friends* illuminated a path for my survival in my *Darkest* hours. *Love* and *Compassion* had shown me a way that I always knew existed, but experiencing it in such a raw, unadulterated form was profoundly incredible. I was *Changed* for the better in a way that altered my *Perception* of what *Life* is all about. In a world governed by a drastic sense of polarity, I was also exposed to harsh realities that most people would rather never acknowledge.

In an attempt to peel back the layers of my onion, I peeped my head behind the curtain of our carefully woven perceived reality. I studied classic and new-age philosophy, psychotherapy, religious texts, books on self-help and spirituality, conspiracy theory, medical texts, quantum physics, paranormal activity, and alternative healing. I looked into books, videos, documentaries, biographies, podcasts, lecture series, Hollywood movies, and the good ol' internet. My brain was hungry for information, and I sifted through a ton of nonsense before stuff started making sense.

I was looking for an underlying theme that connected *Everything*. It amazed me how logical concepts stood strong over time, but what the hell did it all mean? Each investigation into a deeper realm of possibility felt like a piece to a much larger puzzle. There was so much information pointing to something *Deeper* but nothing that connected all the dots. Everyone with a well-thought-out idea had something, but no real answers. There are so many different ways to answer the question why, but only one way to *Live* it. To each his own.

Great! To each his own. As I sat paralyzed in a wheelchair, my ability to create seemed very limited. So I decided to play my circumstances as they were. I needed to figure out how to climb the mountain of *Purpose* without the ability to climb. And I needed to do it with *Patience* that I didn't have. Caregivers were like the wind. Sometimes they were strong and ruthless. At other times soft and comfortable. Either way, it was a necessary staple in my ability to move forward. Getting stuff done meant finding a way to make things work, and it started by securing consistent help.

I posted another ad on the interweb and began interviewing candidates. I was open to finding the perfect person, minus the details of what it needed to look like. After meeting a number of prospects that just didn't fit the profile, in walked a guy that I thought was more of the same. When he sat down, he was tight with nerves like most of the others, but he had a happy-go-lucky mentality to him.

He was dressed sharp in slacks and a button-up shirt, but underneath the clothes was a kid that had been worn down by hard times. He was young with soft eyes that understood struggle. The guy needed to catch a break, but he was dramatically unqualified for the job and had no experience caregiving. After speaking with him for about a half hour, I was ready to send him on his way. Right before I could show him out, he stopped me and said, "Look, man, I know I have never been a caregiver, but I can do this. Just give me a *Chance*. I won't disappoint you."

I'd heard this line before, and the follow-through had mixed results. There was something about the way he carried himself that made me a *Believer* though. I could tell he really needed an *Opportunity*, and I really needed the help. Brutal realities of life had beaten us down, and we were both a bit desperate. One way or another, it was time to move forward, so I chose to roll the dice. The only way to learn to fly sometimes is by being pushed out of the nest. We were both sick of getting pushed around, so I decided maybe we could jump together.

From the Peter Pan perspective, I immediately recognized him as another one of the Lost Boys. Since I was used to being around knuckle heads, we got along quite well. My *Brothers*, who also learned to be caregivers via trial by fire, got him trained and up to speed. He was a quick learner and was adamant about getting things right as soon as possible to prove his worth. He had everything down in less than two weeks. He moved into the extra bedroom and took over twenty-four-hour caregiving duties seven days a week.

The self-declared "unprofessional professional" was one of eight children in an immigrant Romanian family. His father left in his early teens, leaving a single *Mother* to look after a house full of growing children. They quickly learned how to lean on each other instinctually, understanding the strength in numbers. With the lack of a father figure, the oldest boys became scrapper street hoodlums and often found themselves in trouble with the law. After serving time in the juvenile detention system, Romo, as I called him, realized he needed to get his act straight. He knew the time had come for him to walk a fine line because his *Family* depended on him. The opportunity to be a caregiver gave him room to breathe. The pressure of his *Family* and the streets was far enough away for him to work on *Himself.*

Even though the apartment he was raised in was only a for-ty-five-minute drive from my place, it seemed like we grew up in two different worlds. I never had to worry about my next meal or the electricity going out because we couldn't afford the bill. I went to private Catholic high school where my biggest worry was my football coaches yelling at me. Romo and his *Brothers* ran hustles to pay for groceries. His *Mom* and *Sisters* worked minimum wage jobs to pay the rent for their two-bedroom apartment.

Since I was a bit older, I played the mentor role. I left home and received what was considered to be an elite education. I had been places and rubbed elbows with future industry leaders. His education was quite different. Hard knocks taught him how to be a man in a sink-or-swim environment. Being a scrapper taught him the laws of the land. At the end of the day, if he didn't come up somehow, he would go to sleep hungry.

He worked his ass off for me, and we treated each other like *Family.* Romo was the first face I saw in the morning and the last before I went to sleep. He even woke up multiple times every night to the sound of a doorbell and stumbled half asleep into my room to help me pee. In the morning, he showered and stretched me with-out ever being phased by the gnarliness of the situation. He offered me *Dignity* and *Respect* in a pretty hard-core atmosphere. Romo also shopped, cooked, cleaned, and drove me everywhere I needed to go.

We would listen to audiobooks on the way back and forth to physical therapy about how to better ourselves. Once we studied the importance of eating healthy food, we got serious about our diet and began to nourish our bodies properly. I would do the research and pay for the groceries, and he had to learn to prepare everything without killing us. As we slowly figured out ways to grow together, I began to *Understand* on a larger scale how much we as humans need each other.

When we weren't growing with the help of published theories by esteemed authors, we shared stories about life. I filled his head with my adventures about college life, sports, girls, school, and wild parties. And he shared what it was like growing up without a father, being locked up, running hustles, evading the police, and living through violent drug encounters. I took him with me to fancy dinners with successful affluent members of society. And he took me to grungy LA clubs with gang members and wanted felons.

No matter where we went or what we did, there was a mutual *Respect* between us with no judgment. People around us often wondered what the nature of our relationship was because the energetic force that surrounded our interaction was infectious. I'm not saying that we got invited to black-tie parties at five-star resorts or into the inner circle of cartel crime rings, but the *Compassion* we shared worked as a free pass earning us *Respect* everywhere we went.

Months went by, and we started to gain momentum as we got into a rhythm. We were both getting better mentally, physically, and emotionally. Those who *Loved* us started to see major *Changes*. I was physically making gains, and my strategy for finding *Purpose* in my *Life* was rising to the surface. Since most of Romo's living expenses were taken care of, he was able to give half of his paycheck to his *Family*. With the other half, he saved up to buy new clothes and a car.

Right around this time, a wild card was added into the fold. One of my uncles that had been homeless for some time moved into the garage of my *Grandpa's* house. He said it would just be a few weeks to get his affairs in order while he looked for his own place. This was the beginning of a manipulation that would take months to unravel, ending with another staggering hurdle to overcome.

Things started off pretty cool, as he was actually a decent asset to our bachelor pad in the beginning. He struggled with drug addiction over the years but seemed to find a comfortable patch of sobriety. He would shop and cook with us and even came to therapy from time to time. One day on the way home from therapy, he had us stop off at his dive bar hangout to get a bite to eat. He disappeared for a while, but I thought nothing of it. Romo needed to use the bathroom, so he stepped away for a few minutes as well.

When Romo came back, he was sheet white with beads of sweat on his forehead. He was breathing heavy and told me his heart was racing a mile a minute. He said, "This is a creepy place with *Bad* people. I'm freakin' out, man. Can we please leave?"

It was like he had seen a ghost, and I wasn't going to question his instincts because he was obviously aware of something. My uncle walked in minutes later, so we paid the bill and left. When we got back home, I asked Romo to elaborate on his panic attack. It turns out he, too, had a run in with drug problems, and the bar was an all-to-familiar scene. He had been clean for some time, but the creepy dive bar rattled his demons, and it was best for him to get away from that place as soon as possible.

In the following weeks, strange noises and behavior began to develop in the garage-turned-dungeon. People were coming through the side door at all hours of the night. Loud music and rumblings occurred during the evenings for days at a time, then silence while they slept it off in the afternoon. One morning, when Romo came to get me up, he had a huge smile on his face, and I told him to give me fifteen minutes to snooze. He set an alarm and went to the living room to relax on the couch. When he came back to my room, the smile had been replaced by a look of disgust. I immediately made him explain his radical shift of emotions. He said when he first woke up, there was a young half-naked girl walking around the house. She had on thong panties and a see-through shirt with no bra. When he went back to lie on the couch, he heard her throwing up in the toilet. After she left the bathroom without flushing or washing her hands, she went to the refrigerator and drank milk straight from the carton. Needless to say, I drank my coffee black that morning and threw out the milk. About a week later, my uncle decided to tear up the entire backyard in a relandscaping effort. Mr. Green Thumb started his project at 6:00 AM while blasting German punk rock music at full volume in our gated retirement community.

It was obvious what was going on, and my uncle's actions only supported our suspicions. We nicknamed him Tweaky the Gypsy due to his erratic behavior and vagrant houseguests. The healing efforts of Romo and myself turned into a fight-or-flight effort to survive. On another occasion, he mopped the floor early in the morning, and it was still wet when we were leaving. When he came back in from the garage to find wheel marks on the tile, he lost his mind. He chased us out the front door and threatened to throw me out of my chair. He said he would hold my head to the floor until I cleaned up the mess I made. I dared him to touch me. I promised that if he did I would make one phone call and have *Friends* race over with a tire iron to break his legs. We were in no real physical danger, but our efforts had become obstructed by psychological warfare. Money and valuables started to disappear along with groceries and clothing. Even my championship high school football ring went mysteriously missing.

One night, we came home to Tweaky acting all sketchy in the kitchen, and a strange smell permeated the air. He bolted to his dungeon as soon as we walked in the door. We assumed he was just up to his gypsy ways and continued on with our evening. About an hour later, when Romo was cooking dinner, he opened the silverware drawer and found a smoking gun. A foil crack pipe was in with the spoons that had a half-charred bowl of crystallized-looking contraband in it. We called Tweaky's brother, my other uncle, who was a straight and narrow fireman, to discuss our current dilemma. The Gypsy had been occupying the garage for months now, and I thought this crack pipe would be evidence for his eviction. When we sat down to discuss what to do, Tweaky the Gypsy said the drugs were Romo's and cited that he had a known history with drugs.

Romo jumped out of his chair and flew across the room. In a venomous rage, he lunged at Tweaky with intentions on knocking his lights out. The fireman uncle intercepted Romo, which was probably to his benefit. The Gypsy was much larger than him and had been hardened by the streets for multiple decades. The fireman uncle had no clue what to make of the situation. He had no idea what a crack pipe looked like and even if he did, he didn't know whose story to believe. He took the Gypsy to his house for a few days until tempers settled, and the following week, Tweaky slithered back into his dungeon.

As if matters weren't sticky enough, my *Grandpa's* dementia had begun to weigh heavy on the *Family* unit. He spent the past few years at my parents' house with my *Mom* as his primary caregiver. He also spent small amounts of time with my fireman uncle, but the late stages of his dementia demanded twenty-four-hour medical attention. As much as my *Family* wanted to help, the progressive nature of the disease had started to decline rather quickly and required professional assistance. When he was checked into a care facility, there was a significant amount of emotional stress accompanied by a substantial financial commitment.

Romo had taken good care of me for two years, working seven days a week. He hardly ever took time off and was beginning to show signs of fatigue. When the air was clear, things went smoothly, and building ourselves up offered mutual gain for both of us. When reality kicked in, difficult times made an already tough situation somewhat bewildering. The *Family* was in a frenzy, and my *Brother* from another *Mother* was being asked to carry too much weight. I decided to hire a weekend caregiver to ease the tension of Romo's workload.

There was so much nonsense going on around me again that it felt like my wheels were falling off. I recently embraced the temporary confines of Peter Pan living in a chair, and then Captain Hook came along and slashed my tires. I wanted to be there for my *Family*, but it seemed next to impossible to be there for *Myself*. These were typical life problems that every *Family* has a version of, but nothing in my life seemed to resemble any type of normal.

I was Peter Pan with no pixie dust. I wanted to fly, but I just couldn't. I was used to being a fierce leader, but now I was back to struggling with taking care of *Myself*. It was tough to lean on the gains I made because it felt like the drama just kept coming. I was at a new low. I remember sitting in front of my computer, trying to create an ad for weekend help, but I couldn't even hold my body up. I felt like a failure to my *Family* and to *Myself*. I leaned forward onto the table and cried harder than I did in the hospital when I found out I was paralyzed.

Growth

Denial, anger, bargaining, depression, acceptance—the five steps associated with the grieving process. They didn't seem like phases; they felt like a musical playlist blaring at high volume stuck on loop. As I sat there, sobbing at the kitchen table, I wondered if the bottomless pit of drama would ever firm up to crush my bones. Maybe then I would finally splat like a bug on a car windshield, then a little Windex, a squeegee, and some fresh air could offer a new beginning. I wasn't about to give up, but I had no idea where to go from here.

Then something special happened. An opportunity presented itself for me to realize I was on the right track and the work I had been doing was worth the effort. Romo was in the kitchen, doing dishes, when he overheard me crying. Oblivious to my surroundings, I didn't hear him turn off the sink and make his way over to the table. My arms were crossed, and my head was resting in a pool of tears. Without saying a word, Romo wrapped his arms around me and gave me a huge hug.

The table where I was sitting had been a *Family* gathering place my entire life. My late *Grandmother* had been preparing meals on that table since my *Mother* was a child. As my *Grandfather's Light* was fading away, everything he worked so hard to instill in his *Family* was being passed onto me in that moment. It wasn't just that moment; it was every previous moment that led to the *Understanding* of what I was here to do. I realized I had made it. I'd been tested in such an extreme way that I now had the tools to overcome anything.

I was blessed with the *Love* and *Affection* of two sets of *Grandparents* along with a loving *Mother* and *Father*. I have three incredible *Brothers* with another *Stepbrother* that my *Family* absorbed through osmosis. Being the leader of Never Never Land while growing up gave me a fantasy picture of what the world could be. By holding true to the *Values* that were instilled in me, I was able to share something extraordinary that affected everyone I came in contact with. By *Loving Unconditionally* as I was taught to do my whole life, I made a *Difference* in someone else's *Life*. Sharing my *Unconditional Love* with Romo gave him the opportunity to do the same for me when I needed it most.

When I took a *Chance* on hiring him, I did it because I *Believed* in his potential. I saw beyond the details to his true nature. We all have the capacity to express *Love* for one another, but in this fast-paced life of fancy cars and evening news, we get lost in all the commotion. Romo made a lasting impression in my *Life* that I will never forget. The hug he gave me that day was like the icing on a cake. It was the finishing touch that made the *Difference* between something good and something *Great*.

The power of that experience signified a turning point in my quest to get over myself. Rising above what most call problems is really an *Opportunity* to define one's character. Life gets tough for everyone at some point. The question is, how will you respond to it? I sat up in my chair and pulled my computer closer to me. I strapped a pencil to my hand and began to type the best caregiver ad I had ever created. I saw an *Opportunity* to take care of a guy that did a damn good job taking care of me. Getting Romo some time off would diffuse the intensity of the job so he could grow to even greater heights.

I was *Learning* that the best way to take care of others was to first take care of *Myself*. The *Light* said I was to focus on finding *Oneness* within my *Life* before anything else. My previous programming was dialed in to find happiness with and through others. If *Happiness* cannot be found on the inside first, then there is really nothing to give but a false sense of self. So I put together one of the most honest, heartfelt ads I had ever written. I was clear about what the job duties strictly entailed, but I also detailed my emotional struggles as well. It was important for me to inform the next person I would work with exactly who I was in that moment. By doing this, I was creating a clear picture of what they were getting themselves into.

I found a creative way to use the strengths of my personality to offer a humorous, witty portrayal of my life in a nutshell. I was detailed about the struggles my *Family* had been through during the roller coaster of the last few years. I also tried to paint a picture of the emotional hardships I was experiencing and how difficult it was to understand life from a seated perspective. It wasn't a sob story; it was just real. My intention was to send a comedic prayer to the universe with good vibes behind it. I would then *Surrender* to the *Opportunity* to *Grow* and see what happened.

I received some awesome responses, but there was one in particular that stood out above all the rest. It said:

> I come from a crazy family too! I am one of nine kids and am totally interested in this opportunity I ran across that you have proposed. Here is a little about me. I like banana cream pie, spaghetti, tacos, pancakes (but only the outside), strawberry shortcake, ice-cream bars, Hefeweizen, warm Heineken, and baseball. I don't like certain words like "mirror" (use "looking glass" instead, please).
>
> I love my Suzuki 125, and I don't care about the car you drive or the clothes you wear. I don't always like to smile, and I think that's fine, but I smile most often. I don't have a social filter, and it gets me in trouble sometimes. I don't mind drama much. In fact, I'll try to help you fix it or make it worse, but don't make empty promises. There isn't anything I hate more, with the exception of lies. But that's essentially what an empty promise is.
>
> I also REALLY like when things are symmetrical or even. People with lack of empathy make me nauseous, and yes . . . sometimes I DO cry over spilled milk. I love to read and watch clouds, but mostly I

like to laugh. E-mail me if this position is still available and you'd like to meet!

Talk about personality! I had to meet this person, but first, I did some reconnaissance. I copied the e-mail address from the response to my ad and pasted it on a social media site to see what came up. There wasn't much, but there was a picture of a pretty girl that had me deviously considering an interview. I didn't tend to hire women because of the heavy lifting involved with moving a quadriplegic, but I at least wanted to meet this girl. We e-mailed back and forth a few times and scheduled a time to meet.

The interview process was often tense. The nerves of the applicants and anxiety of inviting a new stranger into my life was a complicated affair. I was on high alert monitoring every readable indicator I could in our twenty-minute meeting. The way someone presented themselves offered a wealth of information starting the moment they walked in the door. Their demeanor, personal hygiene, dress attire, greeting, attention to detail, and résumé were the primary points of interest factored into the hiring process. This round of applicants was different though. There was an element of purity present that changed the energy of the transaction. Especially with the "warm Heineken, strawberry shortcake" girl.

The interviews I scheduled with this group of adventure seekers relied heavily upon the personality they shared in response to my heartfelt ad. By this time I understood I was participating in *Life's* version of the knowledge exchange and compensation involved more than just money. I carefully chose half a dozen people to interview and had soulful interactions with each applicant. I was fairly sure I had found my next caregiver, but I had one last interview with the girl that sent the wildly quirky response to the job posting.

When she came through the door, I realized I was right in thinking she was cute, but it might have been wrong to bring her in for an interview. As she glided into the living room, she tossed her résumé on the coffee table with a bag of freshly baked chocolate chip cookies. We talked for close to an hour, but at five feet tall, she was a bit vertically challenged for the position. I explained that I was afraid two hundred pounds of quadriplegic dead weight might crush her pocket-sized frame. She didn't find my chivalry at all compelling. She said, "Don't judge a book by its cover, man. Just because I'm small doesn't mean I can't get the job done. You don't know me, I'm mighty."

Not only was this girl quirky, she was half crazy. I loved it. What was I supposed to say to that? I prided myself in being someone that always found a way to get things done. This girl was basically saying the same thing. She wouldn't let me limit her potential based on what I thought I knew. Since the job was only on Saturday and Sunday, I could always lean on my *Family* if something drastic happened. Who knows, maybe it was time to push my limits a bit more. Besides, not only was she cute, she exposed a personal weakness when she brought fresh-baked chocolate chip cookies. I thought about it for a few days then hired her to start the following weekend.

I was growing tired of having nothing in my life but physical therapy after years of intense training. Athlete-style laser focus served me well in my early years of sports, but my lifestyle was much more balanced then. I needed to come up with something that I could be passionate about that kept my momentum going relating to *Purpose*. Reading books and doing research kept the fire burning, but it was time for action.

As the months passed, my funding to continue long hours of therapy started to dwindle. One evening, a runaway locomotive of thoughts found me struggling to sleep. Smoke seemed to bellow from my ears as my mind churned with uneasy feelings of the unknown. I remember asking God for a definitive sign that things would work out. I said, "Please show me something tomorrow that I will recognize as an undeniable sign that *You* are with *Me*. It can be big or small, just let it lead *Me* closer to where I need to *Be*."

The next day, I showed up to therapy early, which was a miracle in itself because I will most likely be late to my own funeral. While I was waiting for my session to start, I met a couple in the lobby, and we struck up a conversation. The topic of how expensive it was to live life in a chair came up, and I mentioned that I had some tough choices on the horizon regarding funds. I explained to them that the insurance company denied my request for power-assist wheels for my chair. The insurance agent said it was a luxury item because it was not a medical necessity. The add-on was expensive, and if I were to purchase them, it would come out of the money I needed to continue rehabilitation.

They said their son used to be in a chair and they were familiar with the drama associated with insurance companies. I made a joke to lighten the mood and mentioned how important it was to remain positive. I shared stories with them about how my *Family* and *Friends* made it possible for me to go to therapy by joining together and putting on multiple fundraisers. I was grateful to even have the opportunity to pursue rehabilitation. I explained that if it weren't for the *Love* and *Generosity* from all the people that cared about me, I didn't know where I would be.

Before we could finish our conversation, a trainer came to swoop me up, and we were off to the gym. I quickly said goodbye to the couple and was off to begin my workout. About an hour later, the owner of the gym came over and asked what I was talking to the couple about. It turns out that they lost their son due to circumstances associated with his condition. He told me they were so moved by my positive attitude and story that they wanted to buy the power-assist wheels I was considering purchasing.

This was exactly the definitive *Sign* I was looking for. I couldn't deny it even if I wanted to. I asked for something specific, and the offer could've come on any other day, but it just so happened to be the day I asked God to point me in the right direction. It's funny how *Signs* tend to work. If you're open and sensitive enough, the universe has a way of reminding you that there is *Something Greater*. It's not like I had been given any answers. What I had been given was an *Opportunity* to realize that I wasn't alone. I always had *Faith* in a *Higher Power*, but it's nice to get a little reminder every once in a while that my prayers are being heard.

In the following weeks, I had a certain sensitivity that helped aid in my growth process. It was obvious that I was rehabilitating my body to try to overcome quadriplegia, but I had to dig deeper to realize that my *Soul* was on a path to eliminate the *Illusion* I had been

104

living. The emotional weight that I was used to carrying seemed to have been lifted a little. When this happened, creative ideas began to manifest in my mind. I continued the practice of quieting my mind through breathing in the morning and also accompanied it with prayer. When I did this, certain ideas about how to proceed forward started to magically pop into my mind.

Showing up to therapy clearheaded led me to being more social and happy. Being *Grateful* for what I had was an incredible concept, but I really started to feel *Good* about the entire process. I began to listen to the clients' and trainers' ideas about what could be done to maximize our efforts. It wasn't always fairy tales and pixie dust. Most of the knowledge I obtained came from the personal struggles of good people giving their best effort. A lot of the time they would come up short due to things that were out of their control.

There were so many things that went into the process of *Wellness*. I realized that having a stable mind and control over my emotions was a key element toward being okay. I'm not saying by any means that I was a master at doing this. I was just having the thoughts that would lead me in that direction. Finding the *Patience* to work through some of these extremely difficult understandings was the first step toward getting me where I needed to go. *Knowing* truly is half the battle.

There are a lot of positive things that Western science has to offer. There is also a lot left to learn. The rehabilitation clinic that I worked out at developed some groundbreaking techniques that weren't recognized by the scientific community. They started to combine different complementary modalities that worked well with the physical training. When I first had my indwelling catheter removed, I had no control over my bladder. I went to see the acupuncturist after a workout and saw immediate results. I was completely incontinent, and after the first session, I was able to hold my bladder for ninety seconds. After the second treatment, I was able to hold it for almost five minutes.

The more I realized how a combination approach could benefit the rehabilitation process, the more I wanted to learn. Psychotherapy, acupuncture, a healthy organic diet, and physical therapy seemed to be no-brainers when it came to building a life of *Wellness*. Looking at it from this perspective *Changed* my outlook on what I was doing. A coordinated approach could be applied to a variety of different life conditions. If I could use my *Life* to pioneer a synergistic program creating *Value* in people's *Lives*, everything made sense.

I had been referring clients to the gym I was working out at for a while. Therapy was great, but I also believed in their approach toward empowering people. I brought in a massage therapist and some innovative equipment that helped the trainers do their job more efficiently. As the company grew though, so did their desire to capitalize on the niche market that they cornered. When I started to run low on money, management did their best to help, but ultimately, a business decision was made to cut me loose.

I wanted to work with them to integrate more modalities into their program, but their model was growing so fast that I wasn't really needed in that regard. There was a long waiting list to receive therapy from this outfit, and if everyone were to get discounts, they wouldn't be able to reel in large profits. When it came to dollars and cents, their model was locked and loaded. They weren't really looking to add more moving parts at the time.

The demand for a service like this was abundant. Spinal cord injury rehabilitation gyms started popping up all over. Since the main gym was looking to expand its simplified brand in other locations throughout the United States, hybrid versions were starting to gain momentum locally. Since the founding facility's therapists were at full capacity, other businesses started utilizing a multiple modality approach to set them apart from the pack. They were a few gyms willing to work with the funds I had available if I was willing to share my ideas and accumulated resources. The chance for me to continue therapy and learn from the smaller growing businesses was an interesting opportunity.

I continued to train hard and learn as I moved further into what I thought was purposeful action. I consistently wrote in my journal, listened to and read books, ate healthy, prayed, and focused on my breathing practice. With all my heart, I believed that something or another would catch fire, and I would walk away from my seated perspective. I seemed to be doing all the right things. How could it not work?

Funds were really becoming an issue, and each fundraiser I had was generating less and less money. People continued to show up at flag football tournaments and poker games, but my support system was growing tired. There was also some speculation as to whether the funds raised were being used appropriately. The only thing I knew how to do was give my best effort to try to accomplish my goals. I leaned on my sports mentality to keep pushing even when times were tough. That included when others had negative reactions or opinions as to what they thought I should or shouldn't be doing. If anyone ever wanted to question my motives, I had an open-door policy where people could ask any question they wanted. I vowed to answer in an honest and direct way, but in my experience, that's not really how charitable efforts tend to unfold.

I felt an obligation to the people who supported me, to give everything I had to honor their *Generosity*. When people began questioning my motives regarding spending habits, it threw a serious funk into my program. There wasn't a blueprint detailing how to best move forward with a catastrophic life-changing event. Receiving help from others was something that was difficult for me, but I did my best to do it with *Grace* and *Appreciation*. All of a sudden, it seemed like there were expectations that came with the assistance, and I didn't really know how to respond to it. I didn't want to need the help in the first place, but when it was offered to me, I did my best to accept it with a certain moral standard.

Being quadriplegic is a lot of work. What comes with it is hours of additional responsibilities that nobody could ever understand unless they were in the same position. Strategy is incredibly important, and budgeting time is a highly sensitive ordeal. Every action that my able body used to do now either took twice as long or required another person's assistance. Once the person in the chair is ready to go, the one providing the assistance also needs to sort their affairs. I was so sure that I would make a full recovery that I spent all my time focused on achieving my goal. I bypassed learning an adapted skill set because I chose to focus all my time and energy on standing up and walking. I felt like if I did it any other way I would be accepting the fate of living in a chair, and at the time, there just wasn't room for that in my psyche.

It took hours to get ready, hours to drive back and forth to therapy, and hours of grueling work in the gym. When I wasn't rushing to be somewhere, I was reading, researching, grocery shopping, or doing exercises at home. This went on for years, and at the end of each day, I was mentally, physically, and emotionally exhausted. There was no room for anything else. If I wanted to do occupational therapy or try to find a job, it meant something needed to give, and I wasn't ready to face that. I had a goal in mind, and damn it, I was going to accomplish it. My day job was therapy, and my goal for the future was to develop a rehabilitation center that used a community-healing approach. The concept I dreamed up through my many different therapeutic experiences, called for a systematic wellness approach. The concept I wanted to coordinate pooled the *Knowledge* and *Resources* of seasoned professionals. The idea was to get a collective of experts together to design programs that met the specific individual *Wellness* needs of each client.

I tried every modality that I could get my hands on. I threw myself into every type of therapy that seemed to make logical sense. I did massage, deep tissue body sculpting, Rolfing, cupping, acupuncture, acupressure, multiple forms of energy work including, Reiki, adapted yoga, aura cleansing, and spiritual work. I tried bioresonance, EECP, kelation therapy, hyperbaric oxygen, laser and chiropractic care, aquatic therapy, electric stimulation and DMS treatments, sound healing, hormone injections, and experimental progesterone creams. I did multiple forms of gait training, including robotics and a Polish system that utilized a harness and bungee cord apparatus for lateral suspension while walking on a treadmill. I went to numerous gyms, and when I couldn't drive all over town, I lifted weights in a friend's garage. When I wasn't doing things outside my home, I had coordination exercises that I would do in a standing frame while I watched TV. I tweaked my diet numerous times and tried endless supplements to assist my body in the regenerative process. I ate all organic gluten-free for a while, eliminating all dairy, cheeses, sugars, processed grains, and meats. I also bought a juicer and a water ionizer to balance my pH and optimize the nutrients going into my body. With all this going on, there wasn't much wiggle room. I was giving it everything I had, with every ounce of my *Soul*.

When the weekends rolled around, my body felt like silly putty. I ached and burned in ways I didn't even know was possible. No matter how uncomfortable I was, I insisted that it was better than feeling nothing, and I shrugged it off as progress. Someone in their right mind would relax and recover. I needed more out of life, so I did things to keep my mind off my paralyzed body. Sitting around gave me cabin fever. I was so used to going all the time that I felt I was doing myself a disservice by sitting around. When football wasn't on TV, I was out and about. Sometimes I would run into old friends, and they would say, "It's great to see you out." What the hell was that supposed to mean? I think people just got nervous around me, and their brain would malfunction, causing stupid shit to come tumbling out of their mouth. I would just brush it off and make a joke. I'd say, "I'm the worst paralyzed guy ever. I can't move my body, but I continue to have trouble sitting still."

The weekends began to present a new challenge that I wasn't quite prepared for. The "warm Heineken, strawberry shortcake" girl turned my whole perspective inside out. She had a flare for *Life* that I had never seen before. She sat in funny positions on the counter or on the floor and didn't seem to care what anybody thought about it. This tiny girl walked around with the confidence of an Olympic weight lifter. She was like a Little Chicken that scurried about without a care in the world, all bright-eyed and bushy-tailed. It was as if the normal societal rules didn't apply to her, and even if they did, she didn't care. She was all about doing things her own way, and with that came a freedom that was uniquely refreshing. Every time I was around her, I felt like we were wasting time if we weren't doing something fun.

She would say, "You're too serious. You need to lighten up a bit and start living." Who was this "Little Chicken" woman, and where did she get off talking to me like that? I was Mr. Fun, and I took it upon myself to show her I meant business. Every weekend when she came through, I felt obligated to show her a good time. When I did, the wheelchair became transparent, and I started to feel the warmth of the sun again. When the Butterfly flew away, I thought intimacy had failed me for the last time. My heart was shattered, and I couldn't conceive of how someone could make me want to open myself up again. All of a sudden, something was happening inside of me that was like a wildfire that had gone completely out of control.

I kept it cool though, and stayed witty about our "professional relationship." One weekend, our Sunday exploits involved meeting up with my *Family* for a Mother's Day brunch. My *Grandmother*, who was sitting across from me, saw a spark in my eye that was all too familiar. Mummum had initiated her transition toward the *Light* and spent most of her time these days off the reservation. Early signs of dementia had her waving in and out of lucid consciousness for months, offering vague moments of clarity that were few and far between. It was quite a surprise when she leaned across the table, looked me directly in the eyes, and said, "You really like this girl, don't you?"

Everything about that moment blew my mind. My *Grandma* was more connected to what was going on than I was. My process of letting go of the life I once had was standing directly in the way of growing into the *Life* I was currently *Living*. I was so afraid of the terrors that might happen that I wasn't *Aware* of what was going on right in front of me. There were other girls that I was interested in, but none that made me want to give my best effort at being *Vulnerable*. Everything that I loved before was a mirage, and my broken heart was somewhere under a pile of ashes. I didn't have any idea where to begin, but the Little Chicken saw me for who I truly was. I wasn't ready, but who ever is? What does *ready* mean anyway? I couldn't have dreamed up a better place to start. Mother's Day brunch is the day the chase began.

There were things that I did, but nothing that I really wanted. I had an ultimate goal of walking, but that was so I could get back to what I thought was normal. My brain was programmed to chase an *Illusion* and even the act of being able-bodied fit that framework. What I really wanted was to be *Happy*. Since my previous blueprint to achieve such a state was littered with cultural stereotypes, I was cosmically motivated to start with a blank slate. Because of this, I had trouble identifying what was in front of me. What does a *Friend* look like? Where does *Value* exist in everyday life? What does it feel like to *Love* something? Where is the *Purpose* in all this?

I read some incredible books and watched a bunch of thought-provoking documentaries and seminars. But *Living* the principles outlined in all these theories was a completely different ballgame. My *Dad* taught me that half of *Life* is showing up, the other half was what you did when you got there. I had been showing up from the moment I opened my eyes in the hospital. I kept pushing even when I didn't want to. In my opinion, that was showing up. Now I had to figure out what I was going to do, and I found a great place to start.

I'm not a solo rider. I'm a team player. In order to be a *Leader*, I needed a worthy cause to play for. *Unconditional Love* was something that was woven into the fabric of who I was. It wasn't always easy, but nothing worth a damn ever really is. For me to continue to achieve, it was important for me to fulfill a significant *Need* in my *Life*. That *Need* was the pursuit of *Happiness*. At some point, that meant finding a Co-heart in crime that could help me hold down the fort. As Peter Pan, I needed to find my Tinker Bell. She would need to be punk rock though because shit got real in Never Never Land the minute I turned in my green tights and pointy hat for a wheelchair and mini-van with an electric ramp.

The Little Chicken and I had developed a *Soulful Friendship* from the beginning. All our cards were on the table from the moment we met. Things were always honest and straightforward as we both wore our emotions on our sleeve. We laughed and talked for hours with no judgment or expectation. It was the most straightforward relationship I had ever been a part of. This meant before I got thrown into the buddy category, I needed to shake things up a bit. Women are complicated, but there are a few solids that pretty much apply across the board. The minute you let things get boring, it's dunzo.

It was important that I didn't violate the *Friendship*, but I needed to turn up the heat a bit to test the water. There was a little gym hottie that I had been talking to for a few weeks that invited me to her birthday party. She was an actress-singer type that taught Pilates at one of the places I worked out at. She wasn't really my flavor, but she looked good in yoga pants, which worked for my devious little scheme. Since the party was on a Saturday, I needed someone to take me, so I asked the Chicken if she minded escorting me to the get-together.

I had a general idea of what to expect from the actress, but I was really interested in how the Chicken would respond to the whole situation. We made our way to a rooftop bar that overlooked the Pacific Ocean during sunset. I ordered a couple of beers and grabbed a table next to the packed party table. When the actress noticed that I showed up with a girl and sat at the table next to hers, she was miffed. When I didn't make a scene to greet her like a little princess, she chose to ignore me and pretend I wasn't there. I enjoyed the sunset and casually finished my beer.

The Little Chicken was the coolest cat in the whole bar. Nothing about her demeanor changed a lick. When I asked her if she wanted another beer, she said, "Nah, I'm good. This chick is lame. How much longer are you going to put up with her temper tantrum? Let's bail on this place and go get some tacos." The Little One just continued to impress me. The time had come to expose her to my most valuable asset.

My *Family* is definitely an acquired taste. Our social interactions with each other can come off as lewd and inappropriate if you don't understand our personalities. Whenever a new girl is invited over for Sunday dinner, all the Lost Boys have their own way of qualifying a new personality. The running joke is that dinner with the *Family* is like being thrown into a snake pit. If they can survive the heat, it meant they were worthy of being in our sacred circle. Our home was our sanctuary from the rest of the world. We are all loud, quirky, and different. Being normal was a hustle when dealing with the way society expected us to act. When we were together, we might fight, argue, cuss, or blow things out of proportion; but at the end of the day, we *Loved* each other. In a strange dysfunctional way, it felt safe when we were all together. There was no such thing as perfection in Never Never Land. There was always gossip and trash talk, but our core value system led us back to each other. It is the most pure, unconditional thing we have ever known, and no matter what happens, it's something we always depend on.

It's usually not chaos right out of the gate. During the first "act," everyone holds it together to feel things out a bit. As the table is set and the food starts to come out, it's like a calm before the storm. Everyone is nice and cordial to give the impression that we are a normal blue collar family. Usually, after we say a prayer, in come the sex jokes and curse words. The Little Chicken wasn't briefed on the rules, and even if she was, it wouldn't have mattered.

The baked potatoes were served right out of the oven, and approximately ten of them were sitting on a plate in the middle of the table. The Chicken wasn't at all fooled by everyone's best behavior. Since the banter had yet to begin, she chose to take advantage of everyone's guard being down. She casually slipped her butter knife into one of the scalding hot potatoes and left it there for about thirty seconds. One of my *Brothers* seated to her left reached across the table to grab a piece of bread. When his arm was extended, the Chicken seized the opportunity. She swiftly removed the knife from the potato and gently pressed it against the inside of his arm near his armpit. He howled like a dog at the mail man. After feverishly checking his arm for a nonexistent burn, he looked at me and said, "You might have found yourself a keeper."

As the weeks passed, I started to notice subtle changes in the Little Chicken's behavior. She suddenly stopped hugging me at the end of the weekend and instead just bolted out the door. Our playful text messages during the week turned into phone calls that had nothing to do with "work." Soon after, the Sunday dinner snake pit experience, she said she couldn't accept my money anymore for helping out. My response was, "That's fine. We will just spend it on the fun things we do together when you come over on the weekends. But unfortunately, I can't let you go."

We never had a boss-employee relationship. During the interview, it was agreed upon that we were both in a position where we needed a little assistance. She was a single *Mother* that got married extremely young to a guy that she just wasn't compatible with. Years after the divorce, she moved in with a different guy that offered a stable home where she could focus on work and *Family*. After five years of living together, she realized that he, too, wasn't "the one." The bells and whistles of a complicated breakup included cosigning on major amenities that involved cars and a house. When she was back to being a single *Mother* of two kids, the expenses were overwhelming. Since it felt weird to consider this attractive young lady my employee, we decided to call it a working relationship instead of a job. I needed someone to hang out with on the weekends, and she needed help with bills until things settled down during her transition.

When things started getting serious, I found myself in an awkward situation. I was always confident in my ability to generate an interesting chase, but I had no idea how to close this one out. For example, when I saw the opportunity to go in for our first kiss, I totally froze. I was in uncharted waters. I felt like I was in junior high school behind the bleachers. Maybe if I had the ability to sweat, my palms would have been clammy. I had no idea what to do, and I panicked. I started doing stupid boy things, like continuing to stimulate other female interests. That's when I got the disclaimer. The Little Chicken was honest and direct as usual. She said, "Look, I really like you, but I'm not playing around. I've got two kids, and I don't have time for nonsense. Your either all-in, or I'm out."

I wasn't just physically broken, I was an emotional mess. In sports, I learned to disguise my weaknesses by focusing my strategy on another elements of the game. With this injury, it was a lot of the same, and I had pretty much everyone fooled into thinking that I was all right. I wasn't ready for all this, but honestly, when is anyone ever really ready? I liked a good challenge, but I was in way over my head. In the areas that I lacked the ability to take charge, the Chicken just took over. Our first kiss was pretty much an ambush. She knew it was right, so she took it upon herself to just get that out of the way. When it came to sex, I was a deer in headlights as well. One night the Chicken just got us both naked and said, "Let's find out what still works."

I was scared, man; this was a whole new level of being *Vulnerable*. Intimacy was another aspect of the *Illusion* that I had trouble letting go of. I made it tough for the Little Chicken because I was still trying to force things that were out of my control. The pursuit for answers that no longer had relevance to my current plot in life was enough to push any normal person away. Lucky for me, the Chicken wasn't normal. She saw something *Great* in me that not even I was ready to accept. She taught me what *Greatness* is all about by showing me the raw power of *Unconditional Faith*.

Faith is an interesting concept. Most of the time, it is attached to the idea of religion. The way religion is practiced often complicates the essence of what *Faith* truly is. *Unconditional Love* is at the core of what every religious denomination is built upon. Seeing the world for the true wonder of what creation intends to offer is the *Sacred Essence* that all the sages, avatars, saints, gurus, and saviors are trying to communicate to us all. Our inability to see the *Light* in all things is a product of endless distractions that continue to make this simple concept so elusive to humanity.

The Little Chicken saw *Me* for who I was. She saw past all the details that stood in the way of what she knew I could be. The *Strength* it took for her to be *Patient* had to have come from a *Higher* place. At times, I didn't deserve her efforts, but she had an *Unconditional, Unwavering Faith* that beyond all things I was worthy of her *Love*.

Many people saw my strength and determination as some extraordinary thing. The reason I kept pushing is because I *Believed* deep down there was a *Divine* plan behind all the details. I always had *Faith* in a *Higher Purpose* even when I didn't have faith in myself. This warm-Heineken-lovin', strawberry-shortcake-eating Little Chicken was living proof that this plan is very real. The truth is she showed me what *Strength* and *Determination* is really all about.

Together, we began to test the limits of what was possible. The culture that surrounded quadriplegia taught me to accept a limited perspective. There is a lot of discomfort associated with living in a seated position with limited movement. There were very real physical dilemmas that needed to be accounted for that complicate pretty much everything. Because of this, I chose not to venture too far away from what made me comfortable. The Little Chicken wasn't down to put up with limitations that stood in the way of us maximizing our potential.

Simple stuff like close proximity to a hospital and doctors kept me from traveling outside my comfort zone. A bulky shower chair and medical devices like my reclining bed and breathing machine were excuses that I used to justify not leaving my little bubble. The Chicken had a few tricks up her sleeve for this kind of stuff. Since she saw the adventurer in *Me*, she catered to experiences that I couldn't pass up.

She started soft by keepin' it local. It was her way of developing a trustworthy rapport by showing *Empathy* toward my hesitations. She worked long hours as a dental assistant during the week, but it never got in the way of being a good *Mother* or having fun. On a numerous occasions, she took one for the team, and after working all day, we would travel hours to see a concert or comedy show. She was like a finely tuned machine that never skipped a beat. I developed a significant *Respect* for her soldier-like qualities and never doubted when she said we could pull something off.

As our *Love* and *Trust* for each other grew, she ran some shifty little hustles that got me to push my limits. Her intentions were always pure, but she was determined to break the tentative mold of precautionary living that I had grown accustom to. She knew that if my adventurous spirit wanted to pursue an epic version of *Happiness*, it was going to take some creative maneuvering. When the timing was right, her first saucy deployment was a birthday road trip to see the Dalai Lama speak. But there was a catch. It was at Stanford University in Northern California, which was a ten-hour drive from my little comfort bubble. The entire trip was a five-day expedition that had numerous surprises planned along the way. I hadn't been away from home for more than two days since I left the hospital. This voyage was a calculated assault toward bulldozing the walls that had been suffocating my potential.

The Chicken made surrendering to the unknown a no-brainer decision. Making things happen became an *Opportunity* to *Live* beyond the anxiety of what might be, by offering myself to the moment. The gift the universe had in place for us was equally as magnificent. It just so happened that the focus of the Dalai Lama's lecture emphasized giving into *What Is* to get the most out of *Life*. Following the presentation, we experienced the manmade beauty of the Golden Gate Bridge; juxtaposed symbiotically with the natural wonder of the Redwood Forest. That evening, we had an incredible dinner at the Fisherman's Wharf overlooking the San Francisco Bay and went for a tour the next morning of the abandoned jail on Alcatraz Island. I connected with the pain of imprisonment during the crusade and realized that just like the empty cells, the idea that I needed to suffer was now a thing of the past. We concluded the trip with a breathtaking sunset suspended hundreds of feet above the ocean as we drove down the winding cliffs of the Pacific Coast Highway.

Opportunity

H ome was a relative term when it came to having a roof over my head. I got lucky when I was discharged from the hospital because I had a single-level accessible place to go home to, thanks to my *Grandpa*. When his journey on this earth came to an end, my uncles decided to sell the estate. Finding somewhere to stay was no easy task. This was the first time I had run into real-world accessibility issues. I didn't have the finances to afford my own place, nor did I have enough money to renovate my parents' house to make it suitable for wheelchair living. Instead of letting fear and stress dominate my emotional well-being, I prayed for a solution to present itself. Getting out of my own way is something I struggled with, but the demand of necessity can often be an incredible teacher.

My *Dad* was representing a new client in a lawsuit. After discussing the case, they decided to go to lunch. When my name came up, Pops told him I was trying to pull together a wellness clinic, which became a topic of interest to his client. His friend had a nonprofit organization that might be interested in the project I was working on. About a week later, I met with the founder of the nonprofit for breakfast. We hit it off and exchanged stories as if we were old friends. He is an extremely successful businessman that made his fortune through hard work and dedication. He was interested in the project but seemed more focused on my recovery and well-being. When I explained to him my current dilemma with housing, he came up with a two-headed solution.

The serendipitous chain of events reminded me of one of my favorite Coen Brothers' films from the nineties called *The Big Lebowski*. The movie is about how through a random string of notably unlucky events, an average guy finds himself in a situation that is well above his pay grade. The Dude, played by Jeff Bridges, is in an impossible scenario that never would have happened had his life not been shaken up by events that were completely out of his control. A wealthy gentleman referred to as the Big Lebowski comes into his life and changes everything about the way the Dude understands things.

Before this breakfast, I was the Dude. Then out of nowhere, this stranger comes in like a knight in shining armor and saves the day. The Big Lebowski's foundation was dedicated to assisting people with special needs due to unforeseen circumstances. He answered my prayers by solving the most immediate problem of not having a place to stay. In order to create a platform for success, he understood that I first must take care of some basic needs. His second idea was to put me in touch with an extremely gifted homeopathic chiropractor that specialized in neurology.

Once the need for a roof over my head was handled, I went to see the wellness doc. He was no ordinary chiropractor. I was given all kinds of different tests, most of which required no medical devices at all. His advanced studies of the neurological system had him looking for things and testing places that no other medical examiner had bothered to consider. There were no blood draws or pin pricks followed by hours of waiting, and everything we did had some functional component to it. He did ask to see the X-rays and MRI scans in my medical file but didn't seem to spend much time laboring over them. At the end of the exam, he said he would like to try to help but couldn't promise anything. I liked his confidence because he kept it real regarding expectation but left room for *Hope*.

We spent months together trying out different protocols. There was never one approach that he leaned on more than another. Years of advanced research and technical application guided his efforts at trying to rewire my damaged nervous system. He had been using medical grade laser therapy for decades in his practice and was excited about the potential it had to stimulate nerve growth. When we started to see systematic activation below my level of injury, the potential got pretty exciting.

I reported back to the Big Lebowski about the tremendous opportunity that was upon us. I spent years trying to heal my body, and it looked as though all the pieces were coming together. The search to fix myself had revealed some incredible findings, and I was eager to make sense of it all. During our next breakfast meeting, I presented Lebowski with a business treatment. The proposal suggested a facility that offered all the healing modalities from which I had received benefit.

He was impressed by my enthusiasm but explained that he was not familiar with the medical industry. The facility that I was suggesting was a monster project. Since I had no business experience in the medical industry, it would be a huge risk to invest in a project of this nature. He said it was as if I was a bridge builder asking for financing to construct the Golden Gate Bridge as my first project. Since he saw merit in my efforts, he agreed to look into it and get back to me.

The next meeting took place in a board room with attorneys and multiple business associates, but no Lebowski. A considerable amount of legal research had taken place, and there were now details about how things could be accomplished. Since I didn't have a degree to practice medicine, I could not own a business where medicine was practiced. If I were to own a business that collected fees from a coordinated group of doctors, I would be operating similar to an insurance company, and that was illegal. I was informed that the only way I could participate in a business similar to the one I wanted to create was if a licensed practitioner were to own it, and I worked for them.

After spending years trying to make this business concept happen, it now seemed to make sense why I was having trouble pulling it off. The solution seemed simple. It was just a matter of jumping through the right hoops to get things going. The holistic chiropractor was by far the most knowledgeable practitioner I had ever worked with. Not only was his understanding of the nervous system out of this world, he emphasized the importance of supplementing the body with multiple avenues of *Wellness*.

My experience with rehabilitation was that it wasn't one thing that paved the way to *Wellness*. There were many avenues that lead to finding *Balance* on a healing continuum. Each person's journey was *Different*, and every condition deserved a customized approach. In order to do this, it was important to have a few staples in place when it came to knowing where to start. The Chiro Doc built his business on these principles. The freedom to practice the type of *Healing* he *Believed* in was the reason he chose chiropractic care over traditional Western medicine. His practice focused on diagnosing and treating the root of what created disharmony in the body. Dis-ease was a byproduct of mental, emotional, and physical imbalances in people's lifestyle. On paper, he was the perfect person to build this concept around.

I met with the Chiro Doc and explained to him the multimodality, multipractitioner idea that I had in mind. He said it sounded like a great idea, but unfortunately, it just wasn't for him. He spent years growing a successful practice as a solo practitioner. The idea of multiple healing professionals consulting synergistically was too many moving parts for him. In order to play the role I was suggesting, it meant that his license would be liable to those working under him. I wasn't only proposing a risky investment; I was now also asking someone to put his livelihood as a practitioner on the line.

The Big Lebowski and Chiro Doc *Believed* in me so they got together and came up with a plan. The following week, I met with the lawyers again, and they told me how everyone was willing to participate. The Chiro Doc was in favor of expanding his research related to how laser therapy could stimulate nerve growth in spinal cord injuries. The plan enabled him to continue his wellness practice while serving as the director of a spinal cord research project on the side. His protocols had shown so much promise that the Big Lebowski was willing to fund the project. If I was willing to help, they would find a place for me at the facility and cover the cost of my therapy. My job would be to find clients interested in receiving experimental therapy sessions paid for by the foundation. I would also work as an advocate liaison between the patient, the Chiro Doc, and the foundation.

Something about this didn't feel right, but I was so used to forcing things that I didn't know how to respond. Lebowski made a good point when he brought up my inexperience in the medical field. It would be silly to think I could start this business without help. Maybe this was just a different version of what I wanted to create in an unfamiliar package. All Peter Pan saw were pirates. I told the pirate lawyer that the Chiro Doc wasn't the right guy for my master plan. He told me the master plan wasn't what was on the table. He was like, "Look, Dude, if you want to work with Lebowski, you need to start with the one practitioner and modality that shows promise. If things go well, there could be more opportunities down the line."

Since my understanding of the American Dream was pretty much out, I now wanted to pursue a life of *Happiness*. After spending more than six years trying make lemonade out of grapefruit, I just wanted to create something special. I had friends that graduated from college, got jobs, found significant others, bought houses, and started families. I felt like life was passing me by. If I were to pass on the offer from the Big Lebowski, my other option was to get a normal job just like the rest of the civilized world.

Even with an able body, a traditional nine-to-five gig would have been purgatory for my personality type. It seemed futile to attempt it as a quadriplegic. I was so physically uncomfortable all the time, I couldn't imagine adding the stress of meeting quotas as I climbed a corporate ladder. Being an old guy in the rookie bullpen, with an assistant as my hands and feet, just wasn't a recipe for success. On top of this, I developed a certain perspective that changed the way I understood *Life*. Cars, status, money, and "things" had lost their sparkle to me. I wanted to *Help* people and offer significance with the *Knowledge* I acquired. This was somewhat problematic as my experience appeared a bit suspect on a traditional resume.

"Dear future employer. My name is Peter Pan, and I broke my neck six years ago. I no longer have the ability to fly, or move at all for that matter, and I have become surrounded by pirates. I don't understand the current reality I'm drowning in because my earlier perception of life was merely an *Illusion*. I have a degree but no work experience, and I think everyone takes life a bit too seriously. When

I was in the hospital, I saw a *Light* that told me to pursue *Purpose* by *Being* an example of *Oneness*. I'm nowhere near qualified enough to apply for this position, but I look forward to hearing back from you."

One thing that was trending in the right direction is the relationship with the Little Chicken. It was the first relationship I had been in that started as a *Friendship* with no expectations from the beginning. It had grown into something special, and we really started to lean on each other for *Strength*. We spent pretty much all our free time together, and it seemed crazy to live hours apart. She lived two counties over and commuted hours back and forth to work every day. When we decided to consider moving in together, a new adventure presented itself.

The Little Chicken had two kids from her previous marriage, one girl and one boy. She had always lived with both, but as the boy approached his teens, he wanted to move in with his dad. This set the stage for the next episode of the courtship between the Little Chicken and me. The potential of moving in with TWO girls was a marvel that made my heart skip a beat. The only previous experience I had living with multiple women was in college with the pretty little alley kitties. This time, the circumstances were much different. I had no idea what to expect with an incoming high school sophomore.

The Little Chicken's daughter could be loosely described as a teenage punk rock princess. Now when I say princess, it's important that a distinction is made. She wasn't the tacky multi-colored-hair, sparkly-fingernail type of princess. She was a grunge-rock, Black Flag, Misfits type of music princess that loved the movies *Titanic* and *The Little Mermaid*. Since even referring to her as a princess would get me cast off into a gothic hole of blistering death, I will refer to her as the PRP moving forward. Being merely "Mom's new boyfriend," I felt it was important to have a sit-down with this young lady before any decisions were made. I said, "Look, girl, I have no idea how to be a father as I still have a lot of growing up to do myself. I also have zero experience understanding the emotions of a teenage girl, so I'm going to need your help with this one. Since you already have a dad, how about I offer you a deal. If you're cool moving in with your *Mom* and me, I'll do my best to be an understanding grown-up who can offer advice from time to time. In return, I ask of you to be patient with me as I learn the ropes of female adolescence. The only way I'm willing to move forward with this living arrangement is with your blessing."

The PRP was pretty open to the idea and agreed to join the crazy train. She turned out to be an extremely low-maintenance teenager. So much so that at one point I thought something was wrong. On the weekends, she just wanted to hang out with the Chicken and me. She was comfortable just watching movies and reading books. She had a few friends she would hang with, but for the most part, she liked laying low.

I asked her one weekend, "What gives? Teenagers should push the limits and get into at least a little bit of trouble. What about prom, parties, and boys?"

She said, "So what you're asking me is why I'm not drinking and doing drugs like all the other idiots my age. Maybe I should go to a party and make some bad decisions. Get in a car with a bunch of intoxicated, inexperienced drivers. Then there's always date rape. Maybe I should consider some of that action."

Wow! What was I supposed to say to that? She just wanted to hurry up and graduate so she could enlist in the military to serve her country. My biggest challenge was talking her into giving each branch of the armed forces equal consideration. She wanted to be on the front line of the Army Rangers. The spoken word of her idol Henry Rollins had her all pumped up on being machine-gun Mary storming the bunkers of Pakistan. After careful consideration of all the branches, she ended up signing a six-year contract with the US Navy.

When I was young, I planned on having children early so I could enjoy them growing up. I thought it would be cool to participate in their upbringing with my original set of teeth. As they matured into adults, I wanted to have more to offer them than prunes and butterscotch candies. It brought me great sadness to think it might not happen because of my injury. I had so much fun being an older *Brother* that the idea of children was a big deal to me. When things didn't pan out the way I wanted, I thought I might never experience the joy of being a parent.

The mysteries of the unknown continued to baffle me. When the PRP graduated from high school, I sat in the stands with a sense of deep appreciation to have played a small part in her life. When she enlisted in the Navy, I was sad that our time together had come to an end. It wasn't until I had to let go of this little girl I had grown to *Love* that I truly understood how much she meant to me. When I was invited into her confusing teenage existence, I had no idea it would be fulfilling one of my lifelong *Dreams*. Offering significant influence to a young budding *Soul* is one of the greatest gifts I have ever been a part of.

The PRP's first real-world adventure came in the form of military boot camp in Chicago. When she was scheduled to graduate, another *Opportunity* to grow was upon me. This time, it involved a four-hour plane flight in the dead of winter. When we arrived in Chicago, it was during one of the largest snowstorms of the season. The youngest Lost Boy in my *Family* traveled with us as the trip's muscle. He and the PRP were close in age and had developed a special *Friendship*. Her accomplishment was special to him in a variety of ways, and this trip offered the likelihood of *Growth* in his *Life* as well.

As the leader of the Lost Boys, I carried the rally flag growing up. When I needed help, the flag was passed to a boy that wasn't quite ready for it. It created a distorted learning curve for the youngest kid in Never Never Land, turning normal fears into monumental obstacles. Anxiety rattled his bones when an unfamiliar environment couldn't be manipulated. Airplanes and snowstorms were foreign concepts that were outside of his comfort zone. When the idea of control was out of reach, everything in his world was turned upside down.

This crusade presented a complicated algorithm of emotions. The *Life* hack necessary for success demanded *Strength* and *Patience*. Navigating a buffet of psychological complexities was the next phase of my Jedi training. The first time I left my comfort bubble, the Little Chicken acted as a Sherpa, guiding me on a journey where the elements were methodically plotted out. This adventure had a handful of wild cards that demanded I pull more of my own weight. I had an *Opportunity* to recapture the rally flag with a new set of tools that I had acquired with my seated perspective. As much as I didn't want to be experiencing these moments in a wheelchair, I had the chance to resume my role as a *Leader* if I chose to accept the *Challenge*.

I was excited to celebrate the PRP's achievement. Being a part of her success was an incredible feeling, but my role on this expedition was multifaceted. The Little Chicken deserved the right to be a proud *Mother* as her years of pristine *Parenting* were also being rewarded. There was no room for comfort bubble anxiety on my behalf during this campaign. The moment was too important, and I had many areas to focus my strategic attention. My *Brother* was on a mission to offer assistance as my hands and feet but needed direction navigating his fears. Adding value as a *Leader* became my priority, and in doing so, I found a part of *Myself* that had been stagnant for far too long.

Another wild card presented itself on this trip in the addition of another Lost Boy. PRP's father was born in Germany and came to the land of milk and honey as a teenager with his mother. The motorcycle enthusiast was tattooed from head to toe; and with his slicked-back hair, leather jacket, and Chuck Taylor All-Star shoes, he looked the part of a fairly intimidating fella. I only met him a few times previous to this trip because he pretty much kept to himself. He was an important piece to the PRP's puzzle that completed a complex circle she spent most of her life trying to understand. By showing up to her most significant experience to date, her father defined character that revealed potential for future growth.

Axel the Biker is a kind, goofy soul whose quirkiness can be incredibly endearing. The love he has for his family shows up in ways that are often difficult to comprehend. Young love paved the way toward impulsive desires that made it complicated for him to figure out who he was. When children were added to the picture, finding his identity became damn near impossible. Axel fell victim to this common trend and spent years trying to catch up. Once he made sense of the whole ordeal, life had gotten ahead of him. The progression of his coming to *Be* violated the expectations of what it meant to be a father. In the process, hearts were unintentionally broken. All efforts to make things right fell short, and his profound sadness stood in the way of coming up with a solution. I really enjoy the guy. The love he has for his family was obvious to me. Not everyone is equipped with the tools to handle the emotional dramas they find themselves in, but I can appreciate someone who continues to try even when they fall short of others' expectations.

The odyssey to get to the graduation ceremony was no easy task. The frigid cold had my nervous system locked up like an engine with no oil. My muscles resembled frozen rubber bands, and my bones pushed against my skin like the legs of a wooden chair on a marble floor. I would say my body was in extreme pain, but my brain was too frozen to remember. The trip was a textbook definition of Murphy's Law as everything that could go wrong did. Our luggage was lost along with all our medical supplies. They found it a day later after my *Brother* and I attempted to shower in a non-accessible bathroom. Our efforts ended us up having to spend an hour ankle-deep in human feces. We got lost on our way to the Navy shipyard, forgot our money at the hotel so we couldn't eat, and slid through an intersection at a red light because the snow was so thick on the road.

While the Little Chicken focused on supporting the PRP during her emotional roller coaster, my *Brother* and Axel the Biker teamed up to help keep my wheels on. My focus was on controlling the energy surrounding everyone's efforts. As tense as things got, I was the one the guys looked to for guidance. Even though the reason for us being there was the PRP, the Lost Boys were ultrasensitive to my needs. The *Compassion* that went into making sure I was comfortable was a hallmark moment in defining the character of everyone involved. When the chips are down, people's true colors shine through. I found myself feeling incredibly *Grateful* to be in a position to receive such *Love*.

The platform to create *Value* during one of *Life's* surreal fleeting moments had a backdrop resembling a white Christmas. Delicate snowflakes gingerly fell to the ground as families corralled into a frozen airplane hangar to view the graduation ceremony. When the moment came for the PRP's unit to be recognized, time seemed to stand still. Her initiation into becoming an official member of the military also signified a triumph of my own awakening. The universe was providing abundantly, and I was just now figuring out how to receive the *Gifts* it had in store for me. I, too, felt as though I was being initiated into the *Life* I was meant to *Live*.

It's difficult to put into words how proud I was to be a part of the PRP's achievement. She was a soldier in so many more ways than rank and a uniform could possible show. As we celebrated with some of the finest pizza Chicago had to offer, I looked around the room and saw the magnificent perfection that creation was revealing. So much had to happen to manifest the reality I was seeing at this round-table tribute. It involved broken pieces of a marriage, mutated upbringings, disillusioned expectations, and fragmented values to merge in that very moment to equal *Happiness*. The best storyteller on the planet couldn't script a moment this perfect. *The Divine Plan* was present in every detail. All the complexity had come together to create a space for us all to *Learn*.

There were many distractions that clouded my perspective on how I previously understood my life. The project with the Big Lebowski and the Chiro Doc had gone south because of expectations that I had for it. I saw so much potential, but when a narrow focus was applied toward fulfilling the needs of the program, I got frustrated. The Little Chicken was working as the Chiro Doc's front office coordinator, and when she got laid off during the holiday season, I decided to move away from the project completely.

The entire scenario taught me to look at the *Core Values* that surround a situation and not the details. At some point after the Chicago trip and before moving on from the project, I had the best idea of my *Life*. I realized that a huge part of what I needed to complete my *Happiness* equation was right in front of me. Details can often make what matters in *Life* quite elusive, and I had fallen victim to this deception before. Every once in a while, though, something huge comes into the picture that requires immediate action. Regret is *Happiness's* ugly cousin, and I wasn't about to invite that shit back into my existence. It was time to cook up a plan that would invite

Value and *Grace* into every decision I would make for the rest of my days.

The Little Chicken is a bit of an intuitive sage that receives guidance from a variety of unconventional sources. A reliable psychic mentor told her that November 11, 2011, would be one of the most significant and memorable days of her *Life*. When I decided to ask her to marry me, it seemed fitting that my creative efforts should aim to rally around that day. Everything about our relationship was *Different* from the status quo. Thinking outside the box was often difficult because I rolled around in one, but that's not what the Little Chicken saw when she looked at *Me*. It was my turn to create a moment in time that reflected how much I *Appreciated* her *Love*.

About a year before, when our relationship was still growing, we were sitting in bed together on Thanksgiving night. Since I had been injured, my *Family* and *Friends* had coordinated an annual flag football tournament to raise money for the monumental costs associated with quadriplegic living, and it took place the morning after Thanksgiving. Each tournament raised less money with fewer teams participating every year. At this point, my efforts were being scrutinized, and my support team was growing tired. Before every tournament, I would start the day off with a morning prayer. I would follow it with a speech that honored all those in attendance to express my *Gratitude*.

I had reached a point where my physical progress had plateaued. I had little to report to an eager crowd of onlookers, and I was stressed that my life wasn't where I wanted it to be. I was having trouble understanding why people continued to support me when everyone's expectations of what should be happening with my recovery were not being met. I thought I would be walking by now. My plans were to overcome my disability, then turn the fundraiser into an event that could help other people.

When I expressed my thoughts to the Little Chicken, her response caught me by surprise. I wasn't ready to hold myself responsible for the magnitude of *Value* behind her words. She said, "People keep showing up to support you because they *Love* and *Believe* in you. They are not frustrated by the fact that you're not walking, they're confused because they don't understand what's taking so long for you to access the *Greatness* within you. Just let go of what you think you should be, and get on with *Being* the person they know you already are. Show them the person I know you already are."

I had a tough time sleeping that night. It wasn't because I didn't know what I would say, it's because she was right and I knew it. *Believing* in *Myself* meant that instead of just talking about the idea that there was no such thing as an accident, I had to start *Living* like I *Believed* it. I said a prayer, thanking God for all the wonderful things I had in my life, including the Little Chicken. Before I went to sleep, I asked again for an undeniable *Sign* that there was *Purpose* and *Truth* behind all this. I asked the great Creator of all existence to bring forth an example that would confirm I was still on the right *Path*.

The next morning, I showed up. I thanked all those in attendance for *Believing* in me, gave my speech, and closed it with a prayer to kick off the tournament. The *Loving* response of all those in attendance came in the form of a standing ovation with many tear-filled eyes. They then followed with a long hard day of competitive football. After the speech, I made my way to the concession stand for some coffee and a doughnut.

While I was sitting there, enjoying my coffee, reflecting on how *Grateful* I was to be in a position to receive such *Love*, a miracle walked right up to me and introduced herself. It was a little bald girl that wanted to know if I was the man all these people were doing the fundraiser for. I told her yes, and we struck up a conversation. She was only about nine years old with pale white skin and beads of sweat glistening across her forehead.

"Did you have a nice Thanksgiving?" I asked.

"Not really. I'm very sick, and I'm on a bunch of special medications. The doctors said that it wouldn't be a good idea for me to be around too many people," she said.

"You sure are a brave girl. There's a bunch of dirty, sweaty boys here playing football. Why did you decide to come to this fundraiser when you couldn't even see your family on Thanksgiving?" I asked rather curiously.

"My *Daddy* read me the article in the newspaper about how you *Believe* in *Hope* and never give up. Since that's about the most inspirational thing I've ever heard, I made him bring me out here because I just had to meet you," she said.

Her *Dad* was to my left with tears rolling down his face. The Little Chicken was to my right, but when I turned to see her reaction, she had already dashed off. I continued to create small talk, so I didn't burst into tears myself, and before I knew it, the Little Chicken had come back with one of the fundraiser T-shirts we were selling at the concession stand. The girl pulled it over her tiny, frail body and fashioned it to her *Dad* as if she were accepting an Oscar. The *Father* then picked up his little girl in the oversized parachute of a T-shirt, thanked me, and took her home. After they faded into the distance, I was overwhelmed by a flood of emotions. I had been given another undeniable *Sign* that I was right where I needed to *Be*. This time, it came with the added bonus of *Knowing* who I needed to *Be* with.

As the first week in November came to a close, I was still trying to come up with the perfect play. It didn't look like getting down on one knee was the most whimsical option. It's not that I couldn't do it, I just wanted the moment to involve the two of us in an intimate way that was unique to our situation. Each day, from the moment we woke up in the morning until I was transferred to bed at night, I leaned on the help of other people to get things done. It seemed like the only time we were ever alone as a couple was during the evening when were in bed next to each other. We would always joke about how each day brought us such crazy adventures, but if there was one consistent thing that we both looked forward to, it was the moment we lay down next to each other in our bed. Suddenly *poof,* there it was. The answer was so simple. It was insightfully special to our unique bond created in the most unconventional manner.

On November 11, 2011, we were watching TV before going to bed much like any other random night. As we enjoyed the simple abundance of each other's company, I watched the clock tick down to the exact moment that I planned to make my move. Since movement was no longer my forte, the gesture I made physically was subtle. It was the single, most meaningful act of intention I have ever made.

At 11:11 PM I turned to look into the eyes of my *Best Friend*, the most incredible person I have ever met, and I asked her to marry me.

At first, she thought I was joking; but when she saw the look in my eyes, she knew it was real. I told her, "I have nothing to give you but *Myself*." No matter what happens in this *Life*, I can promise you always that I will be yours if you will have me. After she said yes, I explained there was more, but it was important she kept our little secret to herself. I also had a grand charade planned. It was a much bigger deal, but I wanted it to be a surprise. Once the bond regarding the intimate business was secure, I schemed with other key players to help make our dream become a reality.

The plan involved a slow play. I waited until the following year for the flag football fundraiser to come around. Since the Little Chicken was the spark that reignited my pilot *Light*, it seemed fitting to honor our bond where the collective energy could set ablaze a fire that would last our entire lifetime. Everybody that continued to show up to the event had fought the good fight with me for years. My *Faith*, *Family*, and *Friends* had carried me through my darkest hours. It was time for the *Greatness* that had been dormant in my bones to be shared with everyone that *Believed* it was always there.

The *Family* unit was notified a few days before to help get everything in order. Timing was crucial in Never Never Land because hot news was like a pot of boiling water. If you start cooking with it too soon, the food won't come out right. If it is left boiling for too long, it will bubble up in such a frenzy that hot water will spill all over the place. This magical moment was done just right. Everyone snuck around in the dark with extreme stealthy precision. When the moment of truth was upon us, everyone was locked and loaded. All the people that stuck around for the rolling credits of the action adventure, melodramatic feature that was my *Life* were there to see a peak moment of Shakespearian brilliance.

Abundance

At what would be the final flag football fundraiser for my personal benefit, I turned the spotlight to those in attendance. I brought attention to the idea that every donation made on my behalf over the years created something special that I never could have imagined. Each act of kindness, whether it was time, money, or prayers, had served a *Purpose* in my *Life*. I hadn't yet figured out what to do with my life, but I had a pretty good idea how to pursue *Happiness*. I would follow the example of *Unconditional Love* that was offered to me from the moment my unique set of circumstances was put into motion.

The number of people in attendance had dwindled over the years, but there were still hundreds of faces looking at me on the brisk Friday morning following Thanksgiving. After the prayer and speech, I turned to the Little Chicken and asked her to marry me, again. I still hadn't found anything special enough to seal our bond, so I used the only ring available to me at the time. Before addressing the crowd that morning, I peeled the edges off a glazed old-fashioned doughnut, leaving just the circle center. It was a metaphor for how special the moment was the year before when the miracle girl shared a few moments of her *Life* with us. It was also an example of how simple and unique the relationship I had with the Little Chicken was.

Our union was so genuine that the physical component of our *Love* was secondary to the way we felt about each other. Her agreeing to marry me with nothing but a doughnut hole was one small example of that. There would be a succession of many rings to follow, each offering significance in their own way. At the pizza party following the tournament, someone spent four quarters to buy a ring for us at a vending machine. A few hours later, the Little Chicken's son made a ring for us out of a two-dollar bill.

My *Mom* was appalled that the Little Chicken had no bling to show people she was engaged. About a week after the tournament, *Mom* bought her a sparkly little band for $100 so she had something to hold her over. I had no idea what to do about a serious solution for the wedding ring. I didn't have an abundance of extra cash lying around. I had *Faith* that it would all get figured out though. I conspired with the parental units at Never Never Land and came up with a truly special idea.

The *Family* had a jeweler friend that made custom pieces for my *Mom* and *Dad* in the past. For my parents' twenty-fifth wedding anniversary, Pops purchased a much larger diamond and mounted it on my *Mom's* wedding ring. This meant the original diamond from her wedding ring was free-floating in my *Parents'* safe along with a handful of old keepsake jewelry. The safe contained old gold pieces of my *Dad's*, *Mom's*, and both sets of *Grandparents*. My parents offered the unused jewelry to be melted down into a custom band to mount my *Mom's* original diamond. I didn't have much money, but I had a little something stashed away for a rainy day. The Little Chicken once showed me a picture of her dream ring, and I kept the photo just in case. Good thing I did, because the jeweler used the picture to craft a ring made from a combination of my entire *Family's* special keepsakes.

This wasn't the only time our marriage would stray from the traditions of the status quo. Since normal was a foreign concept to our relationship in general, we decided to engineer something that would have a lasting impression for everyone involved. The pressure of what a wedding is supposed to be often distracts the bride and groom from what they are there for in the first place. We both agreed that the ceremony between man, woman and God should be *Sacred* and honored accordingly. If it's done right, the moment when two people are brought together in *Holy Union* is meant to last a lifetime. The reception was something entirely different. It's a party where everyone has a chance to witness the fusion of two souls joined together in *Love*. In order to find balance with our time, budget, and craftiness, we decided to do the two celebrations of *Life* on different days.

We kept the ceremony small. Instead of leasing a massive hall for everyone to be bored to death at during our nuptials, we rented a suite overlooking the ocean at our favorite beachfront hotel. After the ceremony with only immediate *Family*, we took pictures and rolled down to a friend's Mexican restaurant next to the hotel. The intimate setting offered our *Families* an opportunity to get to know each other while munching on tacos and wedding cake. When dinner was over, we retreated to our oceanfront room and fell asleep to the sound of waves crashing on the sand.

We did the reception months later in a country club ballroom donated to us by an incredible new *Friend*. We had a plan to do the after party with a twist as well. Once we saved our *Friends* and extended *Family* from the inevitable dullness of another boring church precession, we came up with a fun concept. We weren't into the idea of sappy tear-filled speeches and drunken dancing that we had to do an adapted version of. Our plan to avoid the stereotypical programming of what a wedding reception should or should not be came in the form of standup comedy.

The entire wedding party did a road trip to Los Angles. Together, we took a one-day, fully intensive, standup comedy course to learn how to compose a routine. The structure of the reception was set up using the template of a celebrity roast. Once a year, Hollywood would throw a party for one of their notorious celebrities. A panel of their friends and colleagues would take turns blasting them with jokes before a final toast was given to honor the star's accomplishments. We loved the irony of a standup comedy reception for a couple that couldn't even stand up to exchange rings. With the cartoon personalities of Never Never Land along with the fragmented perfection of the Little Chicken's peeps, the night was sure to be a calculated mess of epic proportion.

A good amount of thought and planning went into how to we would pull it off. The food was simple but delicious, and alcohol was free-flowing to loosen up the guests for what they were about to participate in. Instead of a *Father/Daughter* and *Mother/Son* dance, the Chicken and I both presented poems to our *Family* chronicling the deep sense of *Gratitude* we shared with our *Loved Ones*. The evening's feature acts were the speeches of the wedding party roasting us with as much dirty laundry as they could recall from years past. After the Little Chicken and I gave our comedic rebuttal, we thanked everyone and closed out the evening with our favorite signature desserts. Instead of wedding cake, everyone got to choose between freshly baked pie or milk and cookies.

The night was sensational. The evening was decorated with laughter, drunken outbursts, crass language, tasteless jokes, and gangster rap. One of my *Brothers* even stripped down to his boxer shorts during his comedy routine. It was everything I could have dreamed of, smack dab in the middle of what most would consider a nightmare. Nothing seemed to work out the way I thought it would, but everything fell into place with a mystical sense of perfection. It was our version of *Perfect*, and we created it *Together*.

Dreams are funny things. We all have this idea about what we think will bring us the maximum level of happiness. Then when life unfolds in a way we are not comfortable with, we're quick to think that dreams don't come true. Maybe there's a reason why every dream doesn't come true. If they did, the creative freedom of the universe would be limited to the linear thinking of our free will. The whole nature of dreams is that they come and go. If one doesn't come true, maybe it's because it wasn't supposed to. If it did, it could very well stand in the way of something much *Greater* happening that reveals a deeper *Purpose*. Either way, I found the natural rhythm of *Life* teaching me secrets of the trade. The only way I could make sense of these secrets was by giving into the flow of the endless possibilities.

Since there were no legal documents drafted during our custom wedding experience, we weren't officially a married couple in the eyes of the Church and State. Traveling to a local courthouse to make it official wasn't our style, so we elected to scurry off to Las Vegas for a shotgun wedding on our first anniversary. After the ceremony and reception with *Family*, life returned to its natural state.

The months leading up to our anniversary were arduous, and we were battle tested. The caregiver carousel was rotating with impressively catastrophic vigor. A revolving door of convicts, emotionally damaged, and clinically unstable characters participated in our honeymoon year of being a newlywed couple. When the project with the Big Lebowski came to a halt, so did the funding for our housing. I always knew it was a temporary solution, but the way it came to a close forced me to reevaluate my goals and aspirations.

I had been rehabilitating an injury for almost ten years. I had been trying to create a multimodality wellness center for just over six years. The whole reason I wanted to recover and create a business to help people is so I could pursue a *Life of Happiness*. I now had a *Family* of my own with bills and responsibilities that extended beyond self-serving goals. I thought my *Purpose* would have something to do with my injury because it was such a dominating component of everyday life. It seemed to make logical sense to create a wellness business while rehabbing my injury at the same time. The problem with this train of thought is that the universe of endless possibilities doesn't always make logical sense. More times than not, it makes no rational sense at all.

My ideas of how life should be unfolding continued to stand in the way of possibilities that could be happening. Once I let go of the need to control things, a creative solution presented itself. Ultimately, the solution was often more desirable than my original idea. The limitation of not having a marriage license turned into another epic adventure with my *Best Friend* to Las Vegas. During our weekend pillage, we made a few huge decisions as a couple.

A three-day intermission from the pressures of reality's natural state gave us some time to review our current strategy toward *Living*. I wanted to walk, but it no longer dominated my way of thinking. I started to have *Different Thoughts, Better Thoughts*. Trying to force my will upon the Lebowski project was one of the biggest reasons it didn't work for us. My inability to let go had left us homeless and jobless. We were back to square one, and we needed to reevaluate everything. It didn't take us long to rally. The Little Chicken found an incredible job, and we downsized our amenities to find a more affordable place to stay.

Everything the Little Chicken did added *Value* to our efforts as a team. My contribution was flighty. I seemed to be constantly focused on projects that would add value in the future. Hanging my hat on the idea of a better tomorrow was exhausting, and it started to wear me down. My health began to suffer which in turn diminished my willpower. I had grown tired of living for something just out of my reach. It had begun to take its toll on the Little Chicken as well. On our little Vegas trip, she asked me if I was okay with the possibility of a never-ending pursuit of happiness. She said, "If your answer is yes, I'm okay with it. I'll support you no matter what. Might I suggest another possible option though? We can both chose to *Be Happy Now* and enjoy every minute of this *Life* the best we can."

When the Little Chicken confirmed she supported any decision I chose to make, it relieved the pressure associated with having to choose a vocation. *Being Happy Now* isn't something I ever stopped to consider. I enjoyed mentoring families that were new to the spinal cord injury world because I had developed a mountain of resources. Giving people *Hope* felt *Good*, but I didn't feel right considering it a career. I felt obligated to offer what I had to people in the same *Unconditional* manner it was offered to me. Once money came into the picture, it seemed to tarnish the value of doing something special.

The same went for public speaking. I'm good at speaking in front of a crowd; it just comes natural to me. Presenting something to three people felt the same as if one hundred people were in the room. On numerous occasions, I was asked to speak in front of large audiences to share my motivational story. When I was called upon, I had no trouble delivering good content, and each crowd I spoke to seemed genuinely pleased with what I had to say. Accepting money to do this was also difficult for me, but for different reasons.

Being a motivational speaker seemed cliché to me. I felt like that's what people in wheelchairs did because they couldn't do anything else. Besides, what was so motivational about my story in the first place? I'm just a normal guy that found myself in a shitty situation and I just chose not to give up. Pretty par for the course, I thought. I felt like quitting all the time; I just didn't. Because of the way I was feeling on the inside, it seemed fraudulent to consider motivating people as a profession. I spoke when I was called upon and was grateful that people got something out of it. Beyond that, it was hard for me to see myself as an inspirational figure.

Another set of thoughts that troubled my melon was the idea that I might have to be in a wheelchair for an indefinite amount of time. Each modality I worked with that showed promise toyed with my emotions. I knew that in order to *Heal Myself*, I had to *Believe* without a shadow of doubt that "this was it." Numerous business owners and practitioners shared the same optimism. They truly believed that with their help and my will power, I would be walking in no time.

It had been "no time" for quite some time now. I put my all into dozens of attempts to heal my body and fell short of my goal each time. Most of the therapies offered *Value* in a variety of ways. Finding *Balance* with a coordinated healing continuum was just beyond my grasp though. I was always off by just a fraction of what was needed to complete a miraculous healing achievement. I had all the tools to make it happen. My approach was just never *Balanced* enough to pull it off. The emotional roller coaster that accompanied each failed attempt took a serious toll on my well-being. When I had the finances, my emotions were way out of whack. When my will was good, my physical health was garbage. When I was given a spiritual lift, I let my physical surroundings keep my mentality bound to the chair.

After nearly a decade of trying to accomplish the unthinkable, I was too tired to wrap my head around where to go next with therapy. Looking back, I wondered if all my efforts had been in vain. Was rehab really what I wanted to be doing? I wanted to help myself and other people, but was I going about it in the right way? Einstein defines insanity as doing the same thing over and over again and expecting different results. Had I let this injury drive me insane?

I didn't really know what I wanted at this point. I had a *Life Partner* that accepted everything I AM, and it made me truly *Happy*. It was *Pure* and *Selfless*. I couldn't have asked for more in that department. Beyond my personal life, it was important for me to find something I was *Passionate* about. I really enjoyed being a mentor because I found *Value* in sharing what I learned about *Health* and *Wellness* with people. The slippery slope of the wellness industry was so elusive that I figured it was time to ravage my brain for an alternative option. I had another skill set, but I hadn't traveled down that road in ages.

My *Passion* for football is an obvious one. I had yet to entertain anything where I could put my knowledge to use though. I was quite stubborn, and my fear-based coping mechanism stood in the way of enjoying certain freedoms. The idea of getting back in the ocean is a good example of where my head was at.

I *Love* the ocean. I had a spiritual connection to the beach that was unlike any other place for me. There were ways for me to accomplish an adapted version of surfing, but I wanted to experience the sea's raw power with an able body. When I couldn't do it the way I used to, I wasn't even interested in putting my toes in the sand. I was so convinced I would walk, I used getting back in the water as motivation to stay focused on my goal. I would see the tide wash over my feet before jumping in and paddling out. I would feel the gentle spray of the breaking waves on my face, and I could smell the salt in the air. I figured I'd hold out to enjoy it the way I wanted to.

I applied the same crappy mentality to football. *Being* a *Mentor* is the same as *Being* a *Coach*. I could have been *Coaching* at my old high school the whole time, but I constantly came up with excuses to avoid the possibility. What if I overheated during a sweltering summer practice because I am unable to sweat? What if I needed to pee and nobody was close to help me? What kind of player was going to listen to a coach in a wheelchair? These are all serious questions that would scare off pretty much anybody. I wasn't anybody though, and the fact that I wasn't acting like *Myself* made me sick to my stomach.

When you're in the middle of a drama circle, it's often tough to see what's going on outside of it. If the circle starts to spin, everything becomes distorted. Dizziness sets in, and the drama circle starts to make you sick. Now you're no longer concerned with what's going on around you, because you've become consumed with the sickness created by your drama. When this happens, all efforts are focused on the sickness and not the problem. When this cycle gets out of control, it becomes increasingly more difficult to make a *Change*. There are really only three options to consider when one reaches this fork in the road: (1) let the sickness that the drama created kill you, (2) get used to feeling this way and learn to live with it, or (3) get the hell out of the drama circle at any cost.

I was sick of spinning. The nausea it created was a bummer. I was tired of the emotional vomit, and I was fresh out of tears to be cried. It was time to move on. That didn't mean I needed to give up *Hope*. It just meant the day had come for me to put down the current tool I was using to navigate my life and pick up another one. When we returned home from our little Vegas interlude, I called the new coach at my old high school and set up an interview.

The previous year, the football team had gone undefeated and won a state title. My old high school *Coach* had left the school years ago, and the team had been trying to get back to their winning ways ever since. The new head coach brought in an entirely new regimen. He cleaned house, dismissing the previous coaching staff, and filled their positions with new coaches that he handpicked. This is not an uncommon practice, but there were a few other moves he made that were a bit questionable in reference to the school's existing tradition. A hard-core, no-nonsense regimen is often what's needed to lead a football team to victory. His on-field efforts produced results that were hard to argue with.

Having participated in the school's longstanding tradition, I was welcomed back to campus with open arms. I got along with the new coach and was captivated by his significant achievement of getting the team back to championship form. The interview went well, and he immediately saw how I could add value to the team moving forward. When he offered me a paid position on his varsity staff, there was something about it that just didn't feel right.

The offensive mentality that he applied to his winning ways was brutal. He didn't seem to care about what anyone else was doing. The playbook was simple with very few moving parts. The only thing that mattered was that his squad stuck to the game plan. Opposing teams often knew what play was being called before the ball was even snapped. This did nothing to alter the shrewdness of his dominating scheme. The military precision that went into preparing the troops created a truly awesome result. The brute force of flawless execution made their offense nearly impossible to stop.

I wasn't familiar with this style of football. Attention to detail is what made this coach's approach interesting, but I grew up playing the game with a defensive mentality. My understanding was that if a team can't score, they can't win. Since the coach had already imprinted his code of conduct onto the entire fabric of the program, I wasn't sure if I was a good fit for his coaching staff. I had no idea how my body would respond to being thrown into such a highly intense demand of my time and effort. Where would I even fit in a dominion that had already proven its merit of excellency? They had established a new legacy that did away with the old-school methods I had learned long ago.

On the other side of town, my old high school *Coach* accepted a job at a new up-and-coming school. He was the head *Coach* of a team that competed in the same league as my alma mater. Since the school was new to the scene, they hadn't begun to attract the high-caliber athletes that some of the more established schools in the area did. For their first few seasons, they got pounded and finished last place in the divisional rankings. By the time I set up an interview with my old *Coach*, they were trending upward and had started competing with the other teams.

I saw an opportunity to be part of their success story. As they moved into a position to challenge some of the better teams in the area, maybe I could develop the skills to be a successful coach. When I met with my old commander in arms, he said unfortunately there was no room for me on his staff. This was the same guy that taught me there is always a strategy for dealing with undesirable outcomes. When I refused to leave until he found a place for me, he told me to take a look at the freshman reserve squad. He said if I was interested, he would bring me on as a volunteer.

The freshman reserve squad was a team assembled to give kids a chance to play football. Usually, only about half the students that showed up to rookie camp had experience playing the game. When the starting lineup was filled on the freshman squad, there was always an abundance of players left over. This was a group of unknowns to the coaching staff. Sometimes there was a diamond in the rough or some raw talent that needed development. That's what the freshman reserve team was for.

It didn't make sense to pass on a paid varsity position with my alma mater, for a volunteer spot on the freshman reserve squad at a rival high school. So I went to check out a reserve game one Saturday afternoon. I wanted to see if being on the field could offer some clarity in the decision-making process. I spoke with a few proud parents between plays to get an idea of what I might be getting myself into. A mother of one of the players mentioned that the team had scattered talent, but there was no telling how they would come together. There was one kid on the starting roster that was absolutely incredible the mother said. At that moment, almost as if it were cued to happen, the boy rushed out onto the field in full uniform without his helmet.

He sprinted right past the huddle to position himself behind the goal post. He hadn't run onto the field to check into the game; he went behind the post to retrieve the ball once it had been successfully kicked through the uprights. Somebody needed to retrieve the ball, but I found it odd that the team's superstar was the one doing it, especially in full uniform during a game where he wasn't even playing. The parents watching just shrugged it off, but I saw the potential of a special football player that doesn't come around very often. There was a *Soulful* component to his efforts, which was a rare find in sports these days. I found the *Motivation* I was looking for. It *Inspired Me* to want to give these youngsters the *Knowledge* I had to offer. It reminded me of why I spent so long playing the silly game in the first place.

I met my old high school *Coach* the following Monday and told him I would take the volunteer position with the freshman team. I felt comfortable in the underdog roll, and by taking a volunteer position as a freshman assistant, I could give my full attention to the team with minimal demands on my behalf. It's not that I wasn't up for the challenge; I just didn't want to be a distraction while I got into an adapted coaching groove. I was familiar with the system my old

Coach was running, which was also one less thing to adapt to while I found my coaching rhythm.

When I showed up to my first afternoon practice, I had butterflies in my stomach. I had no idea what to expect from the players or coaches. When the wheels of my chair transitioned from the rubber of the track wrapped around the field, to the artificial turf of the gridiron, the confident football *Leader* within me subtly rose to the surface. I was introduced as an assistant coach, but no details were given about who I was or what I'd accomplished. There were more important matters at hand. Once everyone was on the field and the whistle was blown, the collective effort was focused on only one thing: becoming the best possible version of *Ourselves* in order to come together as a *Team*.

For the first week or so, I kicked back in the shadows in an effort to wrap my head around where I fit into the organization. I missed summer training camp, which meant I wasn't present for the bonding experience of "hell week." I also wasn't given a specific role because nobody knew what to expect of me. I wasn't even sure what to expect of myself. Until I knew what I was capable of, it would be tough to prove how I could be an asset to the team.

The entire program was still growing, and the numbers of the organization were relatively small. The coaches were understaffed, and the practice facility was still being expanded which forced the varsity, junior varsity, and freshman teams to practice on the same field. This was a huge advantage for me because I got to survey the heartbeat of the entire program. Even though I was technically a freshman coach, I could easily roam the whole field to observe all the levels of the organization.

I spent a majority of my time with the freshman team. The player that nudged me to take the position is where I decided to start my analysis. It was number 21, the kid that was shagging balls that Saturday afternoon for the freshman reserve squad. I hadn't seen him play until the practice sessions, but I was interested in knowing more about a supposed superstar that spent his free time shagging balls for his second-string teammates.

He was phenomenal as advertised. He displayed a rare instinctual ability to be where other players weren't at just the right time. His raw talent helped him take advantage of the opportunities he created. He was able to take a play that was totally stuffed and turn it into a highlight reel that showed up on the evening news. The irony in it all was that he was one of the smaller players on the field. He stood five feet, five inches tall and only weighed about 150 pounds. He had impressive straight-away speed and reflexes, which enabled him to change direction like a cat, but his physical abilities weren't what truly impressed me.

He worked *Smarter* and *Harder* than anyone on the football field. He went full speed on every play, not just during the game but on every single practice rep as well. When he knocked someone down, he would help them up and jog back to the huddle like it was all part of the day's work. When he would score a touchdown, he'd flip the ball to the official and celebrate with his team instead of performing a coordinated dance routine. The most impressive thing I saw him do was when he wasn't in the game. He never missed an opportunity to practice mental reps while watching his teammates execute a play. This encouraged everyone to remain sharp because their *Leader* was holding them accountable for their actions. It made him a *Master of the System* he was leading and encouraged his teammates to pursue *Excellence* instead of just going through the motions.

I obviously wasn't the only one that noticed this. It was a privilege to be around a player with this type of skill set. He didn't need much coaching, just guidance about how to deal with the responsibilities being of a superstar. Instead of latching onto the bandwagon, I did what I thought a *Good Coach* would do. I shifted my focus to the rest of the team. The way to get the most out of number 21's abilities was to focus on the role players that would create opportunities for him. Besides, *One Player* can help win games, but *Champions Transcend the Game* by *Coming Together*.

I started to have ideas about where my skill set could make a *Difference*. Since the coaches were understaffed, it meant they had more responsibilities than they had time in the week. There was a lot that went into a week of preparation, and a team that was more prepared often had the best strategic advantage. Teaching the system to young players was the central focus of the coaching staff. The learning curve is complicated for freshmen because they also need to develop their technical skills. If you combine that with the new educational demands of a private curriculum and the freshly acquired social freedom of high school, the coaches and players had a full plate.

When I was a student athlete, I obsessively studied game film of my opponent in my free time. I studied the other team's system along with the tendencies of their players. Most teams do this together, but only briefly, due to the demands of a busy schedule. After practice, my *Coaches* used to encourage all the players to check out game film to study the opponent on their own. Technology made this process significantly more accessible. Now everything was online and each player was given full access to the other team's previous games.

Since the young program was strapped for resources, the most specific resource being time, film sessions were limited. The coaches mostly focused on watching their own practice film to correct the in-house technical and strategic mistakes. All I needed was an internet connection and a passcode to be a mobile film study station. I could watch our team's practice film and the other team's game film everywhere I went on my phone. I again became obsessed.

I started by quietly pulling number 21 aside to show him specific plays where he could exploit the other team's weaknesses. When the rest of the team started to wonder what I was doing, number 21 explained to them I knew what I was talking about. I started to develop a relationship with other players on the team this way. It wasn't long before I was working with the starting quarterback, a few receivers, a linebacker, and the kicker.

The season seemed to race by. The team finished 6–4 and one of their crowning achievements was winning an away game against my alma mater high school. I learned a lot about *Myself* throughout the course of the season. One time, I got so hot that I didn't know where I was. When my caregiver asked if I was okay, I responded by asking him why I was on a football field. I said, "I don't play football anymore. What's the meaning of this? Why am I on a football field?"

He promptly got me out of the sun and into the air conditioning. On another occasion, I had a bladder infection, which makes it difficult to hold my wiz when I've gotta pee. I needed to go, but my caregiver was on the other side of the field and I was in the middle of watching a drill. There was no way I was going to make it, so I just let it flow. When the drill was over, I met up with my caregiver, and we cleaned up the best we could. I then put a hand towel in my lap to prevent a repeat offense, and rolled back onto the practice field.

When the season was over, I met with my old head *Coach* again. Since the Little Chicken was the only one bringing home money, I wasn't in a position where I could volunteer for another season. I asked if I could be brought on as a paid employee, but the *Coach* explained that he didn't have room to do so in the budget at the moment. After exhausting all other possibilities to get a job somewhere on campus, it turned out that my time with this school had come to an end.

During the previous season, my alma mater went through some growing pains of their own. The all-state quarterback that had led them to a championship the year before blew out his knee, forcing him to miss a majority of his senior season. They ran the offense through him, and when their *Leader* went down, the team struggled. After spending a year coaching, I realized that I could bring benefit to any coaching staff that would have me. It turned out I could have been useful to my old high school after all, and they could have used the extra motivation when their star quarterback went down.

I humbly crawled back to my alma mater and had another meeting with the new coach. One of the first questions he asked was, "Why didn't you take the position I offered you?"

My answer was, "Because I thought I would be a better fit in a system that operated with a defensive mentality."

The real reason is that I wanted to be in an environment where I was comfortable. I questioned myself, and in doing so, things became more complicated than they needed to be. Since you only get one chance to make a first impression, my actions muddied the water. This offensive-minded coach was now put in a position where he had to defend what was best for his program. He again offered me a job, but this time there were many hoops I needed to jump through if I wanted the position. Since quadriplegics aren't best known for their jumping abilities, I was ruled out for the job based on details associated with the hiring process.

Back home, things were approaching a boiling point. We moved multiple times due to tight finances, and we just made a crucial accounting error that caused an eviction from the current place we were living. Right around this time, an administrative *Friend* from the school where I previously coached invited us to brunch one random afternoon. When the topic of how we were doing came up, it was pretty much written all over our faces. We shared our story with him, and he said he might be able to help us out.

I met this gentleman when I was trying to get a job at the rival high school. One of the team *Dads* referred me to him because he was known to *Make Things Happen*. Even though I was unable to secure a job at the school, I developed a rather *Spiritual* relationship to this Mr. Hapnin fella. He *Believed* in the Little Chicken and me. He *Believed* in our *Potential* to create something incredible. Even though there was no telling what this something might be, he had *Faith* that whatever it was would be *Great*.

Since we were living month-to-month on our bills, the immediate problem we were facing was coming up with a first and last month deposit to sign a lease for a new apartment. Mr. Hapnin was interested in *Helping Us*, but wanted to create a relationship that held us *Responsible for Our Actions*. He offered to lend us the money as long as we agreed to a payment plan. Each month, we needed to pay something, even if it were just a small amount. We didn't know it at the time, but this kind gesture was more of a character test to see if we were a worthy recipient of his time and resources.

We moved into a new place and paid Mr. Hapnin each month as much as we could. Sometimes it was only $25, but we made sure to never miss a payment. The Little Chicken was working at a longevity clinic and developed a personal relationship with the doctors running it. When she shared our current dilemma with them, they offered her a small raise if she was willing to take on more responsibility. Part of the deal also included free health care for the Little Chicken and me.

The lead doctor was an old football junkie that had been donating his time to a local high school team for close to thirty years. He was interested in trying an experimental treatment on my damaged spinal cord. His theory was that my lack of normal movement, low hormone levels, and poor calorie absorption contributed to my body's inability to maximize its healing. He was confident he could stimulate nerve growth at the site of the injury by supplementing my body with the right balance of hormones and nutrition. My body's natural healing system would take over once the levels were balanced. There was also scar tissue that was blocking the electrical signals from my brain to the rest of my body. He had some fancy medical theory as to how we could overcome that as well.

The additional workload kept the Little Chicken very busy at the longevity center. She overachieved in a way that baffled the doctors at the practice. Her ability to come up with creative solutions while multitasking numerous responsibilities made her an invaluable asset to the business. Fourteen years of administrative experience in the medical industry also enabled her to work multiple positions at the office. This allowed the business to operate with just one employee instead of three, which saved the doctors a considerable amount of money. The Little Chicken took good care of the practice, and the doctors took good care of her.

Once she established a firm working relationship with the doctors, she suggested a few additional modalities that could be added to the practice to generate further income. The lead doctor was a rogue practitioner that had moved away from the traditional ways of Western medicine. After years of complying with the structural standards of the medical industry, he was forced into early retirement because his vision would no longer permit him to be a surgeon. At this time, he branched off to start a longevity practice of his own.

He was a research geek that had access to medical journals only available to practicing doctors. He developed theories about how to properly move forward with Western medicine combined with proven components of holistic wellness. His trials were conducted at his clinic, and his success over the years made him somewhat of a local legend. When the Little One brought forward a few complementary modalities to aid him in what he was doing, he took the suggestions to his research library. Upon confirming the treatments' functional legitimacy, he gave her the green light to reach out to our contacts.

This new relationship showed serious promise moving forward. I was hesitant to get excited due to my recent decision to move beyond therapy, but I promised myself I would never give up *Hope*. If a solution presented itself directly in front of me, it seemed crazy not to entertain it. *Life* again seemed to be generating a positive organic rhythm, and things seemed to be falling into place. Then a shocking reminder of human impermanence came tumbling into our life.

The Little Chicken's *Mom* had been diagnosed with cancer the previous year. Mamma Hen went through chemo treatments, and the cancer went into remission. When she began to have stomach cramps that prohibited her normal bowel functions, she went to see the doctor. Almost a year after the cancer had been in remission, it had come back. This time, it spread throughout her entire system, and the results of numerous tests were not promising.

The Little Chicken had a troubled upbringing that was littered with divorce and substance abuse. Following a tumultuous adolescent experience, her early twenties mellowed out, and she found peace with the shortcomings of her childhood. Mamma Hen's effort to make up for years lost created an awkwardly strong emotional bond with the Little One. The two developed a *Friendship* that was more like that of sisters rather than mother-daughter. When the Little Chicken found out the prognosis for her *Mother's* cancer was terminal, the doctors gave Mamma Hen approximately two weeks to live before her entire body shut down.

The mixed bag of emotions took back seat to the reality of the inevitable. Our life had been shaken up once again with unavoidable circumstances that were out of our control. I did my best to comfort the Little Chicken, but there wasn't much to say. I had been initiated into the depths of our mortality a number of times in my life, but each experience with the reaper is different. There are only so many grievances that can be given to fill the void of a lost *Loved One*, and none of them is a good substitute. The act of *Letting Go* is yet another

Opportunity to develop moral character. It offers *Purpose* to each individual's *Struggle* with existence.

Mamma Hen left her body behind ten days after the doctors gave her two weeks to live. It was a devastating blow that clouded the Little One's entire perspective. The demands of the Little Chicken's job offered a welcome distraction when Mamma Hen first passed. The intensity of the workload quickly wore her thin though. She was responsible for managing all duties associated with front and back office administration. She also worked as the physician's assistant and accountant for both doctors' personal and business accounts. Weeks before her *Mother* passed, the Little Chicken received certification to become a clinical hypnotherapist. Once she became certified, she started to build clientele at the office to grow her own practice. When she left work for the day, life didn't exactly slow down. Her role as *Mother, Wife, Caregiver* to a quadriplegic, and curator for her *Mother's* funeral made her life dauntingly overwhelming.

This is the stuff superheroes are made of. She accomplished just about everything with flying colors. We worked together to keep everything solid on the home front, and she pulled together a beautiful celebration of *Life* for her *Mother*. She continued to grow her hypnotherapy practice and did an excellent job with her many responsibilities at the longevity business.

In the following months, I started to notice the doctors moving farther and farther away from the daily grind of running the practice. The Little One had proven to be so efficient at running the business that the doctors felt comfortable leaving her alone at the office for days at a time. There were even a few occasions when they left to travel abroad for an entire week, leaving the Little Chicken responsible for running the daily operations alone. She held down the fort like a damn all-star, but she was burning the candle at both ends and was running out of wick.

In a random string of events, the coach at my alma mater high school retired. His wildly successful career generated ten championships with three different schools and multiple state titles. After thirty-plus years of coaching, I guess the time had come for him to ride off into the sunset. He wasn't the only one at the school to turn in his badge and gun. The entire administration was restaffed, bringing in a new dean, and school president. The new president hired was an old *Friend* of mine. He was my senior year history professor and an assistant football coach on our championship team. He was also the former vice president at the school across town where I coached.

With the stars seemingly in perfect alignment, I made an appointment to meet with the newest football coach. He hired me, but the details were pending due to the shakeup at the school. While the paperwork was processing, I decided to be proactive and started attending practices to familiarize myself with the coaches and players. I also began to reach out to a few contacts that might be interested in revitalizing the retired flag football tournament fundraiser. I wanted to turn the event into a countywide fundraiser for a worthwhile charity to include all the teams in our division. I also planned to engage alumni to stimulate a resurgence of tradition at some of the most iconic and influential schools in the area.

Then, one of the most peculiar twists of *Fate* I could have ever imagined fell from the heavens. Seemingly out of nowhere, an *Opportunity* arose that would challenge everything about what the Little Chicken and I were working toward. I got a call from the German kid I befriended at prep school in the training room. It was Jasper the friendly ghost.

We spoke on and off over the years but never with any sense of regularity. I wasn't sure if he was even aware that I was currently using a wheelchair as my undesired method of transportation. It turns out he was more than aware; it was actually his reason for contacting me. He asked me, "Are you still up for that surf trip to Bali, Indonesia?"

I said, "Well, man, my sea legs aren't quite what they used to be."

"I know," he replied. "You broke your neck, right? I've been following your story on the internet. I understand that you didn't sever your spinal cord, correct? Is it still intact?" he asked curiously.

"It is still connected, but there's a bruise that prevents the signals from my brain from connecting to the rest of my body. I'm still quite a bit paralyzed, unfortunately. Surfing might be a tall task if you're looking for a partner to stand on waves with," I replied.

"That's just the thing," he responded with excitement in his voice. "My dad had a congenital heart problem that doctors said required open-heart surgery. For seven years, it got worse and worse. He randomly followed my Balinese stepmother to receive treatment from a Shaolin energy healer deep in the jungle of Jakarta, Indonesia. After three months of treatment, his heart ailment was completely healed. He had follow-up scans in Germany, and the doctors couldn't find any trace of his well-documented ailment."

"I told the healer about your injury, and he thinks he can help. He's healed bruised spinal cords before and estimates that it would probably takes four months to get you standing. In a year's time, he believes you could be fully recovered, and we can go surfing!" said an overly excited Jasper the friendly ghost.

When I hung up the phone, thousands of thoughts raced through my head. Did this voodoo jungle healer have any idea what he was talking about? Where has this Jasper the friendly ghost character been for the last ten years, and why should I *Believe* anything he says? Does he have any idea what it would take for my wife and me to drop everything and transport a quadriplegic to the other side of the world? The idea was outrageous, so I didn't labor over it very hard. It was way too farfetched, and I didn't dedicate much time entertaining the possibility.

A few weeks later, I got another phone call from Jasper. This time, he was in California an hour up the road from my house. He asked what I was up to and wondered if it was cool for him to swing by. I all but ruled out his preposterous plan, but I figured that brainstorming a pipe dream wouldn't hurt anything. When he arrived, it became obvious how hell-bent he was on making this idea a reality.

He did most of the talking for the first hour of his visit as he seemed to have it all figured out. I tried to remain open while entertaining his brainchild, but my gut feeling continued to reject the possibility. He presented himself as a natural problem-solver, and each time I countered one of his ideas, he responded with a reasonable solution. I explained to him that close to a decade of rehabilitation had beat me down, and I was tired. I had objectively entertained dozens of "this is it" opportunities, and when I fell short of my goal, I experienced a deep sadness, and the failure was difficult to live with.

The Little Chicken and I had just begun to gain some traction moving beyond an existence centered around rehabilitation. Her job was solid, and I started to move in a direction that showed real promise. I explained my wellness clinic idea to Jasper and told him that the Little Chicken was making small moves toward making it a reality. Jasper brought up another reasonable counterargument that got me thinking.

"Have you ever considered that you might be trying to set this clinic up on the wrong side of the world? Western medicine seems to have its strong points, but what about ancient traditions that have stayed relevant over the course of the last thousands years?" the friendly ghost asked.

Jasper was an engineer by trade, but he had become bored by the redundant confines associated with the job. Since moving away from the profession, he had been pursuing a career as an entrepreneur, dabbling in a handful of startup ideas that he created. Creation of custom tea kettles had brought him to the US, this time to meet with some friends in the designing field. He had no experience in the wellness industry, but he brought up some pretty intriguing points about the current demands of the marketplace in Indonesia.

He said, "It sounds like there is too much red tape to accomplish what you're trying to do here in the States. In the East, it's far less developed, and they invite Western practices to be used with their wellness concepts. Bali is currently trying to move away from party tourism and into wellness travel accommodations. It's the perfect place to set up a business like the one you guys are trying to create."

All of a sudden, this Bali, Indonesia, idea started to sound interesting. I was *Learning* that the logical framework of expectation often limited my thinking in the past. Was this *Opportunity* here to challenge that mind-set? If it was, I needed to be *Sensitive* to everything else going on around me. The cues to move in one direction or another were previously overlooked because my entire approach was out of *Balance*. If this plan had any chance of manifesting, I needed to be *Aware* of the trail of bread crumbs the universe was dropping.

Jasper grabbed a pen and paper and began composing a budget for what it would take to make this happen. After reviewing the numbers, he suggested a plan of action.

"I'll save up the money to pay for the first four months of treatment. That will include everything from treatment cost, plane tickets, room and board, transportation, and food. We will shoot a documentary of the entire process, and when you're up walking, we will use it to promote the wellness center we will create together. We will be 50/50 partners. How does that sound?" he asked.

This didn't actually sound like a bad idea. I told him that the Little Chicken and I would need to do some serious thinking about it. An astronomical amount of maneuvering would need to be done by us to make it happen. Since it was going to take some time for him to save money, we had a few months to think about it. In the meantime, Jasper would find a way to lease his flat in Europe and move to his dad's place in Bali.

What a crazy *Life* this was panning out to be. I was still in search of a paying job while the coaching gig was pending. I also wasn't sure how to structure the fundraiser I wanted to pull together. I didn't know if it would be better to start small at my alma mater high school with the current following or to get the entire league involved to make it a county-wide event. I decided to make that decision once I found out whether or not I got the job at my old high school. Since the administration was going through a full restructuring, there was no telling how long it would take before I would know about being a contracted employee.

The Little Chicken's *Light* was growing dim. The high-intensity demands of her time and efforts were pulling in too many directions. She was working her ass off. Under normal conditions, she wouldn't have trouble doing so, but she never took time to process her *Mother's* passing. There was a deep void that she had yet to deal with. She just kept pushing forward, but in doing so, she was overextending herself. At the end of the day, when work was finished, we would spend a few hours together before she collapsed from exhaustion. Something needed to give. Without the physical ability to take over, I needed to come up with a creative solution before she ran herself into the ground.

Holiday season was upon us. Under normal conditions, this is a joyful time of year. Since this was the first year without Mamma Hen, things were a bit tense. The Chicken was working more than normal to try to scrape together extra cash for Christmas presents. Since time was of the essence, most of the Christmas shopping was done online. The convenience of having it delivered to the front door was a huge relief.

In an effort to save the longevity practice time and money, she purchased office supplies online. When she did so, all that needed to be done was to switch credit cards and user information on her account to make purchases. At some point between shopping for Christmas presents and ordering office supplies, she forgot to switch accounts. This resulted in over a thousand dollars being charged to the business account for our Christmas presents.

Right around this time, I got a call from Jasper the friendly ghost. He was excited to share with me that he had moved to Bali and saved enough money to pay for the first four months of the master plan. He booked a ticket to California and was scheduled to arrive just after Christmas. His plan was to live on our couch for as long as he needed to until we were motivated to travel with him to Indonesia. It was a bold move, but if this idea had any chance of happening, something drastic needed to take place.

I hadn't made a decision yet about what I wanted to do. The plan was so outrageous it was tough to wrap my head around how it could be pulled off. I found myself waiting around for something to happen. I was tired of my life being in a constant holding pattern. I had a few low-paying jobs pending, and I was still waiting to hear back from the high school about the coaching position. I was at a serious fork in the road. The only thing that seemed like it was definitely going to happen was some crazy German guy was flying in to live on the couch.

Nobody was going to make any decisions for me. The Little Chicken was in full support of whatever I wanted to do, and Jasper was more than welcome to stay on our couch as long as he would like. I was currently trying to figure out where I fit in this *Life*. My decisions to date felt like they were burdening those I cared about, and I didn't feel like I was actively fulfilling my *Purpose*. The question that needed to be answered was, "Is the risk worth the reward?"

In the past, comfort was one of the things that stood in the way of going outside my little bubble. It wasn't just physical comfort that I would be giving up if I chose to move forward with this global field trip. I had to be willing to throw caution to the wind if I was going to make this happen. Able-bodied folks struggle with fears of the unknown when making a drastic change like this. As a seated crusader, I needed to be willing to leave Western medical amenities behind along with *Friends* and *Family* that could come to my rescue if something bad happened.

A lot of promises were made that felt a bit inflated, so the first thing I needed to do was strip the idea down to its bare bones to see if it was worth it. This was a once-in-a-lifetime experience that was hard to just dismiss. It's not every day that someone calls you up and offers to pay for a journey to the other side of the world. The experience alone seemed to have enough to it for me to roll the dice to see what would happen. I was done rolling the dice on stuff though, so I needed to go *Deeper* in my search for *Value* if I was going to consider this.

The pressure of disabled living had worn the Little Chicken and me pretty thin. It seemed like we were always swimming upstream. We had yet to find our identity as a couple because we were constantly playing catch-up. We both had some internal stuff we needed to deal with, and detaching from the grind that constantly held us down might be just what we needed. We are both adventurers at heart, and a grand adventure was right at our fingertips.

I had always wanted to write a book and make a movie. By going with this extreme idea, I would have the time and content to create something truly special. The potential of walking, surfing, and creating a wellness center were also possibilities that stretched my imagination. I was open to giving myself completely to the experience. In my heart, I knew it was the only way to successfully accept an incredibly rare chance to heal myself. I *Believe* in the universe's ability to provide, and this felt like something far beyond linear programmed thinking.

Now that I was seriously entertaining this, there were many logical realities that needed to fall in place for it to actually happen. It seemed like a long shot, but with all things considered, I would be crazy to pass on the *Opportunity* if everything lined up. The Little One would need to leave her job. We would need to find a caregiver to come with us. We'd have to stockpile supplies and equipment, plus find someone to house-sit with our two dogs.

I had two reliable caregivers at the time. One was a musician who recently moved back home to attend college, and the other was new to California that took the odd job as a caregiver because he needed to make extra money. The musician was transitioning into a focused effort to get serious with his life. The other guy was looking for an adventure, and that's what brought him to California. I immediately saw where the two might fit in the plan. I asked the musician to look after the place and the other guy if he was interested in coming to Bali. With zero resistance, they both agreed to help make this nutty idea work.

It was almost too easy. Informing the doctors at the longevity practice wasn't nearly as pleasant. At first, they were very encouraging about the experience as a whole. They even helped us create a poker fundraiser to help raise money for the additional costs associated with the trip. Both doctors had their reservations about the healer, but they saw the overall value in the opportunity. When the lead practitioner got to thinking, he realized how important the Little One was to the practice. He knew that if she were to leave, there would be a major disruption in his practice.

When we decided to pull the trigger, the shit hit the fan. At first, the doctors tried to come up with accommodating solutions. They suggested the Little One travel to Indonesia to help get me set up for a few weeks then fly back to resume work. When their idea of leaving me on the other side of the world with the friendly ghost and a caregiver was rejected, things got complicated.

To make a long story short, they accused the Chicken of stealing from the practice and slandered the two of us to everyone they knew.

Since the Little One made an accounting error at Christmastime, it didn't look good on our behalf. One of the reasons I believed it was necessary for us to go was because the Little Chicken was under so much pressure. She needed to patch the holes *Life* had poked into the fabric of who she'd become. She never had it easy, and her *Mom's* death was the straw that broke the camel's back.

The longevity clinic doctors had already made up their minds that we were irresponsible people with poor moral standards, and the die was cast. Despite our repayment of the funds to rectify a mistaken accounting error and their acceptance of the payment, they then threatened to prosecute the Little Chicken for theft. It was safe to say the bridge was burned and all that was left was another pile of ashes.

The final hurdle was to run this by the residents of Never Never Land. I chose to bring up the whole ordeal three days before Jasper was set to come in town. It also happened to be on Christmas morning. As expected, everyone was shocked, and *Dad* had his classic look of disapproval firmly intact. Pops was always the voice of reason, but this time, I prepared for the conversation I was going to have with *Dad*.

He voiced concern and listed all the problematic issues standing in the way of the idea's success, and I had solutions in place to offer him peace of mind. I know that term is somewhat relative because I'm not sure any *Father* of a quadriplegic would have peace on their mind when his wheelchair-bound son says "Hey, *Dad*, I'm dropping everything to go on a surf trip to Bali, Indonesia!" But *Dad* had been doing this for a while. He knew I was an adventurer, and if he told me not to go, that would be a definite way to get me all fired up on doing it anyway.

As worried as my *Parents* were, there was something about this idea that brought a smile to their faces. Their firstborn son had his fire back and was ready to take on the world again. The Lost Boys saw their fearless *Leader* ready to fly, and they had little doubt that something amazing would come of this. Once we took care of the last few details needed to make this journey happen, *Mom* and *Dad* dropped us off at the airport, and the adventure of a lifetime began.

Adventure

I 'm not much for the pharmaceutical game. There's really no way to tell how certain synthetic chemicals will react with our organic *Being*. With that said, there's a time and place for everything. Our journey from Los Angles, California, to Jakarta, Indonesia, was a total of thirty-two hours' travel time. Just the thought of being trapped in an airplane seat unable to move for what seemed like forever gave me anxiety. My reservations about ingesting toxic chemicals got put on the back burner when I put myself in a drug-induced coma for a good portion of the flight. When I woke up, I was in a whole different world.

We were greeted by a thick, wet, tropical heat that was radiating through the island air. It made the entire airport feel like a locker room sauna. People were going about business as usual, but the buzz of ordinary life was nothing like I had ever seen. The energy that went into people's casual affairs was astoundingly different. There was a chaotic order to the flow of sporadic living going on in every direction I looked. It was as if I were a child experiencing Disneyland for the first time. Everything was magnificent. I tried to quantify it somehow, but I had never experienced anything like it. The only thing that seemed to matter to the locals was what was going on in each moment.

Our travel team consisted of the only five white-skinned people in the entire airport. We were three Americans, one German, and one amateur filmmaker from Switzerland. The Chicken and I were accompanied by our *Friend* and caregiver Georgio, Jasper, and the cameraman we all referred to as Nëvil. Once we gathered our belongings from the baggage claim, we went out front to wait on the curb for our car.

The twilight associated with coming off the meds I had taken, coupled with severe jet lag, distorted my understanding of what was going on. Between the suffocating heat and deafening sounds of taxi horns and street vendors, it was hard to tell if this was really happening. Was I dreaming, or had I really gotten on a plane and traveled to the other side of the world? Before the euphoria had time to settle in, a VIP bus rolled up to the curb with a paper sign in the window that had our names on it. Georgio went behind my wheelchair and bear-hugged me from the back, while Jasper stood in front of me, grabbing my legs. They picked me up, counted to three and swung me into the passenger seat of the bus. Everyone else loaded up our stuff, and we were off.

Just looking out the window had a cinematic feel to it. As we left the airport, each turn of the makeshift roads moved us farther and farther away from any familiar reality. I had never seen so much traffic. Our journey to the clinic in the jungle was only eighty kilometers from the airport, but the driver said it would take us approximately five hours to get there. An outrageous number of cars and trucks littered the two-lane roads, but I was in sheer amazement at the number of motorbikes. They outnumbered the cars ten to one.

Hundreds of scooters and motorcycles dominated the road like a swarm of bees. All movement was conducted through herd mentality. If there was space to be filled, it was immediately occupied by the next motorbike in line. Both sides of the street, including the sidewalks, were flooded with cars and motorbikes. Cars were a luxury item reserved for people with significant means, but that didn't stop entire families from getting to where they needed to go. It was common to see five or six people on a single motorbike. If it wasn't three generations of family members occupying a bike; it was a goat, wheelbarrow, mattress, or mobile food cart known to the locals as a *Warung*.

As we journeyed deeper into the jungle, the roads narrowed, and the potholes in the pavement continued to grow in size. After close to forty hours of total travel time, we arrived at the base of a volcano in the village of Sukabumi, Cisaat. We turned onto a narrow one-lane road that was half gravel and half dirt, then traveled to the top until it came to a dead end. The road bottlenecked into the entrance of a national park that was guarded by military officials. Just outside the entrance to the park, there was a gated medical clinic on the right-hand side of the road. When we pulled up to the gate, a middle-aged local came to the window of the bus and muttered something to the driver in their native language. Once the gate was open, the guard flashed us a sincere smile, exposing the few teeth he had remaining. We finally made it to the place we would call home for the next four months.

I didn't really know what to expect. A surf trip to Bali, Indonesia, somehow turned into a four-month voyage to the jungle of Sukabumi on a completely different island. I'd eventually come to learn that my first real lesson of *Surrender* started the moment I got on the plane in Los Angeles. I knew that expectation would do nothing to serve me on this journey, but my brain was programmed to reference familiarity in everything I did. The only reference material I had were the stories that Jasper and his father shared with me before they bought our plane tickets. Having a general idea of what was going to happen was about as relevant as the airline meals I slept through on the flight over.

To say I experienced the feeling of culture shock is an extreme understatement. I was freakin' out, man. What had I done? Everything I knew was ten thousand miles away, and I was stuck at the top of a volcano in the middle of the Indonesian jungle. I knew when I made the decision to come to Indonesia that I would be facing a considerable amount of discomfort, but I hadn't put much thought into the mental and emotional struggles that were ahead of me. The jungle isn't exactly a wheelchair-friendly place to be. My van with an electric ramp, the shower chair custom-built for my needs, and my motorized reclining bed were only a few of the things I had literally cashed in for this wild adventure. There was no telling what was in store for me now that I was in the middle of the jungle.

All the "things" that were supposed to offer me comfort did nothing to silence the noise I had going on in my head. After everything that I had been through, I still felt inadequate and like a sizable burden to everyone around me. No matter how hard I tried, I couldn't get over how difficult it was to manage the hand I had been dealt. I had so many people that cared about me, and I was married to my best *Friend*. Why was *Happiness* still so damn illusive?

Before leaving, I did some *Soul-searching* to weigh the benefits of the *Opportunity* ahead of me. For the previous ten years, my focus was self-serving, and it didn't help me fulfill my desire to be significant. The act of not giving up rewarded me with *True Love* and an undeniably loyal support system, but I didn't feel like I was honoring these gifts the best I could. Underneath the positive attitude and refusal to let a difficult situation get me down was an emptiness that followed me everywhere I went. It didn't have enough momentum to get in the way of my daily activities, but it haunted me at night before I fell asleep. This trip was a chance to put all that behind me. The way I intended to do so was by cutting all ties that disabled my way of thinking. By removing myself from the influences that controlled my thoughts, I could establish a new way of understanding who I was.

Since the Chicken constantly made sacrifices to accommodate my needs, the first thing I thought about when pondering the trip was her. This wasn't just my life anymore; it was our *Life*. I could tell that the way we were living in the States was wearing the Little One thin, and something needed to be done. She would just keep grinding until there was nothing left, and I wasn't about to let that happen. She, too, needed a release from the stranglehold that was oppressing her thoughts. We let ourselves become boxed in by the demands of a culture that was limiting our potential. Nobody but us was responsible for letting this happen, but the drama circle had begun to spin out of control, and something needed to be done to stop it. In order for the Little Chicken to process the reality of her *Mother's* passing, it was important that she cut ties with her current way of thinking as well.

The caregiver we brought was also in search of a *Deeper Meaning.* Georgio grew up in a highly conservative part of Utah that was predominantly Mormon. Even though he wasn't a practicing member of the faith, the region was heavily influenced by a strict moral code enforced by the church community. He moved to California to focus on his music and to develop himself as an independent thinker. His adolescent years were the subject of a pretty animated divorce. When his parents separated, it gave rise to an internal conflict that led to some serious anxiety issues. Just like my youngest brother, he struggled with situations that forced him out of his comfort zone. When I asked him if he was savvy on coming with us, he confirmed his interest based on the potential for self-improvement. Having another Lost Boy on the island adventure was just what the doctor ordered.

The clinic was set up in two tiers. Up top was the parking lot with a large waiting room attached to a kitchen and a single treatment room. The bedrooms were below at the end of a long cobblestone path that overlooked the entire jungle. The rooms were perched at the top of a valley where we could see for miles below. The cool mountain air caressed our faces when the wind blew through the five-hundred-year-old trees that surrounded the clinic.

All the rooms were the same, except for the master suite at the end of a long corridor. The only room that had a proper shower was the master bedroom, which the Little Chicken, Georgio, and I were promised before leaving the States. We were told the suite was reserved for us to stay in, but when we arrived, we found that Jasper's father, Gargamel, occupied the room. There was a king-sized bed, a television with a set of speakers and a table large enough to seat four people. Attached was a small dressing room with an armoire and a bathroom with a tub, a toilet, a small shower and sink.

Upon our arrival, we found out that Gargamel had been staying in the suite for about ninety days and planned on sticking around for another month. This meant the three of us needed to share one of the standard rooms, which was about ten feet by twelve feet. Three people plus a wheelchair was an extremely tight fit. There was only room for a queen bed for the Chicken and me, with an additional single mattress smashed against the footboard for Georgio. We kept all our belongings in suitcases and stashed them under the bed. Once I transferred out of my wheelchair for the evening, we put it outside our front door so it didn't block the bathroom. There was a small broken toilet, a hose, and a bucket in case anyone was inclined to tidy themselves up a bit. But hey, we were in the jungle on the other side of the world. Our job was to figure out a way to make it work.

There wasn't much time to collect ourselves because therapy started right away. I was to be seen three times a day, four days a week. Our mornings started with one of three different rotating meals that were left in front of our bedroom door. It was either a bowl of noodles, a piece of white bread with a thin layer of strawberry jam, or rice porridge with a pouch of local sugar. If you got to it before the ants or stray jungle cats, it was destined to be a good day. We then made our way up the cobblestone path to a waiting room, where we lounged around until we were called into the treatment room.

Sometimes the waiting room had as many as thirty people from all over the island lined up to be seen. Other days there were only a handful of Cisaat locals. Anywhere between five and ten people were called into the treatment room to be seen at once. Jasper's father translated for us for the first few weeks because nobody at the clinic spoke English. After days of travel and months of anticipation, it was finally time for me to be seen by the mystery jungle healer.

The Master Guru that founded the healing clinic was trained by Shaolin monks at a monastery hidden in the Taiwanese mountains. The Shaolin are known for their superior combat skills, but the essence of their mastery is rooted in a sacred knowledge about how to harness energy. *Chi* energy is the fundamental *Life Force* that flows through all things. The ability to manipulate this energy is one of the coveted skill sets protected by the Grand Masters of ancient traditions. In order to acquire this *Knowledge*, a special individual must be *Chosen*. Once they were considered worthy, the rigorous training began.

The Master Guru of the clinic was a military-trained special ops agent that had experienced the gruesome horrors of war. Once his time in the army had come to an end, he began his search for salvation. He had an extensive background in martial arts and had been a student of *Chi Gong* since he was a child. After all he had seen, he wanted to dedicate the rest of his *Life* toward healing the human condition. This is when the Shaolin way embraced him.

He studied the ancient healing art of Totok therapy for six years while secluded from all other factions of life. Totok therapy is a series of neck grips used in combination with acupressure to stimulate blocked energy meridians. The neck grips are used to rush fresh oxygenated blood to problematic areas of the body. The treatment starts by assessing the body's energy system to locate the places where energetic blockages exist. The practitioner stimulates the meridian points that have become stagnant by harnessing *Chi* energy into his fingertips. He then transfers *Life Force* energy from his physical *Being* to the patient with extreme precision. Once the blockages have been activated, he moves to the neck and uses one of a hundred different holding techniques. Each grip is associated with a different part of the body, and each treatment varies depending on what ailment is being treated.

In the Western world, we refer to these blockages as knots. It's common to dismiss tense muscles as a structural problem that can be fixed with a good massage. The Eastern traditions have a much more intricate understanding of the human vessel. They see the body from more of an organic perspective as opposed to the mechanical approach adopted in the West. They believe that the source of disease is an energetic imbalance brought on by diet, stress, spiritual impurity, guilt, sadness, and a slew of other emotionally distorted living conditions. It's what motivated the Master Guru to start the clinic thirty years earlier.

Jasper's father had a degenerative heart condition that had been healed by the Master Guru, and he came for annual tune-ups. When Gargamel asked if it was possible to heal a spinal cord injury, the Guru confirmed he could help, as he had healed a number of people with spinal cord injuries during his thirty-year career. There was a small kink in the program though. In the months that Jasper was saving the money to make the trip happen, the Master Guru suddenly died.

The Guru had chosen an apprentice that he had been training for seventeen years. He didn't receive the direct teachings from the Shaolin Masters, but he had been studying the art for almost two decades. He had a background in martial arts and had also been training in *Chi Gong* since he was a boy. He graduated from a prestigious acupressure school in Jakarta and was handpicked by the Master Guru to learn the ancient Shaolin healing practice. When the Master Guru passed, his apprentice took over the clinic that had developed a legendary rapport in the local community.

The apprentice, Pak Heru, had been running the clinic for about six months by the time we showed up. He was able to keep the business operational, but his Guru passed before the final stages of Heru's training was complete. He had become a skilled practitioner but had yet to master the art of Totok therapy. He still needed to iron out the fine details to perfect his craft, which required time and hands-on experience. Without his teacher present to guide him, he was left to figure it out on his own.

Pak Heru only stood about five feet tall and couldn't have weighed much more than a hundred pounds. The first time I rolled into the treatment room, it was with a large group of people, and I would end up being the last patient treated. I was able to watch numerous people's sessions before it was my turn, and I asked Heru's assistant, Larno, a bunch of questions with the help of Gargamel's translating.

It didn't seem to matter what was going on in the room because the healer used his hands to explore each person's energy system. He usually started between the shoulder blades or on the patient's feet. After a minute or so, it was almost as if something clicked, and he got into a rhythmic groove applying aggressive acupressure. It was pretty eerie how precise he was at being magnetically drawn to certain problem areas. Most of the time, the patient didn't say a word about what was bothering them. After about ninety seconds or so, Pak Heru was already addressing the issue. It was usually the most painful part of the treatment.

Once he activated the entire meridian channel, he moved to the neck. Using his pointer finger and thumb, he positioned himself in place the same way a sprinter would at the starting line before a race. He would then channel *Chi* energy into his fingertips and apply firm pressure to neck region. What happened next was different for every person. During the time when pressure was being applied to the neck, it was almost as if Heru would go into a trance. He would read each patient's energy system the same way a blind person reads Brail. Before I could make sense of anything I was seeing, it was my turn to be treated.

Heru had a soft, jolly demeanor that made his presence light and cheerful. The idea that he was channeling *Life Force* energy through himself into other people seemed like it was no big deal. He had been doing it for years, and healing the needy was all in a day's work for him. His confidence put me at ease, and before I had the chance to mentally ready myself for what was about to happen, he was already tuned into my body.

He started between my shoulder blades and began poking me in areas that were incredibly sensitive. In just seconds, he knew right where to go. It felt like he was jabbing holes into my *Soul*. I winced and groaned like a small child receiving vaccination shots for the first time. Pak Heru just chuckled and continued to torment my most sensitive areas. Everyone in the room smiled and laughed because they had just experienced a version of the same thing. After about ten minutes of having my most vulnerable areas violated like I was participating in a medieval torture ritual, he moved to my neck.

He adjusted his grip a few times then clamped down on the area he was searching for. I felt my blood slow down and my heart rate increase. When he let go, I felt a warm rush surge through my body like a runaway freight train. I could feel my body shaking, but mentally, I was somewhere else. My body was obviously still in the room, but my spirit seemed to step out for a moment. Right then, Heru gently tapped me on the shoulder, and I came to.

What the hell just happened? I was at a total loss for words. What just went down was a bit scary. I wasn't a part of myself for a second, and at the same time, I had never been so whole. I was flabbergasted. I had no idea what to think of what I had just experienced. Heru communicated to Jasper's father that he wanted me to try to unlock the brake on my chair. When I went to hook my wrist around the brake to unlock it, he corrected me and pointed to my fingers. I was a bit confused because after twelve years of therapy, I wasn't able to activate my fingers enough to wrap them around anything. Since the healer just gave me an order, I wasn't about to argue with him. I reached down, wrapped my fingers around the brake, and pulled it back.

Holy shit! Was this really happening? I had just activated my fingers and used my hand to unlock the brake! It was incredible. After one session, I was able to activate my fingers, something I hadn't done in over a decade. I was a bit lightheaded, and I was mentally and emotionally drained. Once the session was over, it was time for lunch. We gathered our belongings and made our way to the kitchen.

All this was a bit too much for me to wrap my head around. As I sat at the table, waiting for the Chicken to grab our lunch, I began to entertain some foreign thoughts. Maybe I wasn't supposed to understand why things were happening the way they were. Maybe my job was just to react to my surroundings in the best way I could. What was the best way for me to respond? How was I supposed to know if I was doing the right thing?

I was all over the place. The more I tried to collect myself, the farther away I seemed to get from any answers. Then something amazing happened, something simple. Lunch arrived. Everything I needed in that moment was right in front of me, almost like it was supposed to be there. And it was a good thing, because I was starving. I wasn't in the mood to try to figure things out. I was just incredibly hungry and there was food on the table. I had everything I needed, making the moment absolutely perfect if I was willing to see it for what it was.

I had two more sessions with the healer that afternoon. At the end of the day, Heru explained to me that his focus for the next six to eight weeks would be on healing my *Spirit*. He said my body couldn't heal until my chakras were functioning properly. One of the reasons I was having trouble with poor energy circulation is because I had a spiritual entity attached to my *Being*. He explained that when the *Spirit* becomes separated from the body, it is vulnerable to other dimensional influences. Heru said a Native American *Spirit* had attached itself to my body when I had my near-death experience.

This jungle healing ordeal went from being a little trippy to off-the-wall bonkers real quick. I never told Pak Heru anything about an out-of-body experience, but somehow he knew I had one. Years ago, I had done some research about the area where I tweaked my neck and found out it was on an Indian burial ground. Supposedly, the lake where I was injured was built on land where a Native American tribe was massacred. When I was at the hospital in Colorado, some wooey-hooey Reiki therapist also told me I had something funky attached to me. At the time, I thought nothing of it. My Western conditioning couldn't comprehend the information I was being exposed to. Now there was talk of out-of-balance chakras and Indian spirits attached to me. This was full-on, man.

We had no internet or phone service for the first couple of weeks. The cell towers and Wi-Fi situation in the jungle was a bit dodgy, but eventually, we came up with a solution. During the evenings, we would all pile into the master suite to watch whatever bootlegged DVD Jasper or his father picked up at the local market. Other than that, life was pretty quiet in the jungle. We had ample time to ponder our existence and relax without any distractions from the outside world.

As the days turned into weeks, we settled into a pretty structured routine. The unpredictability of the jungle was balanced out with a few fairly consistent daily benchmarks. Indonesia is a predominantly Muslim country. We woke every morning at 4:30 AM to the sound of multiple Muslim mosques blaring morning prayer on speakers designed for stadium rock concerts. The entire community took the ritual quite seriously. They prayed five times a day and had numerous different celebration rituals that would shut everything down for days.

The dedication was quite impressive. The entire region came together in a collective manner that expressed a genuine *Love* for *Life*. It was amazing how happy everyone was with very little financial means. It didn't matter that we were foreign to their way of life and religious ways. We were always welcome to eat and pray with them, and they always had something to share with us.

The clinic provided us with food the four days a week that we received treatment. The cuisine was simple and redundant due to the limited finances they had to work with. We ate a ton of rice, fruits, vegetables, chicken, and fish. Fried tofu and tempeh (fermented soybeans mashed into small cakes and deep fried) were the go-to side dishes we had with every meal. I particularly enjoyed the tempeh and the occasional corn fritter that squeaked into the routine on special occasions.

Jungle life frequently provided us with an abundance of special visitors. Mosquitoes where the number one staple that we could count on seeing every day. Before leaving home, we were bombarded by horror stories about how the evil vampire pests carried life-threatening diseases. Every time one of us got bitten, there was a feverish panic that coursed through our veins. We were certain we had just contracted malaria or Dengue Fever. Though this is a very real possibility, so is a heart attack. We learned real quick that mosquito bites were just part of living in a tropical jungle. Since it came with the territory, the hysteria quickly became white noise.

There were also many different types of winged friends that we would encounter fairly often. There were beetles the size of baseballs, blue bees, and large butterflies in every color imaginable. There was also an ongoing battle between bird-sized moths, and these strange black pincher bug creatures equipped with a Kevlar-style shell protecting their backs. It would also be a shame not to mention the cockroaches the size of sewer rats that liked to hide in our shoes.

Then there were our ground-dwelling comrades. Stray jungle cats were everywhere. They were like village vagrants willing to do just about anything to secure their next meal. We befriended a small family of them by gaining their trust with our chicken bone scraps. Once they came close enough, we would engage in a bit of social banter by enticing them with an old shoestring. It wasn't long before they were smitten.

Soon after the shoestring came out, they began scratching at our door in search of a dry, cool place to sleep. Once they became part of the *Family*, they brought us jungles prizes like dead birds and lizards that they would leave as offerings on our doormat. Our jungle *Family* grew when one of the female cats had a litter of kittens. The Little One found the kittens on Mother's Day, which felt a whole lot like Mamma Hen was watching over us. One by one, the momma cat brought them into our room and nursed them under the bed. Before Mamma Hen passed, we asked her to give us some definitive *Signs* from the other side that she was still with us. Since she was a sincere cat lover, it wasn't hard to make the connection when we were gifted a litter of kittens on Mother's Day.

Then there were the not-so-social little creeps that were as shocked to see us as we were to see them. We found lizards, snakes, frogs, and spiders in all shapes and sizes. Occasionally, we would see a rouge monkey or a family of otters that would come try to eat the catfish living in the pond outside the kitchen. The otters were greeted by a hostile snapper turtle that shared the pond with the fish. Once they met the grumpy-shelled security guard, they didn't come back to our quite jungle sanctuary again.

Finally, there was the clinic mascot. A few months before we showed up, a luwak cat was rummaging through the office treatment room when Heru showed up for work one morning. The luwak is a tree-dwelling jungle mammal that resembles a cross between a possum, monkey, and jungle cat. They are a highly-sought-after animal in Indonesia due to their ability to produce rare coffee beans. They would eat the cherry off a coffee plant and digest the beans. Once it went through their digestive tract, the enzymes did something to make the coffee beans age to perfection. Once they were pooped out, the beans were washed and roasted into some of the most expensive coffee in the world.

This particular luwak wasn't having the best morning when Pak Heru showed up to work. When Heru tried to assist the little guy out the door, it attacked him, leaving some fairly severe bite and scratch marks. Because the animal attacked the village's sacred healer, the tradition was to put the varmint to death. Heru wasn't about to let that happen. Even though he was scarred for life, Heru decided to keep the luwak in a large cage on the property. The luwak avoided certain death but was sentenced to life in prison without parole. He was to live out the remainder of his days in a minimum-security prison on a diet of leftover chicken and wild bananas.

During the four days of treatment, the entire staff lived at the clinic. It was a special opportunity because we got the chance to really get to know everybody. We got rather close to a diverse set of Indonesian personalities. During the downtime, Georgio and I would play chess with Heru's assistants. Larno, Agus, and Bang Bang took us to school on the chessboard. It was a game that the locals started playing as little kids, and their craft was finely tuned. Every once in a while, I found it in me to pull off a win, but they were few and far between. Larno was a grand master. Nobody ever beat Larno, not even the local Indonesians.

When we weren't playing chess with the locals, we would practice learning the language with them. We would teach them English and in turn they taught us Bahasa. There were thousands of islands in Indonesia and hundreds of different dialects. When Dutch colonization came about, the locals got together to form one dialect that everyone could use to communicate. It was common for certain regions to speak multiple dialects, but Bahasa was the universal language used to bridge the gap between the locals and foreigners.

The Indonesians kept things pretty simple. They would spend most of their free time eating and praying. They played chess, smoked their cigarettes, and occasionally brought out a guitar to sing traditional songs together. Another thing that most of the men were into was making precious gemstones.

They would buy rocks in bulk form that came from the local mines. They had a special machine that they took turns using to grind the rocks down to expose the jewels embedded inside. During all hours of the day and night, the buzzing sound of grinding rocks echoed throughout the compound. Once they exposed the gem, they would spend hours sanding and polishing it. Then they would go out into the jungle and cut down fresh bamboo. They would pull it apart and use the twine to intricately design braided rings and necklaces. Upon completion, they were put on display in a showcase outside the treatment room and were sold to the clients at the clinic.

Pak Heru utilized his free time much differently. He too fancied smoking cigarettes and making gemstones, but the rest of his day was spent alternating between two different worlds. He acted as a beacon between the physical and spiritual dimensions. Twice a day, he would go into deep meditation drawing in *Chi* energy from the jungle. The *Life Force* energy was stored within him, and he used it to treat patients throughout the day. He would only sleep a couple of hours a night, spending the rest of the time in meditation. In the mornings, he would go on a ten-mile run through the jungle after meditation and a yoga routine. When he returned, he would practice Tai Chi or Chi Gong until it was time to start treating patients.

The guy was a beast. The yoga poses he did defied normal human anatomy. Every once in a while, he would do a demonstration to show us how the power of harnessing *Chi* worked. He would send *Chi* energy to his throat chakra and put a rope around his neck then hang himself from a tree. He could hang there for well over a minute with his legs crossed and his hands touching in a prayer position. Another time, he sent *Chi* to his fingertips and did push-ups with nothing but the tips of his two index fingers touching the ground.

He taught me all about the chakra systems and coached me on how to bring *Chi* energy into my body. In the mornings, I was instructed to wake up before the sun and meditate facing the jungle, where I could see the sunrise through the trees. Once I got comfortable doing this, he prescribed a specific regimen to release the entity attached to my body. It would happen over a four-day period with each day offering a different theme to release my Indian travel partner.

The week I attempted the exit strategy is something I'm not sure I will ever be able to wrap my head around. If I hadn't directly done it myself, I'm not sure I would believe that it happened. Each day I had a different theme that I was supposed to execute to get the *Spirit* to leave my body. On day one, I focused on the *Earthly* elements that I was in contact with. I offered them *Thanks* and *Praise*. I accepted all the things that had come into my *Life* whether I agreed with them or not. I took slow deep breaths, feeling the earth's atmosphere moving in and out of me. When I opened my eyes, I was in awe of how green the jungle was and how closely connected I felt to all the *Life* that was surrounding me.

On day two, I focused my meditation on the *Water* that was in and around me. I offered it *Thanks* and *Praise*. I felt the fluidity that composed my *Being*, and I shared a connection with all aspects of *Life* that depend upon this critical element. I opened myself up to the *Flow* of *All There Is* and asked it to cleanse me of any fear and regret that I might be holding on to. When I opened my eyes, it had started to rain, and each drop that touched my skin was a reminder of how lucky I was to be experiencing a new beginning.

On day three, the meditation was directed toward the *Wind*. I offered it *Thanks* and *Praise*. As I was breathing in and out, I felt the *Wind* float through me. It was the same *Wind* that made the trees dance and sing with ancient wisdom. It came and went as it pleased without ever wondering where to go. I asked the *Wind* to take me with it to places I had never been so that I could soar to heights beyond my imagination. When I opened my eyes, I saw the jungle swaying back and forth. The *Wind* touched each and every living thing in a way that invited all creation to bend without breaking.

On the fourth and final day, I called upon the element of *Fire*. I offered it *Thanks* and *Praise*. I felt the warmth of the sun breathe *Life* into the entire jungle as it poked its rays of vitality through the trees. As I breathed in, I invited *Passion* into my *Being*, the same *Fire* that I had misplaced for so many years when I lost my way. I asked for the energetic vibrancy of all that was *Good* to ignite my *Soul* in a way that would set *Fire* to my *Purpose*. When I opened my eyes, the sky looked like the volcano in the background had just erupted. The brilliance that illuminated the jungle had set *Fire* to all *Life* that it touched. The day was alive, and something inside of me was burning with a desire to demand more out of my efforts.

Suddenly, my body began to shake. I got dizzy and felt like I was about to pass out. I started to see stars, followed by tunnel vision, and then everything got blurry. Just before I was about to faint, a euphoric rush passed through my entire body, accompanied by a tingling sensation in my hands and feet. All at once, I felt a release, and my heart seemed to skip a beat.

A single dragonfly that was perched on the ledge in front of me took a long deep stare into my *Soul*. It was as if a chariot had arrived to escort a would-be traveler back to where it came from. When it flew away, so did a heaviness that I had been carrying with me for far too long. I felt a warmth within me and a sense of *Gratitude* suggesting that everything was going to be okay. As I watched it fade into the distance, I knew that a difficult chapter of my *Life* had come to an end. A shift in consciousness was upon me. Now all I needed to do was let it in.

I was pretty quiet the rest of the morning, reflecting on what had just happened. It felt weird to discuss what transpired with anyone because I was still having trouble *Believing* it myself. I had a cup of coffee then traveled up the cobblestone path to receive my first healing session of the day. When I came around the corner, Pak Heru was silently sitting by himself, smoking a cigarette. He was deep in thought, staring at the five-hundred-year-old trees as if they were engaged in a telepathic conversation. When I got closer, he put out his cigarette and walked toward me. Once we made eye contact, a huge grin lit up his face. He then shook both of his hands in the air and with excitement in his voice shouted out, "Good, Damien. Good work! You make Indian go home."

The healing sessions began to intensify as Heru took us deeper and deeper into his program. We were all receiving treatment, but each of us responded differently. The therapy had a way of bringing the ugliness we struggled with come bubbling to the surface. I was short-tempered and highly irritable. My body was constantly burning with nerve pain, and my muscles relentlessly ached.

At night, my body pulsated, and it kept me up for hours on end. Muscle spasms would make my arms and legs twitch nonstop, and I spent long hours in bed staring at the ceiling. When I did sleep, I had incredibly strange dreams that didn't seem to make any sense. Amid all the chaos, I found myself moving closer to a *Self* that was much easier to understand. A simple existence that was centered in the *Now*. The past and future were only a process that my mind was used to entertaining. As I continued to give into the *Now*, I found myself developing a clarity that did away with the need to question everything.

Georgio was an emotional mess. He was so far away from anything that resembled a comfort zone. His fears of being left out intensified to a point that he felt completely alienated. He struggled with thoughts about being insignificant and worried that he wasn't doing anything to move his life in the direction he wanted it to go. It was ironic because he was doing exactly what he left Utah to do. He was exploring himself intimately and working on improving the things he didn't like about who he was. The sessions forced him to focus on areas that were easy to avoid in the States. Countless distractions made it possible to hide the broken parts so well that he never had to deal with them. The isolation of the jungle, combined with the energy healing treatments he was receiving, was a potent blend of *Wellness* medicine that challenged him to the core.

The Chicken was on a whole different level. She seemed to breeze through the treatments with almost no physical reaction at all. Every once in a while, she would come out of a session describing certain visions she had, but nothing extraordinary. Then one afternoon, a session hit her like a ton of bricks. After her treatment was finished, she described seeing a vision of her *Mother's* eyes, followed by dizziness and an upset stomach. She passed on lunch and went to the room to lie down.

When Georgio and I were finished eating, we went down to the room to check on her. We opened the door and found her curled up in a blanket, crying hysterically. This was odd because she never cried. When Mamma Hen passed, I only saw her tear up maybe once. She was a stone-cold emotional gangster who took on the world like a championship boxer. Nothing really ever got her down. The emotional complexity of her childhood calloused her to normal everyday nonsense. What she was going through was not normal though.

I guess having parents pass away is part of life, but the process of dealing with grief is *Different* for each person. It's a reality that challenges the very *Essence* of our existence. Mortality isn't something that most people sit around and ponder daily. When the person that brought you into this world leaves the earthy plain, each individual finds themselves at a crossroad. The Little Chicken trained herself to keep going no matter how difficult things got. The time had come for her to slow down and finally deal with how she felt. Once the genie was out of the lamp, there was no chance it was going back inside.

She cried for two days straight. When she wasn't bombarded by emotions, she was sleeping. Treatment continued, but it was right back to the room as soon as the session was over. I felt so helpless. My superhero was in incredible pain, and there was nothing I could do about it. What she was going through had nothing to do with me though. It was a dragon she had to slay on her own. I was there to offer support in every way I could, but the time had come for her to shine *Light* on a dark reality.

On the third day, she woke up, and it was like nothing ever happened. It seemed as though the pain had just vanished. The Little One described it as being set free. The emotional burden she was carrying had been lifted, and a certain order was restored. When Mamma Hen passed, it changed the Chicken forever. I was afraid that a part of her died as well, and maybe it did. Cleaning out the skeletons in her closet created the *Potential* for something *Great* to develop in its place. The space for her to *Grow* without suffering is a gift Mamma Hen would be proud the Little One was now finally able to experience.

Traveling into the great unknown can be intimidating. I was *Grateful* that I had a team of people to do it with, so I didn't need to go about it alone. Knowing who was a part of this team was a bit hazy though. The Little Chicken was my ride-or-die girl. She had nothing left to prove at this point. I would roll my chair into oncoming traffic to save her if I needed to. The feeling was obliviously mutual, considering she willingly dove into this pot of boiling water with me headfirst.

Bringing Georgio with us was a gamble that definitely paid off. He was far from perfect and just the right amount of weird to add *Value* to our team. He pushed himself daily to become a better person. When he made mistakes, he dusted himself off and kept pushing. I would often tease him, saying he had a disorder that wouldn't let him give up even when he was in way over his head. He did everything in his power to offer himself *Unconditionally* to the cause. He's my *Brother* from another mother and the type of *Friend* I consider myself lucky to have.

By this point in the trip, we had moved into the master suite, and things began to establish a sense of normalcy. When the excitement of jungle living died down, a clear picture of what surrounded us began to take shape. The shock value of being in a foreign country was good footage for the documentary, and the Swiss director had his camera rolling to catch the honeymoon period of us getting settled. Occasionally, he would pop into the treatment room to catch a session, but with twelve appointments a week, he felt that it was redundant to be there all the time.

Filmmaking caught my attention in college, and I was excited at the opportunity to get back to it. I longed for a creative outlet, and the platform to formulate a beautiful motion picture was tremendous. Every time I tried to involve myself in the production though, I was subtly pacified. It was frustrating to not be involved in the creation process, and it didn't make sense to me why my opinion was not valued. When the idea to create a documentary first came about, it was agreed on that it would be about friendship, healing, and perseverance. That's not at all what it felt like.

Jasper the friendly ghost and Captain Nëvil the Swiss were partners in another business venture. Jasper's father had financed a 3D media company, and Nëvil was the lead animator and co-owner. The original game plan was that the documentary would be a project of their media company, and it worked well for multiple reasons, including the fact that they already had licensing rights to create media material in Indonesia based on their current work visas. Since Nëvil was already working on 3D assignments, it seemed reasonable to have him also direct the film out of sheer convince. I understood the arrangement and knew flexibility was key for everything to unravel smoothly.

Captain Nëvil the Swiss came equipped with an incredibly peculiar personality. He did and said whatever he wanted no matter what the circumstances were. He was brash and opinionated with little regard to what anyone else thought. His passive narcissism made him a bit of a loner, and he preferred to be alone in his room, working on the computer. When he wasn't working on 3D projects, he was incessantly focused on watching skateboard videos on the internet.

Jasper had a way with him. Nëvil respected him above all others and followed Jasper's lead in all business affairs. I liked Nëvil even though he had a tendency to be a bit of a spaz. Sometimes creative geniuses were difficult, and I learned this when I was involved in production work during college. I tried to give him space, but he had a way of rubbing me wrong. Once he figured out which buttons of mine to push, he liked to set me off. This was a difficult environment to heal in and somewhat problematic as he was trying to shoot a biography of my life.

Jasper was becoming less and less present at the clinic. He's a slippery fella that constantly jumps from continent to continent. He is a rolling stone that never really stays present in one place for too long. It was hard to get any momentum behind the numerous projects he was involved in, which created complications for all his business partners. His aloofness brought a certain ambiguity that was tough to be confident about. Since he was the catalyst for most of what was going on, his absence left gaping holes that became missed opportunities.

When he was off to other lands, he took the car with him. This limited our mobility, and we were subject to public transportation. The jungle didn't exactly have a coordinated bus system or subway. There were gutted minivans operated by locals with the seats removed in favor of wooden benches to promote maximum occupancy. It wasn't uncommon to see twelve to fifteen people crammed into a van. The hand-painted vans were color-coordinated according to the route traveled. In order to make trips to the local market, it was important to know the proper rainbow of colors needed to reach each destination. It was also smart to communicate with a trustworthy local to find out the appropriate faire. *Bules* (a slang term designated for foreigners with white skin) had a tendency to get charged double or triple if you lacked crafty negotiation skills.

The rainbow adventure transit system wasn't something I desired to participate in. A noodly quadriplegic isn't set up to travel on a sketchy minivan bench stuffed with locals. I had to pick and choose my battles in the jungle. Being there took just short of a miracle to pull off in the first place. I had to find *Patience* with what I could and couldn't do. I really wanted to experience all the mysteries the jungle had to offer, but accepting my limitations was another *Learning Opportunity* for me. I began to train my mind to give in to the *Lessons* this *Life* was offering me.

The Chicken and Georgio would go on hikes in the jungle and would come back with incredible stories about the things they had seen. Luckily, the Little One was exploring her *Passion* in photography, and she would come back with incredible photos and video segments. It was a cheap stand-in for actually experiencing the real thing with my wife, but what was I supposed to do? I couldn't exactly stand and hiking was certainly out of the question. It was an exercise in *Accepting* things as they were, and I was *Grateful* to have people in my *Life* that found ways to include me in every way they could.

Weeks seemed to fly by in the jungle, and I was making gradual physical and emotional improvements. On the days the clinic wasn't operational, we had the whole compound to ourselves. The opportunities to absorb the culture around us were truly humbling. I felt the way I understood *Life* start to *Change*. Simple pleasures like clean clothes and a warm shower were amenities I learned to *Value*. There was only one bathroom that all of us shared in the master suite. At times, there were up to eight people that needed to share hot water and a single mirror to get ready.

The kitchen we used to prepare our meals looked like something that would be found on an eighteenth century pirate ship, and so was dubbed the pirate kitchen. We had to fight off jungle cats, beetles, mosquitoes, spiders, sewer rats, and vast array of other critters just to get the food cooked. Then there was no guarantee that the food wouldn't kill us. The walls were infested with mold, and the plates and cutlery looked like relics rescued from an abandoned prison. There was only one cutting board that was used for everything. Chicken, fish, fruits, and vegetables we are all prepared on the same slab of mold-infested wood. On the days the staff went home, we tried to clean up a bit, but our efforts were wildly unsuccessful.

As our four-month journey came to an end, we were happily surprised with the therapeutic gains that had been made. In a relatively short time, we had become *Different* people. Being exposed to a completely *Different* way of *Living*, *Changed* the way we *Understood* our existence. Before getting on the plane back to the States, we found out that the clinic would only be open for another four months. When the clinic closed down, Pak Heru committed to Jasper that he would travel with us to Bali to set up a new healing clinic.

We had no way of telling what the future might bring, but the potential looked incredibly promising. My body was healing, and Pak Heru estimated that I could make a full recovery by the end of the next calendar year. The plan was to go home for a few weeks to reevaluate our options. Jasper held to his promise of covering the first four months, and it had been an incredible journey. There were a few bumps in the road, but it was expected considering our outlandish plan.

Upon our return to the States, we had some serious *Soul-searching* to do. Coming back to continue what we started seemed to be a particularly enticing option. We would need to go back to the drawing board to iron out the details, but returning to Indonesia seemed like an exciting idea worth entertaining. Once we boarded the plane, a certain reality hit us. We did it. We just completed an unbelievable journey against all odds. Now the question was, should we return to the scene of the unthinkable and continue to push our limits?

Decisions

The comforts of home felt incredible. We slid right back into our old life almost like we never left. Something was *Different* though. As we sat in our adjustable electric bed, watching our big screen TV, something was off. It was eerie how nothing had changed. It was almost like our life got put on pause and we hit the resume button like nothing ever happened. But something did happen, something major.

Our *Awareness* had grown in a way that made it impossible to see things the same. To say it was the same but *Different* doesn't even come close to capturing the significant shift that had taken place inside us. I had been wearing the same two pair of shoes for the last four months. Now I had a closet full of shoes. What did all this mean? How was I supposed to find *Balance* with all the things that were completely unnecessary just the week before?

Both the Chicken and I also noticed stuff about our *Friends* and *Family* that we never bothered to pay attention to before. It was so amazing to be in the presence of people that truly *Loved* us. The emphasis that *Families* in the jungle put on the people surrounding them was like nothing else mattered. We now realized there was nothing more important than the people we *Loved*.

At the end of the day, each person only has a certain amount of energy to distribute in whatever manner they chose. We had a new appreciation for how to prioritize our energy output. I found myself feeling overwhelming *Grateful* for just about everything I came in contact with. Simple pleasures like coffee with an old *Friend*, or a conversation with my *Grandpa* took on a whole new meaning. I even began to appreciate little things like warm showers, clean paved roads, and the world-famous California weather.

We also noticed a different side of things that wasn't as pleasant. In the jungle, life was simple. Since distractions were minimal, the opportunity to express one's love for life wasn't so complicated. At home, there seemed to be so much going on. It was difficult to sift through all the nonsense to get to what actually mattered. Our *Friends* and *Family* appeared to be hung up on all kinds of energetic vacuums that drained their vitality. With so many different things pulling in every direction, it made sense why everyone was so easily distracted by stuff that didn't seem to matter.

Everything about the way I understood my *Life* had *Changed*. I was no longer plagued by the same obstacles that got under my skin before leaving for Indonesia. That doesn't mean that nothing got to me though. I found myself getting caught up on how frustrating it was that people couldn't see the source of their own unhappiness. Now that I had begun to experience my life with much less resistance, I wanted to share it with everyone I *Loved*. Just because I had experienced a shift in consciousness didn't mean that the world around me had changed. Now that I was able to see things in a *Different Light*, my eyes were open to how far away from the *Self* that our entire society had become.

I was experiencing distance between others and myself that surprised me in a way I had not prepared for. The jungle educated me about the power of *Oneness* that is shared with *Everything there Is*. Now that I was back home, I felt more detached from everything than I ever did before. People seemed to be quarreling about stuff that just didn't matter. They were striving for things that would only make their lives more complicated. The path toward achieving stuff and attaining goals was so complicated that even when a desired endeavor was complete; it just led to more searching.

This sucked, man. I expected to come home to a life that I could appreciate more and have endless gratitude for. With all the meaningless nonsense going on around me, how was I supposed to go about doing that? Then it hit me. It was the very process of expectation that was generating the cracks in my energy system. I was falling victim to the same process that was draining the energy of everyone around me. I had again fallen ill to a Western sickness that suggested a four-month trip was the pill that would fix everything. I still had a lifetime of cultural programming embedded in the fabric of who I was. There is no pill, no Band-Aid, and no road trip that will make that disappear.

If I wanted the lessons I had learned in Indonesia to stick, I needed to make *Conscious Decisions* to expand my *Awareness* every day. I found myself getting discouraged about how easy it was to fall back into the same patterns of thought that I had previously struggled with. It was important for me to be *Patient* with the *Process* though. I read that every time we have a thought, it strengthens the pathway in our brain. I had been reinforcing my old way of thinking my entire life. The road my thoughts were used to traveling on, the only ones they knew to take, were ten-lane highways congested with rush-hour traffic. This new way of thinking was more difficult to travel, a scant dirt road only containing trace footprints reminding me where to go.

As I looked at all the "stuff" around me, I caught myself not caring much about it at all. It was great to be around all the people I *Loved*, but my training was incomplete. If I really wanted to enjoy the bliss of what I learned, I needed to find a way to make it last forever. I knew the only way I would be able to share what I learned was by embracing it fully without a shadow of doubt. My frustration meant that my eyes were now open. The question was, Now what was I going to do about it?

One of my favorite quotes of all time is by martial arts master Bruce Lee. He said, "Empty your cup so that it may be filled. Become devoid to gain totality." I had let go of my *Suffering*, but when I came home, I filled my cup with frustration. *Letting Go* was a new concept for me, and I still needed to learn the totality of *Surrender*. Everyone has a different gauge when labeling things as right or wrong. Good and bad. *Surrender* doesn't deal with that type of currency. There is no duality when it comes to *Acceptance, Compassion, Forgiveness,*

Humility, Surrender, Understanding, Valor, and *Love.* They stand alone, and you either have them or you don't.

One night when the Little Chicken and I were sitting in bed, zoning out in front of the television, I suddenly shut it off. We sat there quiet for a moment, both pondering the same thing. It wasn't necessary for either one of us to speak right away because it was obvious what was on both of our minds. I was the one to break the silence.

"Should we go back?"

"I think we have to," she said.

"How? We don't have the means to make that happen," I replied.

"It doesn't matter. If we are supposed to go back, it will just happen. I feel like we need to finish what we started. There's more out there for us to discover about *Ourselves.*"

"We need to go all in then. Sell everything. Our car, all our belongings, everything. I don't wanna come back to this same life. If we're going to do this, we need to put everything on the line and never look back," I said with zero hesitation.

"A lot would need to happen for everything to fall into place. Let's put it in motion and see what the universe has to say about it," commented the Little One.

She was right. A mountain of things would need to be considered if we were going to leave our entire lives behind and move to the other side of the world. This wasn't a four-month sabbatical; it was a *Life-changing* decision. It didn't exactly make a lot of sense on paper. We were grown adults with serious responsibilities that demanded our attention. There was more to this than just returning to the jungle to see if a healer could help me walk again. It was an exciting possibility, but there had to be more to it if we were going to put all our chips on the table.

We both felt the transformation that had taken place inside us. A *Light* had been switched on that showed us a version of what we could *Be.* We began to understand a limitless *Potential* that was beyond our current way of thinking. Wellness comes from within, and scratching the surface wasn't enough for us. It was time for us to start playing with the creative *Possibilities* readily available within all of us.

The next day, the Chicken and I created a spreadsheet detailing the costs of what it would take to make this happen. We learned that one of the first things needed to create something incredible is a clear and distinct plan of how to make the vision happen. There were a number of costs we needed to evaluate that had nothing to do with money. We had two dogs that we *Loved* dearly that we needed to find a permanent home for. *Family* looked after them the first time we left, but we needed to find a more permanent solution for our indefinite leave of absence.

The stability of our son's home life was also currently in shambles. Axel the biker was working long hours trying to keep his shop together and pay the bills associated with it. He also had certain obligations to his biker gang that didn't exactly provide the best influence for a teenager to develop pristine morals. The bottom line is that Axel was preoccupied with numerous responsibilities that made it difficult for him to be around very often. For Jayko to avoid becoming a full-time pirate, we reached out to offer him the adventure of a lifetime.

He was going into his junior year of high school but described his life as less than desirable. He's an old *Soul* that was frustrated with the stagnation of his daily affairs. We explained to him that there was no way to accurately describe what he would be getting himself into. But like most teenagers, he was sure that anywhere was better than where he was. Since it would take stern discipline to stay on top of his studies doing home school, we put the ball in his court. We told him if he was serious about coming with us that it was up to him to figure out how he was going to finish high school.

After totaling up the possible money we could make selling our car, television, furniture, and appliances, we were still well short of what it would take to make the trip happen. We were going to need to come up with a sponsor. There were so many people that helped make my life incredible over the years that I didn't feel comfortable asking my support system to continue to nickel and dime our way toward another pipe dream. I really *Believed* in this opportunity though. I just needed to find someone that *Believed* in it as much as I did.

I set up a meeting with Mr. Hapnin to share our travels with him and to explain the opportunity we had in front of us. When I came to him with our detailed plan he could see how serious I was. I explained that the healing sessions were working, and the treatment looked like it was going to take another year. I also explained to him that the clinic was closing down and the healer was interested in starting a clinic with us in Bali.

Mr. Hapnin was intrigued by the project but was more moved by the *Changes* he saw in the Chicken and I. He could see that I was hungry and that something about me was *Changing*. Mr. Hapnin is a seasoned professional, and he knew a good thing when he saw it. He *Believed* in the Chicken and I and knew in his bones that something *Good* was going on. Since he wasn't quite sure what part of our plan had the most *Value*, he kept things simple and chose to invest in our *Process* of *Coming to Be*.

He saw a *Higher Power* at work with what the Chicken and I were looking to create. He also *Believed* in the approach that the two of us were taking. We were investing in *Ourselves* so that we could give back to the world in a major way. He understood the importance of becoming whole and knew there was only one way to go about it—all in or nothing. This is something he could firmly get behind. When he saw our plan and the fire in our eyes, he agreed to finance our healing expedition. As for the wellness center, he agreed to meet with us about it once we got all our ducks in a row.

Jasper was incredibly optimistic. He believed once the healer confirmed his interest in creating a clinic, everything would be smooth sailing from there. It looked like that was exactly what was happening. When I expressed a few very realistic concerns, he assured me that the hard part was over. He painted a picture for the Chicken and I that was hard to argue. So far, all his outrageous ideas had fallen into place in quite a surreal fashion, so it was tough to doubt him at this point.

He yanked us out of our comfort zone and delivered on one of the most miraculous experiences that we had ever participated in. There were a few speed bumps in the program, but how could there not be? Taking a quadriplegic to a Third World country on the other side of the world was bound to have a few hiccups. He was also responsible for coming up with a director and equipment to shoot a documentary just like he said he would. The treatment was offering benefit, and it looked like it would only continue to do so.

Jasper encouraged us to go all-in. "This is bound to work," he would say, "and if it doesn't, I'll be there to help you. We're in this together, partners. Just like we discussed in the very beginning. It's great that you have a sponsor," he said. "Now you have a safety net, but you won't need it. Soon enough, we will be making money in Bali. Once we secure investment capital, it's game over. The idea is a hit, and it's just the right place in the world for a business like this to explode. Damien and I will produce and market the whole thing, and the Chicken can do all the social media. She can also help Nëvil as a second cameraman, and when the film is finished, the two of them can edit it together. Once the clinic is open, we will all be so busy running it that we will hire staff to do all the grunt work. This way, we can focus on the things we want to do. Damien will be the director of the clinic, because once he's on his feet, it will shock the whole world. Everybody will be a believer in what we are doing, and Damien will be there to walk them through the whole process. The Chicken will be the lead hypnotherapist and do all the media production work on the side. It's a brilliant, fail-proof plan."

Things were looking up, and I was pretty excited to say the least. I was driven and truly *Believed* we could make this all happen. Everything was lining up perfectly. We put our stuff for sale on the internet, and *poof*, it just disappeared. Someone called about our car and said they would be there the next afternoon and pay cash for it. Before we knew it, we had a fist full of dollars, and our car was gone.

Mountains were moving, and everything was falling into place like it was meant to happen. It was hard not to see what the universe was telling us to do. We just went with it, man. We were caught in a whirlwind, and things were unfolding almost effortlessly. Sixteen-year-old Jayko even found an incredible online school all by himself. The strangest part about it was it was free. All we needed to do was pay for books. Georgio was in for round two of the Indonesian experience, and everything seemed locked and loaded.

The last thing we needed to do before shipping out was meet with Mr. Hapnin about the potential of him getting behind the wellness clinic project. While we were getting our affairs in order, Jasper was working on the business plan for the healing center. He was super excited and wanted to wait until he was finished before showing it to me. He promised it would be brilliant and wanted me to trust in the plans we made together. He said most of it was already done, he just needed to make a few tweaks so it would cater to Mr. Hapnin's specific interests.

The Chicken and I were so overwhelmed with getting our lives together to move across the globe that we had no choice but to have faith in our partner. I set up the meeting with Mr. Hapnin two days before we were scheduled to get on the plane and set off for the next leg of our journey. We were to meet at a coffee shop to have a casual look at the plan, and if things went well, we would make another meeting with the appropriate professionals to get the project off the ground.

When we met at the coffee shop, our heads were still spinning. We were so excited about the adventure ahead of us. Our focus was on dotting all the *i*'s and crossing all the *t*'s. We knew that once we got on that plane, there was nothing to come back to. Our life as we knew it would be *Changed* forever. No dogs, no car, no apartment, no job. My *Family* let us keep our bed and a small TV in the room I grew up in so we had a place to stay when we came to visit, but that was it.

We showed up at the coffee shop before Mr. Hapnin to grab a drink and go over our strategy about how to present the plan. When Jasper slid the business plan across the table, I noticed the bound stack of papers looked a little light. As I started to flip through it, I noticed that Jasper didn't find it necessary to dot his *i*'s and cross his *t*'s. The plan was a PowerPoint treatment at best with typos from front to back. It was mostly pictures and concepts with only a brief snapshot of financials.

When I first read through it, I finished and asked him where the full business plan was. He told me that was it. I said, "You're joking, right? We have a business tycoon about to arrive in ten minutes, and this thing isn't even spell-checked." He assured me it was just a first run-through. The concepts were intended to dazzle him so he would get excited to eventually see the master plan. He muttered that this was a coffee shop meeting, not the meeting with his board of directors.

Sliding down in my chair wasn't an option because I would have ended up on the floor. I did feel like I just swallowed one of the Kevlar-style jungle beetles with the long pincher-looking things though. I froze. The confidence that I had about what we were doing went from feeling like an alpha lion to a field mouse in about ten seconds. I wanted to call the meeting off and reschedule for a different time when we had our shit together. Right then, Mr. Hapnin pulled into the parking spot in front of the table where we were sitting.

I didn't panic; I just changed my strategy a bit. I shifted my focus to the excitement surrounding the healing opportunity we were about to embark on. I didn't want him losing confidence about the asset he saw so much potential in. What the Chicken and I were doing was an epic adventure that Mr. Hapnin truly *Believed* in. I *Believed* in myself and the support system that was around me. Everyone thought I was crazy, but in a way, that showed *Value* in how it was being approached. As for Jasper's end of the bargain, I let him speak for himself.

I would say he put his foot in his mouth, but it was more like he did a mound of cocaine then swallowed his entire leg. He was sweating like a whore in church and rambled on and on like he was selling secondhand paintings at a swap meet auction. Once Mr. Hapnin had enough, he broke up the conversation by inviting us to his home just up the road. He asked the Chicken to ride with him and suggested it was so she could drive his car. He just so happened to be putting around in the Little Chicken's dream car.

When we got to his house, it was more of the same. I believe he wanted to give the situation a moment to cool off, because he could tell Jasper was nervous and he needed a moment to collect himself. When we were all seated in Mr. Hapnin's living room, he took the lead this time. He began asking questions to try to clarify what the core concepts of the plan were. He wanted details about how we were going to execute our strategies. When I tried to slide in to do some damage control, Jasper chimed in with more fast talk super strategy.

The time he was given to collect himself was used to reload his gun to continue firing away like a drunken cowboy. It was as if he were a spinning top going around and around in circles. Right when it seemed like he might be getting to a point, he would bounce off in another direction. This meeting session was much shorter, and when Mr. Hapnin's wife and kids came in the house, he excused himself to go eat dinner with his *Family*. On our way out, Mr. Hapnin put his hand on my shoulder and winked at me. He wished us safe travels and told me to call him once we got settled in.

I wanted to throw up. I'd crashed and burned in a business pitch before, but Jasper just took it to a whole new level. It was more like a nuclear bomb just hit, and it was only a matter of time until all the survivors died of radiation poisoning. There had to be a silver lining; everything felt too good for there not to be. Right before I rolled down the windows of the car to alleviate the feeling of suffocation, the Chicken told me about what Mr. Hapnin said to her on the car ride over.

When she got behind the wheel of the beautiful machine Mr. Hapnin was cruising around in, she realized what was going on.

"What are your thoughts on this Jasper guy? Do you trust him?" Mr. Hapnin asked.

While trying to avoid yanking the wheel into a head-on collision with the nearest tree to end her embarrassment, she replied, "He's followed through on all the promises he's made so far."

"That's not what I asked. Do you trust him?" he asked again emphatically.

"I have no reason not to. He's done everything he said he was going to," she replied with a sliver of confidence.

"How do you like the car?" he asked her.

"It's unbelievable. It's everything I thought it would be and more," she said.

"It could be yours. Everything you could ever imagine will be yours if you *Believe* in *Yourself*. You and Damien have everything you need between the two of you to be *Great*. Just *Believe* in the way God can work through you, and all your dreams will become a reality."

My brain was like scrambled eggs with no butter, man. I didn't have the *Life* experience behind my travels to process everything that was going on around me. All I knew was that I had a plane to catch and *Life* was going to unravel the way it was supposed to. I put my *Faith* in a *Higher Power* and trusted in the *Unconditional Love* I had all around me. The rest was up to the universe to figure out. I had a good feeling about what was ahead, but it definitely looked like it was going to be a wild ride.

When we arrived at the jungle clinic in Sukabumi, it was a lot of the same with just a few variations. The word got out that the clinic was shutting down and there were significantly fewer local patients showing up each day. Most of the staff had been laid off, and only the critical players were still around to keep the clinic operational. This made our stay a little more comfortable because most of the rooms were no longer occupied. Georgio and Jayko got their own room at no extra cost, which gave the Chicken and me a bit of space. We all still needed to share a bathroom, but it was a serious upgrade.

Upon our return, Jasper left with the car to pursue a romantic interest followed by a lengthy "business" trip. We were left to fend for ourselves with the rainbow minivan transit system for six weeks. We were confident in our jungle survival skills at this point, and not having a car was just another minor inconvenience. It was probably better that we put some space between us anyway after the coffee shop debacle.

Having Jayko with us was another significant upgrade to our jungle healing team. We got to completely relive the excitement of being in such a shockingly incredible new place. He was blown away, just as we were when we first arrived. As he tried to wrap his head around the intensity of the decision to come with us, jungle life provided him with the same mysterious allure that we had grown to *Love*.

I had another miraculous *Opportunity* to participate in the development of a young man's *Life*. This was different than with the Punk Rock Princess because it was more intimate, and the time we shared was void of all the distractions that come with living in the States. Part of me felt bad that he wasn't able to figure himself out by making dumb teenage mistakes with his friends. But another side of me was happy to be exposing him to raw *Life* lessons at such an influential age. Jungle life would show him the *Value* of the human experience and help him *Understand* the importance of what really matters. This experience was hard-core but pure in its *Essence*.

Within a week of our arrival, we all came down with an Indonesian flu. The sickness in the jungle is no ordinary cough and sniffly nose. We were all filthy sick. It lasted about a week. Treatments continued, but some of them took place in our beds because we were not well enough to leave the room. Pak Heru chuckled as usual and offered us herbal medicine to soothe our stomachs. Right when we thought we had made it through the thick of it, another unpleasant surprise was right around the corner.

With the decline in clients at the clinic, it meant funding to run things was also minimal. The food selection went from limited to vastly meager. This was a rude awakening for young Jayko. The lady that ran the kitchen did what she could to put food on the table, but she had to cut corners to make it work. We ate vegetable soup, chicken, rice and tempeh twice a day. In the mornings, it was either white bread or rice porridge.

One afternoon after treatment, we bellowed into the kitchen completely famished. We all inhaled the chicken, rice and soup, except for the Little One. For whatever reason, she wasn't in the mood for fried chicken. Jayko immediately pounced on the opportunity and promptly scarfed down the extra portion. It turned out the chicken was a few days old. The power in the kitchen had also gone out the night before leaving the poultry to stew in its own warm juices. I don't know if it was the chicken that went bad or if the filth of the pirate kitchen finally got to us, but Jayko, Georgio, and I all became violently ill.

Liquid fire was coming out of both ends nonstop for days straight. It felt like the demons of all the bad food we ate back in the States were being purged from our bodies. Georgio and I recovered in about three days, but poor Jayko spent the next two weeks incredibly sick. At one point, we considered taking him to the hospital because he couldn't even keep down rice and water. The poor guy had been sick for three weeks of the first month of our trip. Following his most recent brush with death, he swore off anything cooked by the clinic staff. All of a sudden, the minivan transit system wasn't such a sketchy option. Georgio and Jayko would team up to execute grocery missions to the local market once a week, and the Little One began making our meals.

The therapy sessions had been kicked into high gear, and Pak Heru added an exercise routine to go along with his treatments. At the end of the day, I was so exhausted I could hardly feed myself. Just lifting a spoon to my mouth took tremendous effort. I continued to improve, but the progress was slow and painful. With fewer patients came more quality time with the healer. His laser focus intensified, and I got all the healing energy this Indonesian jungle healer had to offer.

Our days at the clinic also started to change. Pak Heru joined Georgio and me during our morning meditations. He would teach us ways to better our technique and gave us pointers on how to harness our *Chi*. His assistants, Larno and Bang Bang, would go on long walks with the Chicken through the jungle. They would enjoy the morning air and take pictures of the rich culture and natural beauty. After our healing sessions, we spent more personal time with everyone exchanging language lessons and playing chess. We shared laughs while eating together as we stumbled on our words, desperately trying to communicate with our limited vocabulary. On the final day of treatment, Pak Heru's *Family* and *Friends* started coming to the clinic. They would bring with them traditional Indonesian food and decorate the table with large banana leaves. We would feast together while enjoying a bond between two different cultures coming together as *One*.

One night, we were invited to a large Muslim gathering that took place in the waiting room area of the clinic. Members of the community all came dressed in elaborate ceremonial gowns to pay their respects to their Guru that had passed away a year earlier. There were food, drinks, children, and elders. When the village's high priest showed up dressed in all white, with an epically seasoned beard that must have been a decade in the making, the ceremony began.

Everyone sat on the floor in a circle on prayer mats. The high priest said something in Bahasa, then in unison, they started chanting a Muslim prayer. The Chicken and I positioned ourselves just outside the door to avoid creating a distraction. When Larno noticed us outside looking in, he motioned for us to join their prayer circle. We were no longer strange white people here to be served by the locals. We had been invited into the most *Sacred* part of their *Lives*. It made us feel like we found *Family* on the other side of the world.

When Jasper returned with the car, we had an opportunity to visit Pak Heru at his home for dinner. We heard stories about his astonishing pet collection that we couldn't wait to see. He had a ten-foot python, two luwak cats, a crocodile, piranhas, a snapper turtle, and a couple of flying squirrels. When we arrived, we were greeted like royalty. They lived in a good-sized home by Indonesian standards, and all the animals were offered the same *Respect* as the humans, even the aggressive alligator that chased the children around the house.

After a tasty meal of sautéed goat kebabs, locally grown vegetables, tempeh, tofu, and rice, we all sat in the living room to share stories. We learned about how they grew up in extreme poverty with little to no food or shelter. Pak Heru also told us about his yearlong pilgrimage into the jungle. He and a meditation Guru traveled deep into the thick woods in nothing but loincloths. They would meditate for weeks straight, only stopping to eat and sleep. All they drank was rainwater, and the only food they ate was cassava (tree roots). They spent their time tuning into the vibrations of nature and harnessing the powerful *Chi* of the jungle.

His wife, Nuli, told us different stories about before Pak Heru decided to become a healer. She said he had a serious affinity for tuwak and arak, which were the locally brewed alcohols of choice among the locals. Nuli swore she saved him from an alcoholic life of mediocrity. He would also go on hunting expeditions with his friends in Sumatra. They would hunt lions, tigers, and bears with nothing but a hunting knife. After this story, Pak Heru darted up the stairs to grab his trophies.

He brought back deer antlers, tiger pelts, and a venomous cobra he caught and preserved in a bottle with homemade formaldehyde. He also carried with him a small showcase that had twenty-five miraculous gemstones on display beneath a glass cover. He made thousands of stones over the years, but this case contained a collection of his personal favorites.

They were all unbelievable, but one in particular caught my eye. When the light would hit it, a kaleidoscope of colors cascaded in every direction. It was a white opal that seemed to have all the mysteries of the universe embedded into one small stone. Pak Heru explained that whoever wore that ring created a relationship with it. If you knew how to listen to it, the stone would accurately reflect whatever emotion the person was feeling.

He unlocked the box and pulled the stone out of the case. He grabbed my arm, put the ring in the palm of my hand, and wrapped my fingers around it. It was the only one he had like this; I felt uncomfortable accepting such a generous gift. I tried to put it on, but it didn't fit any of my fingers. I tried to tell Heru it was a sign and I couldn't accept the only gem from his collection like this. He said, "I'll have one of my assistants make you a ring that fits when we return to the clinic. The stone called for you, Damien. You must take it. It's my gift to you. It's the way it's meant to be."

When the evening was over, we thanked the entire *Family* and set off into the night on the long broken roads back to the clinic. The next morning, one of the groundskeepers went into the jungle to retrieve some fresh bamboo. When he returned, it was stripped down and braided into a ring to mount the stone Heru gave me the night before. I put it on and never took it off. Each morning when I came into therapy, he would take one look at my hand and know right away what type of day it was going to be.

In the meantime, the water had begun to boil between Nëvil the Swiss and me. His utter disregard for people's privacy and personal space got on my nerves, but that wasn't the issue I was most concerned with. Before Jasper left on another journey abroad, I expressed my concerns to him. I told him that if our film was going to reflect *Love*, *Friendship*, and *Perseverance*, that footage of special moments like a dinner with Pak Heru's *Family* was important to capture. Since we had been back, Nëvil hadn't picked up the camera once. He specifically said that what was going on every day was boring, and nothing significant was happening that would be good material for a documentary.

I'm far from being a professional filmmaker, but I know that magic can happen at any moment. When I worked on creating a television show in college, we would shoot hundreds of hours of footage for a half-hour episode. We would shoot great ideas that came out crap on film and garbage ideas that ended up being brilliant segments for the show. The rule of thumb for our production staff was to shoot as much as possible and sort it out in the editing room. We had been back at the clinic for just over two months, and Nëvil never took the camera out of the case.

Jasper's response was that Nëvil was under a lot of pressure creating content for the 3D company. He also needed to do side projects so he could make money to continue to donate his free time to the documentary. Jasper suggested that if I had a problem with his process, I should bring it up with Nëvil. He didn't have time for a production meeting because he had a date with a new girl and her two kids in Jakarta. He promised to take the whole family out for dinner and the movies before he set off on another business trip.

What Jasper didn't know was that I was well aware of what Nëvil was doing with his free time. He decided that his room was too congested and it didn't have enough natural light. He liked the table in our room because he felt less cramped and there was a much better internet connection. He would barge into our room while we were still sleeping and open all the windows, claiming that the natural light inspired his creativity. He claimed to be rendering animation projects, but I mostly saw him surfing the web and watching skate videos.

On our trip back to the States, the Chicken and I decided that part of our extended growth plan involved shooting an incredible documentary, and I would finish my book. This way, no matter what happened we would have something that we could call our own to share with the world when we returned home. We sensed the relationship going south with Nëvil, and we put some backup options into place in case we needed to call upon them. The next order of business was discussing our concern with Nëvil to see if moving forward with him as our director was a realistic plan.

With Jasper off doing his thing, we approached Nëvil in the most *Compassionate* way we knew how. The Chicken and I didn't want him to feel like we were ganging up on him, so we had our meeting in a neutral setting and let him speak first. He complained about feeling boxed in and that we were expecting too much from him as a filmmaker. He didn't agree with the way we wanted to capture emotion with the movie. The concept he signed on with Jasper to film had a fairly simple plot as far as he understood it. Guy breaks neck. Guy sees healer. Guy makes miraculous recovery and goes surfing with an old friend. When the film is complete, it becomes a marketing tool to launch a wellness center.

We explained to him that even if that were the case, it was important to have the camera rolling as much as possible. When we went all-in selling our belongings and moving to the other side of the world, it was proof that we were fully committed to the project. In our opinion, he didn't seem to share the same dedication to creating something incredible. I had seen dozens of doctors and healers over the years, and I was still in a chair. We wanted the film to reflect the efforts of never giving up *Hope* and how important it is to *Believe* in the endless potential of the human *Spirit*. Our interest in making a film was to show the world how the journey is often more important than the destination. If for some reason I didn't end up walking, we still had the desire to share a remarkable journey about *Love, Friendship*, and *Perseverance*.

It was almost like it was the first time Nëvil had heard where we wanted to go with the film. Isolated production meetings removed any input that the Chicken and I had to offer. Nëvil was taken aback by the flood of new information offering an entirely different perspective. Once the meeting came to an end, we agreed on some fairly reasonable terms that respected the needs of everyone involved. Well, almost everyone. Shortly after our discussion, we overheard Nëvil speaking with Jasper on the phone. To this day, we have no idea what the two of them talked about, but a permanent energetic shift had been etched in stone. Nëvil collected all his belongings from our room and became a complete recluse for the rest of the time we were at the clinic.

More clarity was on the horizon, and it came in the form of Jasper's father returning to the clinic. He reappeared as a liaison for a friend and decided to stick around to get a bit more treatment himself. One afternoon after lunch, Gargamel struck up a conversation with the Chicken and me. He had a belly full of harsh criticism that he felt the need to unload on both of us.

The first few missiles were aimed at the Chicken when he claimed that the followers she generated on social media were fraudulent. He called her an idiot and said her efforts were embarrassing. He said, "I told Jasper that you ignorant Americans were good for nothing when it came to getting things done. Jasper doesn't know a single thing about wellness. You can't believe a word he says because he's a total failure. He hasn't been successful at anything in his whole life. I just keep giving him money because I'm his father and I don't want to crush his spirit. He's totally worthless, just like you two."

He continued, "As for you, Damien, don't think anything you're doing means a damn thing. Your effort toward therapy is meaningless. We could have brought any cripple in here to take your place. There's nothing special about you. Pak Heru is the miracle man. I have no idea why Jasper is wasting his time and my money making a movie about a fat, lazy American. My wife is a real professional that should have been in charge of this project from the beginning. You might have some crap marketing degree from a private school in the States, but she's run successful businesses in the real world. She has highly influential connections all over Bail, which means a lot more than the silly little games you played while being babysat at a university."

I thought to myself, *Wow, that sure is one way to get a point across.* There was so much hate and frustration behind his outlandish comments that there was no chance I was going to give him the satisfaction of letting it get to me. It affected the Little One quite differently though. In that very moment, if the Chicken would have had a sharp object or gun in her hands, I would be telling a completely different story. Her face turned bright red, and I'm surprised I didn't see actual smoke coming out of her ears, because she was fuming. I gently put my hand on her leg and asked her calmly to leave the room. I assured her I would handle it.

When she stepped out of the room, I looked at this haggard old man directly in the eyes and politely said, "Sir, don't ever talk to my wife like that again. I have no idea what makes you think you can speak like that to anybody, but if I ever hear you speak to her like that again, we're going to have a serious problem. If you think that because I'm in a wheelchair you can do and say whatever you want, you are sadly mistaken."

A few months earlier, before my healing trip to the jungle, I would have probably spent every penny I had to fly one of my hoodlum *Friends* over from the States. I have a handful of buddies that see life much differently than the average Joe. I *Love* them and *Accept* them for who they are, and in turn, they would do pretty much anything for me. There are some sick people in this life that get joy out of hurting people. For a plane ticket and a six-pack of beers, all I would need to do is point this old sorry bag of rocks out, and they would attack him like a wild animal.

But I was in a *Different* place now. I had become a *Different* person. His words meant nothing to me. Why would they? They weren't true. I was giving everything I had, and I knew it. I *Believed* in *Myself*. I *Believed* in the Chicken, Jayko, Georgio, and everyone else that *Loved* me *Unconditionally*. I was participating in something that most people never get the opportunity to. There was so much to be *Grateful* about, and it felt much better than letting myself be angry. By dodging the emotional drama that could have been attached to it, I was able to get a clear picture of what I was dealing with. It was critical information that would help me navigate some tough times ahead.

The day the clinic closed was a little bittersweet for everyone. A few tears were shed by both Eastern and Western *Friends* alike. So many amazing things had happened while we were there, and years of magic had taken place at the clinic before we knew it existed. The Chicken had a final request for Pak Heru before we departed for the last time. The approach was stealthy, and she had been working the angle for months. Her final wish was for the luwak cat that had been sentenced to life in prison on the compound to be released into the jungle. She had been feeding it and playing the ukulele next to its cage since we arrived. Heru offered his classic chuckle and agreed to drop the life sentence and release the luwak under the designation of time served.

Learning

We stayed in Jakarta for a few days while our temporary villa in Bali was being prepared. The jungle was an amazing experience, but it was nice to drink a fancy coffee and eat some legit pizza. We even caught a movie at one of the super mall's luxury theaters. Our short stay also reminded us about a very obvious but important lesson: we were privileged foreigners in a strange land.

As a single mother with a full-time job, the Little One didn't have much time for hobbies. At a young age, she fell in *Love* with photography. Once she became a *Mother*, her *Passion* got replaced by maternal demands. The jungle gave her the *Opportunity* to reconnect with *Herself*. Part of the process included finding her eye through the lens of an old friend.

She saw something special in the suspended moments that often go unnoticed in everyday life. Her eye as a street photographer got better every time she picked up a camera. Once the photos were uploaded to her computer, she would spend hours manipulating them. The art of getting the moment just right was an activity that inspired her to be *Great*.

The day before our plane left for Bali, she was in downtown Jakarta with Nëvil snapping some photos. Without warning, two hooded locals raced by on a motorbike and snatched her camera right out of her hands. It happened so fast that the lanyard attached to the camera yanked her to the ground. Before she could even look up, the shady culprits dashed off with her most prized possession.

The rest of her day was ruined, and the excitement of being in a new place had become grossly tainted.

Of course, she was bummed that her camera was gone, but her innocence had been violated. We were sheltered by the jungle, but the time had come for us to recognize how much of a privileged life we had in the United States. Sure, crime went on back home, but having white skin in this foreign land put a target on our backs. In the jungle, we were like celebrities. We were stopped at the market, and entire families would huddle around us so they could take a picture. Sometimes people even wanted an autograph, thinking we might be someone famous.

Things were much different in the city. From here on out, we needed to watch our backs. A camera like the one stolen from the Chicken could be easily sold on the black market. A local family could eat for a month with the money they would make selling it. Protecting ourselves was now a serious priority, and it was important for us to be *Aware* of our surroundings.

We landed in Bali just in time for the sunset. The moment we got off the plane, we could feel that we were in a special place. The locals called it the Island of the Gods. Bali is primarily Hindu, which was a different vibe than the Muslim locals we lived with in the jungle. The pace of life was significantly different, but the locals connected to their land in the same *Sacred* manner. It made sense why it was such a heavy travel destination. The energy of the whole island was extremely laid-back. It had a *Spiritual* buzz to it that was curiously inviting.

The drive to our villa wasn't quite as shocking as when we first arrived in Jakarta, but seeing a new place for the first time was still an exhilarating experience. I had dreamed of coming here since my conversation with Jasper the friendly ghost back in prep school. I had finally made it. Since we hadn't yet secured permanent lodging, Jasper had a friend that offered us a temporary solution. His friend was looking after a property while it was on the market to be sold. He said we could stay there until escrow closed on the estate.

The villa looked like something out of a travel magazine. Upon entering the front door, there were two flights of stairs leading down to an open-air common room. The traditional Balinese architectural style divided the property into multiple private bungalows offering each person their own slice of heaven. To the right of the common area was a separate dining space next to a stand-alone kitchen. Each cabana-style hut was surrounded by perfectly manicured natural grass and banana trees.

Two master suites were located on the level below, separated from the rest of the bungalows by another flight of stairs. Between the two cabins was an infinity pool that had a breathtaking view of the island landscape, with a peekaboo glimpse of the ocean in the background. Each of the master suites had a king-sized bed and two couches with a small living room. We had our own bathroom with an outdoor shower and a Jacuzzi tub. There was even a massive closet, almost as big as the first room we stayed at in the jungle. By this time, we hardly had any belongings to put in it, but the Chicken enjoyed the privacy and full-length mirror.

The villa itself was motivation for me to get back on my feet. The Bali mansion was one of the most incredible places I had ever seen. It was also the least accessible wheelchair dwelling I had ever rolled into. The staircases were long and steep. There was also at least one step surrounding each hut and in front of every bungalow. I had *Grown* beyond all the things I couldn't do, but I was literally land-locked at whichever hut someone pushed me into. I was finally ready to *Accept* the *Opportunity* for what it was. I was motivated to make a full recovery and surf the waves of Bali

With all the amazing things going on around us, it was a shame the Little One didn't have her camera. She was bummed about it for a few days but moved right on to a solution. Anytime we had money left over from our monthly trip allowance, we put it into a rainy-day account. There was no telling what might happen in this strange land so far away from home. We made sure we always had a safety net.

After our fallout in the jungle with Nëvil, the Chicken and I realized we needed to be more proactive when it came to capturing moments on film. When Nëvil completely abandoned his promise to be more involved, the Chicken and I took matters into our own hands. I had connections in the States that could help us make the film incredible. We just needed to capture all the moments that supported our vision. The Little One's camera took beautiful photos, but it had significant limitations when it came to shooting movie clips.

Most of the film she shot in the jungle was captured using her iPhone. Her Nikon camera was an older model, so the quality of the movies wasn't too much better than her mobile phone. Once we got the internet up and running in Bali, she found a newer model of the same Nikon that was stolen in Jakarta. The camera was used, but it was in excellent condition. It was also within our price range if we tapped into our rainy-day fund. The upgraded edition was perfect for shooting movies. It also had many technical improvements that would enhance the Chicken's ability to take beautiful pictures. There was only one catch. It couldn't be delivered to Bali, which meant somebody would need to pick it up in the United States.

When the Little One left the room following the meltdown Gargamel had at the clinic, the first thing she did was call the friendly ghost. She was really upset about all the things that were said about us but was astonished that a father would speak that way about his son. She told Jasper that she *Believed* in him and trusted that our plan was amazing. We had all put in a good amount of time and effort to get this far, and the Chicken wanted to let Jasper know that we had his back.

Jasper shrugged off his father's outburst and explained to the Little One that his dad gets that way from time to time. It was something he learned to deal with because it had been happening his whole life. It was usually instigated by his Indonesian stepmom throwing a tantrum for not getting what she wanted. It had a way of setting his dad off like a stick of dynamite. Jasper calmed the Chicken down by assuring her there was nothing to worry about. He reinforced that our team was stronger than ever by telling her that he had been diligently working on the business plan the entire time he was away. It appeared to soothe her in the moment, but the ruthless rhetoric and eruption of emotion by Gargamel made it difficult for her to take anything useful away from the encounter.

Now that we were in Bali, it was time to put our plans in motion. Pak Heru began to see new clients at the villa, and I continued to work hard on my own healing program. While we searched for a permanent location for Pak Heru to work from, the marketing plan was to create an underground buzz about a mysterious healer that just arrived in Bali. The initial friends and family approach seemed to be working, and it didn't take long for Pak Heru's client list to grow.

The treatments were performed in the common area that provided a spectacular view with a soothing ocean breeze. Since I was treated three times a day, it made sense for me to stick around and greet all the new clients between sessions. I did my best to answer everyone's questions and shared success stories that I witnessed while I was in the jungle. When people asked if I had experienced any benefit from my treatments, I had video evidence to show them my improvements. Jasper asked the Little One to create a website with a short bio on Pak Heru that included directions to the villa. The Chicken and I understood how critical it was to make a good first impression, so we aimed to add a certain degree of professionalism to everything we did.

Jasper met an American doctor on one of his trips to the States who was doing a project involving sucralose research. He convinced the doctor over a few pitchers of beer to sell all his belongings and move to Bali. The friendly ghost explained that he owned a media company that could shoot a documentary about the project the doctor was doing. Jasper also invited him to be part of the wellness project he was working on.

According to Jasper, he was putting in a considerable amount of work on the business plan for the wellness center. He said he consulted with numerous business professionals in Bali to help him perfect the plan. He claimed to have a world-famous architect on board and another friend that just finished building a luxury boutique hotel. The hotel owner offered Jasper a template to help calculate proper financial projections. He had used it for the business plan of his hotel. Once Jasper plugged all his numbers in, he had the hotel owner look it over.

We established a general timeframe to revisit the wellness project with Mr. Hapnin after we had prepared a comprehensive business plan. When the Chicken purchased her camera, Jasper offered to pick it up the next time he traveled to the States. He mentioned needing to go to California to pick up a doctor that agreed to do the nutritional programs for the wellness business we were creating. He asked me to reach out to Mr. Hapnin and set up a meeting so he could present the plan to him.

After purchasing a new camera for the Little One, we didn't have anywhere near enough money to buy plane tickets to the US. Not only would the absence interfere with my therapy schedule, we were expected to stay in Bali to run the clinic that was still in its infantile stages. Jasper said he wasn't sure when he would leave, but it would be within the next few weeks. In the meantime, there was plenty for everyone to do in order to keep a steady flow of new clients visiting the clinic.

There were a number of things going on that smelled funny to me. I had never met this architect or hotel owner who was consulting on a project in which I was supposedly a partner. Jasper said he would bring the plan to me once things were tightened up but said for now it was best if I focused on running the business and my own rehab. Now there was a doctor added to the program that I also had no knowledge about. Out of nowhere, I was just told he was part of the team. On top of this new addition, we were informed there was also going to be a second documentary being shot. Our current director rarely even took his camera out of the case!

When I called up Mr. Hapnin to revisit our wellness idea, he was completely slammed negotiating deals for his own business. He said he couldn't imagine taking on another project at the time. Since he agreed to take a look at the plan once we got everything together, a quick meeting might be a possibility. The chances of making it happen didn't look very promising though. Even if he could find some time, he wasn't in a position to give us his undivided attention.

When I told this to Jasper, he somehow interpreted it as a green light. Two days later, he knocked on the door of our room around 10:00 PM and asked if he could speak with us for a minute. We just finished watching a movie and were about to turn off the lights to go to sleep. We invited him in, and he sat down at the end of the bed.

He told us he was leaving for the States early the next morning and wanted to show me the business plan before he left.

I was completely caught off guard and didn't really know how to respond. The last time we spoke about him going to the States, I was given the impression that it wouldn't be for a few weeks. He promised to show me the business plan before he left, but I figured we'd have a few cracks at revising it together to iron out the kinks. Now all of a sudden, it was sitting in my lap at 10:00 PM the night before he was leaving.

If I had been thinking straight, I would have stayed up all night and gone through the plan with a fine-tooth comb. The fact that I didn't was a rookie mistake that would be followed by many more in the weeks to come. I went directly to the financial documents to see how the friendly ghost planned on spending the investment capital he was about to ask for. I'm definitely not a Fortune 500 CFO, but the numbers just didn't add up.

The build-out, staffing, cash flow, and returns looked completely out of whack to me. Jasper said it was because it had been scaled to reflect the Balinese economy, which was much different than in the States. Since everything was considerably cheaper in Indonesia, it changed the entire structure of the financial landscape. Jasper said the hotel owner and architect both looked it over. Neither of them said anything about the numbers being off.

When I turned to the section that broke down ownership percentages, Jasper quickly changed the subject. He interrupted me to tell us about a few executive decisions he made that were important for us to know before he left. Jasper said when he told Nëvil that the Chicken was in charge of creating the website for the clinic, he completely flipped out. To avoid mass hysteria in both his business projects, he decided to let Nëvil create the website. Nëvil just secured an opportunity to work on a 3D gig in China, so he would work on the website remotely during the month he was out of the country.

While Jasper was gone, he wanted the two of us to find a new villa to work out of, because escrow had just closed on the one we were staying in. He sent the Chicken a few listings via e-mail and asked if she would schedule appointments to go see them. Since we only had a week left to stay at the current place we were in, he made arrangements with another friend up the road for us to rent rooms until we found a new place to stay. Pak Heru would be working out of Gargamel's place until a new location was secured. Since Jasper would be gone during the transition, we were asked to redirect all the clients to the new location. He also requested for us to move all his personal belongings to his father's house as well.

When Jasper grabbed the business plan out of my hands, I asked him for another copy to look over. Since his plane left early the next morning, he explained there wasn't enough time to get another one printed. I was so appalled by everything that just went down that I was speechless. I didn't even know where to start. Before I could get two words in, he slipped out the door in the same snake-like manner that he slithered in.

In the weeks that followed, everything started to fall apart at the seams. Bang Bang, one of Pak Heru's two assistants, is something of a clairvoyant. He would go into deep meditation and receive information from unknown sources that were not part of our physical dimension. He was noticeably shaken up one morning and got into a heated argument with Pak Heru. I asked Pak Heru's other assistant, Larno, what all the commotion was about. He said sometimes Bang Bang was a little crazy and that he was always a bit weary when it came to white people. He was also scared to death about flying on airplanes, and Larno said he probably wouldn't come back.

Later when I spoke with Bang Bang myself, he had a much different story. He said the gods communicated to him that the energy surrounding our efforts in Bali was impure. There was a *Dark Spirit* attached to our project, and he no longer wanted anything to do with it. He pleaded with Pak Heru to pay attention to the *Signs*. Pak Heru told Bang Bang to relax and urged him not to jump to any conclusions. Before Bang Bang left, he said he *Loved* the Chicken and me and gave us both awkwardly long hugs. We never saw him again.

I met interesting characters from all over the world that came to the clinic to be healed. Later in the week, I met a guy from Italy whose best *Friend* was in a wheelchair due to a stroke. He was interested in what benefits I received from the treatment, and we talked for close to an hour. He told me he just finalized a deal to start building a luxury boutique hotel and construction began the following week. A buddy of his named Jasper recommended the healer, and that's what brought him there.

I immediately realized who I had been talking to. I told him that Jasper was my partner and thanked the Italian guy for helping with the business plan. He was a bit shocked because Jasper never mentioned anything about having a partner. When I told him he was in the States, presenting the plan to a potential investor, the Italian's whole demeanor changed. "If it's the same plan he showed me, he will be committing business suicide," commented the Italian.

He told me that Jasper just plugged a bunch of numbers into a generic template without doing any of his market research homework. The Italian said, "Do whatever you can to stop that meeting, or you might never speak to your investor again."

It was already too late. Mr. Hapnin's office declined the first meeting because there was no time in his schedule. Since Jasper was persistent and stuck around an extra week, Mr. Hapnin agreed to fit him in as a favor to me. If there was any wind left in the sail of our plans, it no longer mattered because Jasper sank our ship to the bottom of the ocean.

We were also currently in the process of transitioning caregivers. Georgio put in a heroic effort, but the trip was no longer serving him in the way it was before. There was a lot going on around him, and certain dramas began to affect him in a negative way. Since he was such a trooper, there was no chance he would ever throw in the towel. The Chicken and I could see it wearing on him, so we made a tough decision to let him go. He *Learned* a lot about *Himself* in the process of *Caring* for me. It was now our turn to take *Care* of him.

We *Love* Georgio, but the time had come for him to start pursuing his own *Happiness*. We encouraged him to take the *Lessons* he *Learned* back to Utah and chase his dreams. He is a *Good* dude and had a bright future ahead of him. We would definitely struggle to replace him because he brought significant value to our team. But we needed to do right by him, the same way he did for us. It was tough to see him go, but it was in his best interest to take *Care* of

Himself as well as he took *Care* of me. Another *Friend* of ours from the Philippines flew over to help us while we searched for a local Indonesian caregiver.

Shortly after we moved out of the first villa, Nëvil approached us about the documentary. He said his heart was no longer in the project and that he was stepping down as the director. He accepted a six-month job in China, and he would be leaving in a couple of weeks. It was obvious he was over it, so it came as no surprise to the Chicken and me. The Little One had been shooting footage for months with her phone. When the friendly ghost returned, she would have a proper camera to film with.

Between Nëvil and the Chicken, we had some amazing footage for a documentary. The way things were transpiring though, the direction everything was going had become unclear. The guy that owned the villa where we were renting rooms thought our story was extremely compelling. He had a close friend from the *Surfer's Journal* that was interested in doing a feature story on the project. When word of the story got back to Jasper back in the States, the opportunity suddenly vanished. Coincidentally, so did the owner's interest in our cause. He went from being a keen supporter of our courageous journey to aggressively annoyed by just about everything we did. What was supposed to be old friends working together on a common goal was starting to look like a chess match with an "us versus them" theme.

Gargamel had a really nice place for Pak Heru to work from. While the clinic was being run from his home, we saw more signs suggesting things weren't quite what we envisioned. We were led to believe we were partners in a wellness business. But remember, in the jungle, Jasper's daddy offered us a much different understanding of what was going on. And now we were on his turf, playing by his rules.

The alpha leader behind the curtain began to make his presence known. Gargamel began flexing his muscles so that everyone at the clinic knew who was boss. A simple difference of opinion turned into a shouting match with one guy, and he made a woman in a wheelchair refuse to come back. Apparently, she didn't appreciate her willpower being questioned by a grumpy old German dude. The chess game was set, and each move now revealed details about the other team's strategy.

The rental arrangement for villas in Bali is strange. Owners want all the money up front for a year lease. We found a great villa that was divided into two different bungalows. It was a sweet setup for what we were trying to accomplish. The entrance area had a lobby with staff housing and a large statue of the Hindu God, Ganesh, guarding the pool. Each two-story bungalow had its own kitchen, living room, and dining room. The one we would stay in had a master bed and bath downstairs with another separate living area upstairs for Jayko.

The other side was set up well for Pak Heru to see clients. The living room was a bit larger, and it was connected to a small bedroom with a bathroom that patients could use. There was plenty of waiting room with a large open space for Heru to do treatments. Upstairs, Jasper had a larger room with a bathroom and an extra room with two beds that Pak Heru and Larno could use when they were in town.

The first time we met the landlord was at his restaurant up the street from the rental property. Billy69 is a Balinese local that owned properties all over the island. He also owned two restaurants and just finished building his third. We told him the story that brought us to Bali and what we planned on doing while we were there. His property was a perfect place for us to live and see patients until we transitioned to a larger clinic.

Billy69 had become highly successful by using good karma in all that he did. His *Father* was a high priest that taught him to treat everything with *Respect* and *Dignity*. By doing this, the Gods blessed him in ways beyond anything he could have ever imagined. Billy69 liked the Chicken and I. He was interested in helping us in any way he could. When we told him that our partner was out of town and we couldn't pay him all the money up front, Billy69 said it wasn't a problem.

There wasn't another property like Billy69's anywhere near our price range. It was perfect for what we needed, and someone had to pull the trigger if we wanted to make it happen. Since Jasper wasn't back from the States yet, the Little One and I were in a tight spot. We offered Billy69 all the money we had allocated toward rent for the entire year. This locked us into the property, leaving us with very little spending money left over after all the utilities were paid.

When we decided to move to the other side of the world, there really was no looking back. We were there to make something *Great* happen. Taking risks was part of the program, and somebody needed to step up and be a *Leader*. We were being told to focus on playing our role, but nobody else was doing the things necessary to run a successful business. Locking down a place to build our clinic for the next year seemed like a fairly significant priority, but our "producer" that called all the shots was out of the country again.

Being in a strange place isn't that big of a deal, but we were given the impression that our partner would guide our efforts. Almost two years went into preparing for this trip, and critical details that should have been sorted in advance were being figured out on the run. If this were the plan, then flying by the seat of our pants wouldn't have been such a surprise to the Chicken and me. Being told that this stuff was already worked out made it difficult for us to improvise. The way it turned out, none of the so-called preparation ever took place. After the camera was stolen in Jakarta, it was important for us to have our heads on a swivel so we didn't get robbed or hustled. It was becoming increasingly more evident that being in a Third World country wasn't the only thing we needed to watch out for.

For thirty-five years, I celebrated Christmas with my *Family* at home in Never Never Land. The type of dysfunction I was used to involved arguments about who got to open their gifts first, drunken outbursts, and gluttonous feasting that took place while we all awaited present time. After dinner on Christmas Eve, we all gathered around the tree to see what Santa brought to reward us for another year of naughtiness. This year was much different.

We were far away from home in a country that didn't celebrate Christian holidays with much enthusiasm. Jasper was scheduled to return a few days before Christmas with gifts from home. Our *Family* shopped diligently to find all our favorite things so that being away during the holidays wasn't such a bummer. It would have been nice to be with our *Loved* ones, but this year, a package from home would have to do. The friendly ghost decided that comfort food from the States didn't fit my healing program, so he handpicked a few items and left the rest behind.

Before Jasper left for the States, he invited us to have dinner with his family on Christmas Eve. After giving us only a quarter of our holiday gifts, another revision was about to shake up our seasonal festivities. Apparently, Jasper's dad and stepmom decided that this year's Christmas meal was for immediate family only. As a consolation prize, Gargamel offered to buy us lunch the next day at a restaurant of our choice.

I was now more comfortable in a foreign country with complete strangers than I was in a room with the friend that brought me there. It was disappointing to have all our plans turn into something completely different than what we set out to do. But having the friend that created the plans uninvite my family and me to Christmas hurt in a way that I couldn't have prepared for. The *Healing* that had taken place within me turned this experience into another *Opportunity* to *Learn* a *Valuable Lesson*.

Everything happens for a reason. If emotion can be stripped from matters that aren't exactly desirable, discomfort can be an incredible navigator. Nobody makes plans with the intention of failing. If something doesn't work out the way it's intended, it's either a bad plan or something about the execution is faulty. There were *Signs* from the inception of the healing-surf journey that pointed to potential disaster. Now that everything seemed to have gone up in flames, the real test was upon us. The way we responded to this adversity would be the defining factor as to whether or not the Chicken and I had learned anything on our grand voyage.

Emotions are very important components that need to be factored into personal growth and healing. Thoughts can be just as addictive as heroin and nicotine. Once neural pathways have been conditioned to fire in coordinated patterns, the brain remembers the connective pathway. This means that certain thoughts will create a familiar connection in the brain, causing specific physical reactions in the body. If someone is constantly worried, it generally leads to hypertension. If a person experiences mostly *Happy* thoughts, there's a good chance that their physical demeanor will be relaxed and their health tends to be pretty good.

My sabbatical to Indonesia made me *Aware* of harmful thought patterns that had been governing my entire way of *Life*. By forcing my impulsive will upon things in the past, I would approach certain life situations with a feverish EGO that clouded my intentions. By doing this, I not only sent the wrong signals to those I was trying to work with, I also made things more difficult on myself. I found that I was my own worst enemy. My emotional self-control was often the very reason I fell short on a good majority of my goals.

It all started with not being *Aware* of my thoughts. The pathways that I created when responding to life's nuances were burned into the fabric of how I understood things. This meant the way I reacted to certain peak moments in my life literally defined who I was and how I would behave in the future. Without *Being Aware* of the *Power of my Thoughts*, I was making the same mistakes over and over again. If the *Healing* I experienced had any chance of becoming permanent, the *Lessons* I *Learned* needed to be put in motion immediately. It was the only chance I had to create the *Life* I knew I was meant to *Live*.

Gratitude

66 J asper is a weasel, and I don't like him. I'm not interested in
being involved in any business he is a part of. I *Believe* in you
and the Little One, but as long as you continue to associate yourself
with people like Jasper, you will continue to struggle in business. I
will sponsor you until the end of the year like I promised, but after
that our business is through."

Mr. Hapnin is one of my most *Valuable Resources*. His comments following the meeting he had with Jasper helped me understand the *Difference* between help and assistance. Only *Life* experience can develop the *Awareness* to know the *Difference* between the
two. *Patience* with the *Learning Process* is one of the only ways to
absorb the *Lesson*.

Desperate people need help. Nothing is wrong with being desperate, but the way one responds to an impossible situation defines
their moral character. There is a codependency between a person that
needs help and the person giving it. Assistance, on the other hand, is
guided by *Intuition*, *Faith*, and *Belief*. Jasper was desperate for something to work. The pressure he put on himself to please his father
created an emptiness that I was completely unfamiliar with.

My *Dad* is hard-core, but behind his gnarliness is an underlying
Compassion that lets me know he *Loves* me. Jasper's dad thought he
was a total failure. In order for him to deal with the internal conflict
he felt, certain defense mechanisms needed to be in place. I wanted
to succeed but not so bad that nothing else mattered.

When Jasper presented the business plan to Mr. Hapnin, the Chicken and I were penciled in as 5 percent owners of the idea we helped create. Jasper was so focused on how the end result would make everyone happy that he never stopped to realize how poorly he was representing everyone involved. Or maybe he did. Maybe sabotaging the investor I brought to the table would give him the power and control he desired. Either way, it didn't matter. What was done was done.

When Jasper approached me with the idea to go on a surf trip to Bali, he was under the impression that I needed to be saved. After spending a few years with him working on making the project happen, I finally understood why. I know what it feels like to be desperate. In my attempt to create value with my life, I needed to figure out how to accept the help of others. It didn't always feel good. There is an internal conflict that goes on when people accept others' help, and it puts a strange pressure on the one needing to catch a break.

Nobody wants to need help, but everyone could use a little from time to time. Practicing *Humility* and *Accepting* a person's charitable efforts means opening up to *Vulnerability*. Modern society suggests that suffering or needing help equals weakness. It's all in the cognitive programming. Welfare, refinanced home mortgages and bankruptcy are all frowned upon because it means your affairs are not in order. People immediately assume you're "less than" or that you are doing something wrong. Needing help can be associated with pity and failure, which are feelings that nobody voluntarily invites into their life.

People help others because it makes them feel good. That's usually what they want—to feel good about doing something positive. In this day and age, that's a complex ordeal. Most people have no idea what really makes them feel *Good* or why. The golden rule has nearly vanished, and EGO has found its way into the act of doing something kind. *Jealousy, Envy, Pride,* and *Vanity* have all become part of the philanthropic landscape.

Jasper was so focused on needing to succeed that he cut corners thinking it would be okay in the end. If the miraculous healer could get his buddy in a wheelchair to walk, his business ideas would sell themselves. Then he thought the hard work would be over and we could just sit back and collect money. Everyone that ever doubted Jasper could then kick rocks while he drank victory champagne, including his father.

I'm all too familiar with this tendency. I've gotten ahead of myself countless times in the past. It looks like the plan or surrounding assets are failing you, but really, it's a faulty approach. In this situation, communication broke down because the integrity of the plan was garbage. Jasper's fear of failure was so great that he was willing to do anything it took to feel successful. Even if it meant misleading a couple dealing with a serious disability to believe they were his partners.

Suddenly, I realized that being physically paralyzed wasn't that big a deal. Some people are completely able bodied and *Suffer* from a paralysis much more extensive than my own. Everyone is struggling to make sense out of his or her own existence. Feeling *Good* has a lot to do with *Surrender*, *Acceptance*, *Compassion*, *Humility*, and *Learning* how to *Love*. Receiving other people's *Love* is a skill set that first must be developed within. You must plant the seed of *Love* in your heart first before you can offer the harvest to others.

I had a tough time falling back in *Love* with *Myself.* I had it all before I snapped my spine. Well, at least I thought I did when I believed in my *Illusion*. When I became quadriplegic, I was forced into a time-out for over a decade. It helped me slow down so I could see the world for what it actually is. Not everybody is *Blessed* with such an extreme opportunity to study existence. With this *Knowledge*, I have a *Responsibility* to do the right thing.

When I spoke with Mr. Hapnin a few days after Christmas, we discussed an exit strategy. Mr. Hapnin wasn't giving me help; he was offering me the *Gift of Assistance*. When he decided to sponsor a portion of our trip, he did it because he *Believed* in *Us*. There was no expectation attached to his investment. He found his rhythm in business and pushed himself to find *Balance* in all that he does. I *Believe* in him as a mentor, and he *Believes* in the *Potential* that the Little Chicken and I brought to the table. By offering his *Assistance*, he gave us what we needed to pursue our best *Selves*.

Life is an incredible situation once it can be seen for what it *Is*. I will spend the rest of my *Life* helping people *Value* the opportunity to *Believe* in *Themselves*. Each one of us is strangely unique. WE ARE all here having individual experiences, but WE ARE also here for each other. I want to bring people closer to their *True Selves* so they don't miss another moment of this incredible theme park we call Earth.

It was clear that Jasper and I were on different pages concerning what we wanted out of a wellness business. When he sank the ship on the business deal with Mr. Hapnin, the writing was on the wall for where things were going to end up. Mr. Hapnin knew how bad I wanted to create an amazing wellness center. I'm sure it wasn't easy for him to walk away from making it happen. I blew it though. I made a rookie mistake by exposing a successful investor to my "partner" who didn't have his affairs in order.

If it were just business, Mr. Hapnin would have been dust in the wind. Successful folk don't have time for rookies flailing around in the shallow end. Mr. Hapnin had a positive read on the situation the first time he met Jasper. That's when his business experience, *Faith*, and *Intuition* guided him to secure the asset he *Believed* in. It was a tough blow to lose the confidence of someone who *Believed* in my ability to succeed. The way he went about passing on the wellness project is a *Lesson* I will never forget.

Jasper shook things up when he offered the Little Chicken and me the opportunity of a lifetime. It gave us the *Chance* to permanently better *Ourselves*, and Mr. Hapnin was quick to point that out. Even though things didn't work the way we would have liked, that didn't mean the entire trip was a wash. Mr. Hapnin understood the disappointment we were experiencing after making critical mistakes. I'm pretty sure he knew the trouble we were getting into long before we did. Instead of telling us what to do, he was there to offer *Assistance* when we needed it most. When the business venture no longer interested him, he stuck around and was *Patient* with our *Learning Process*.

Holding strong to high morals and soulful integrity can be tough when you're pissed. Maintaining your cool when the shit hits the fan is mandatory if you want to play with the big boys though. Mr. Hapnin did this daily in his line of work. Practicing a solid exit strategy when everything is on fire requires ice in your veins but warmth in your heart.

When Jasper left Mr. Hapnin's office, he was under the impression that Mr. Hapnin was too busy to take on another project. In all honesty, he probably was. Jasper didn't do anything to sway him into believing that the wellness project was worthy of any "free time" he "might" have. The numbers were bonkers, and the plan had too many moving parts. It also didn't work well for Jasper that he was trying to screw over the *Friends* of the person to whom he was pitching the plan. Either way, Mr. Hapnin respectfully declined in a business-classy, ninja-like manner.

Since I was his guy, Mr. Hapnin didn't hold back when he spoke with me. He told me how he felt cut and dried, and I'm glad he did. The way he responded taught me the *Value* of a *Good* asset, which is a person that will tell it *How It Is*. My poor *Dad* will rip out his hair when he reads this, because he's been trying to teach this to me my whole life. It took failure and embarrassment to *Learn* the *Lesson*, which is exactly what my *Dad* was trying to help me avoid.

It felt *Good*, though, to feel this *Bad* after crashing and burning so hard. It meant I would never forget it. We were running out of funds because we spent all our rent money for the year on a bungalow at Jasper's wellness clinic. I obliviously wouldn't have drawn the plan up this way, but the moment I heard from Mr. Hapnin, I was immediately *Aware* of what I had done wrong. I could finally see it for what it was. It sucked, and everything about it stung, but that's it. *Life* went on.

My mind had previously been programmed with so much clutter that when a high-intensity moment flipped my life upside down, my reaction was to freak out. This caused my emotions to spiral out of control, and I would look to chop off heads. Strangely, I was only a little bummed about this one. I was more confused than anything else. How was I supposed to navigate my way out of this?

Lucky for me, I had a superhero for a *Wife*, and a mentor who still *Believed* in me. From here on out, the game needed to be played much *Differently*. Our previous strategy wasn't going to put us in a position to win. The chess game had changed, and key pieces were lost due to our careless mistakes. Mr. Hapnin had some great advice for us moving forward. He emphasized the need for us to *Respectfully* move away from all future business with Jasper. It was important that we did so with *Gratitude* in order to pay homage for the opportunity. We could do this by communicating our stance effectively and creating boundaries while living in such close proximity.

It was a tall order, but even though I was in a chair, I was finally up for the challenge. It would test the areas that were most damaged in my psyche and force me to break through walls that took my whole life to build. I wasn't just equipped with the *Knowledge* to *Change*; I also was in tune with how I was going to do it. The *Light* told me to start by fixing *Myself*, and it was now clear to me why it was so important. *Leading* by example is often the most effective way to create *Change* in any situation.

The Little Chicken was devastated. It wasn't because we needed to move three times by ourselves in a foreign country with rotating caregivers. And it wasn't because the friend that brought us here was never there to help. It wasn't even Jasper's dad and evil stepmother that hated us for a hundred different reasons. It was because she trusted Jasper and *Believed* he was somehow going to pull off a miracle.

The Chicken and I know what *Miracles* look like. We find ways to see them all the time in our daily lives. She wasn't looking for a magic Shaolin wizard to snap his fingers and, voila, I go skipping down the street. She was looking for a friend to pull through on the things he said he would do. Anything is accomplishable in the Little One's eyes even when things don't work out as planned.

A bit of communication among friends is all she was looking for. She doesn't trust many people, but she trusted Jasper. He gave her the *Opportunity* to deal with the pain of her *Mother* passing when we were in the jungle. Now she'd been scorned by the dude that brought her to the other side of the world with her son and paralyzed husband. It was my *Responsibility* to stay centered so I could guide us through the tough times ahead.

The Little One saw something in *Me* that sometimes I didn't even see. Her blind *Faith* and *Unconditional Love* put me in the position to *Realize My Potential*. Relationships are a lot like the tides. There is always a delicate balance going on as life constantly pulls from every direction. In order for a union between two people in *Love* to last, both individuals must be open to the *Changes* going on around them. As the *Grand Charade* unfolds one day at a time, *Partners* need to *Learn* how to lean on each other. The time had come for the Chicken to lean on me for support, just like I did when I needed her.

The Chicken helped save me from myself. She guided me in times when I didn't feel like I had what it took to be *Great*. It was my turn to be strong for her. I already knew she was *Great*. I now needed to convince her that she was *Great* as well. For whatever reason, her *Beauty* is a foreign concept to her. It's one of the reasons I *Love* her so much. She's a bear claw and doesn't even know it. Actualizing my *Potential* included treating my *Best Friend* with the same *Patience* and *Compassion* she showed me when I was *Learning*.

She was my *Partner* in every way one could imagine. Her *Patience* with my *Learning Process* offered me the type of *Assistance* I needed to absorb important *Life* lessons. She also helped me find *Value* in my most *Vulnerable* moments. I had been making the same mistakes over and over again for years. Countless people gave me excellent advice. If I would have followed half of it, I wouldn't have had to suffer so much. When I couldn't receive the advice and I would fall, she was there to catch me. The Little One always seemed to find ways to make everything better.

If my mind weren't busy with so much nonsense all the time, I probably wouldn't have made so many mistakes. The Chicken understood why I continued to make the same errors and stuck by my side anyway. She had *Faith* that I would overcome the mechanisms that were rupturing my efforts. It was time for me to be that person for her. *Learning* how to *Appreciate* something as incredible as the Little Chicken taught me how to act when someone I *Love* needs me.

It always seems easier to pinpoint other people's issues. Maybe it's because you're not blinded by the emotions that are getting in the way of the solution. Being there for someone involves an acute *Sensitivity* to the areas where they struggle. If this is done right, it gives the person room to grow in their own way. Trying to change someone is a waste of time. Nobody is going to *Change* until they are damn well good and ready. The best chance anyone has at influencing the actions of others is by *Being Aware* of what the situation *Needs* them to *Be*.

Sometimes it's important to listen. Sometimes it's necessary to take action. Other times, just *Being* there is enough. Every situation requires a level of *Sensitivity* that is unique for each individual. Now that I was no longer standing in my own way, I was beginning to *Accept* the role others needed me to play. The Little Chicken needed to do everything she could to try to make the wellness center idea work. My job was to *Support* her while she processed what was going on in her own way.

We had a great plan that made so much sense. What didn't make sense was that everything seemed to be falling apart. The Little One wanted to show Jasper how much we could accomplish as a team. She was in utter disbelief that he could really be such a selfish wanker. The Chicken understood why Jasper was suffering and believed if we could show him a better way, he would surely do the right thing. Either way, we *Believed* in Pak Heru's abilities as a healer and saw him as extended *Family*. Since I already committed to Pak Heru's healing program for the next year, it made sense to continue promoting the healer I *Believed* in.

Shortly after we moved into the villa that would double as Jasper's wellness clinic, Gargamel approached me to speak on behalf of the business. He wanted me to do a presentation for his golf club. The group of wealthy business professionals was well connected in the Balinese community. He knew I had a public speaking background and wanted to utilize my skill set to entice his affluent cronies to drop by for a treatment.

The Little Chicken and I had two options. Pack our shit and fly home with our tail between our legs or use the situation to practice what we just *Learned*. *Leading* by example only worked in this situation if we took *Care* of *Ourselves* first. The tricky part was we needed to do it while tiptoeing around the selfish motives of people trying to maneuver around us.

Doing the right thing is something both the Chicken and I wished Jasper would do for us. Since he wasn't capable of doing it for himself, we took it upon *Ourselves* to offer him an example of what it looked like. If *Being* my *Best Self* meant seeing the game for what it was in the moment, then I needed to make the best strategic move to put my team in a position to win. I want to help people. Helping *Myself* in this situation was an exercise that would put me in a position to do just that.

Before we sold our stuff to make the Indonesian experience an all-in gig, I needed to be confident in a plan B. Walking after being paralyzed for twelve years was a long shot. Starting a wellness business on the other side of the world in a country I knew little about was also a pipe dream. I asked myself one very important question before deciding to embark on this epic journey: if nothing went according to plan, what *Value* would the experience offer to my *Life*?

I never had the opportunity to travel once I finished college. The trip alone would help me prove to *Myself* that *Anything is Possible*. Just because I was in a wheelchair didn't mean I had to compromise being an adventurer. Picking up and moving to the other side of the world is a big deal for an able-bodied person. Doing it as a quadriplegic is a pretty impressive endeavor. My plans to write a book and shoot a documentary meant I could use the experience to share my story with others. The *Chance* to find my mojo along the way made all the risk worth the hassle.

When the Little One's *Mom* passed away, it marked a fork in the road concerning her own mortality. The peak experience changed her in a way similar to how my spinal cord injury affected me. Both situations were complete game changers. It forced a perspective shift that offered a whole *Different* way to exist. The way we responded to these circumstances redefined our *Understanding* of *Everything*. The things that mattered now demanded our attention, and bettering *Ourselves* was mandatory if we wanted to *Be Great*.

The last thing I felt like doing was putting together a presentation for Jasper and Gargamel's benefit. Impressing a group of rich suits to stimulate Jasper's business and his father's EGO made me want to vomit just thinking about it. So the Chicken and I came up with a plan that would challenge us to be *Great*. The only people that would ever know if we were giving our best effort were *Ourselves*. A victory in this situation meant that we put our emotions aside and aimed our talents at maximizing the ability to better *Ourselves*.

I understood what it felt like to have no control over my life. I also know what it feels like to be so desperate that I would do anything to succeed. Jasper was putting so much energy into trying not to fail that he wasn't *Learning* from the mistakes he was making. The friendly ghost was also financially dependent on a father that seemed nearly impossible to please. By bringing the two of them together in a positive way, I had the ability to affect a relationship between a father and his son.

Gargamel was a successful chemical engineer that could have given up on his son a long time ago. He didn't need to continue to dump money into everything Jasper was doing. He wanted to pass his legacy onto his son but didn't know how to stimulate his success. His iron fist put a wedge between them, and now everything Jasper did frustrated Gargamel into a dysfunctional frenzy. Presenting the wellness business at the golf club gave me the ability to better *Myself* while helping others along the way.

I saw a father that wanted to love his son and a son that wanted to succeed, but neither of them had the skills to do so. They needed each other. Presenting a healer that I *Believed* in to a group of people that might need his help was a way for me to express my *Gratitude*. If it weren't for those two crazy German dudes, I wouldn't have been there in the first place. Moving beyond my emotions maximized my ability to offer *Myself* to the situation.

I wrote a speech and coordinated it with an incredible visual presentation that the Little One made. We focused the discussion on Pak Heru and backed our claims about how incredible he was with video evidence. Then I switched gears to Jasper and Gargamel. I said that if it weren't for the love and trust between a father and his son, I wouldn't be in front of everyone exposing them to a gifted healer.

It went over well. More than half the people in attendance stuck around after the lecture to ask questions and inquire about the clinic. As for Jasper and his dad, there were plenty of attaboys and introductory handshakes. There wasn't much in it for the Little One and me, except that we overcame ourselves to do what we thought was best for the situation. After everything we went through, it felt incredible to overcome it in this way. We gave it everything we had, and it felt *Great*.

We had to leave the country every few months when our visa expired. Once we got a stamp confirming that we left Indonesia, we could come back. Since the closest neighboring country was Singapore, we would just take a day trip to get our passports taken care of. On one of our trips to Singapore, we met a buddy of Jasper's that was a retired pro surfer turned film director. During our trip, we mentioned needing an extra set of eyes on our documentary. When Nëvil ducked out on the production, we needed a new director altogether. The surfer guy seemed legit, and everyone got along pretty well, so we asked him if he was interested in taking over as the director of our film.

Brutus agreed to sign on to the project if we could give him a place to stay and leads for more work. Since Jasper recently committed to doing the sucralose documentary, he had multiple projects to offer Brutus. Brutus was also willing to work together with Nëvil on the post-production process of our documentary. This helped us avoid a conflict of interest regarding who shot what footage.

When Brutus moved in, the small amount of time we saw Jasper turned into almost never. He and Brutus were always off "working." Brutus did one interview with the Chicken and me, and that's the last time he recorded anything for our project. It wasn't a big deal. We had been shooting our own footage for months, assuming we would be left to make the movie on our own. It was just more evidence supporting Mr. Hapnin's advice to get away from any future business with Jasper.

Brutus had a good read on how to hustle the situation for maximum personal gain. He immediately figured out where the money came from and became best pals with Gargamel. When he figured out that Gargamel was not in favor of the project Jasper was working on with us, Brutus shifted the focus to the sucralose documentary. When it came to making a documentary about healing, Brutus agreed with Jasper's father that the focus should be on the healer and not my journey. This was music to Gargamel's ears.

Right around this time, the sucralose doc moved into the villa. Jasper gave him Heru and Larno's room, then told the healer and his assistant to share the caregiver's room up front. This meant my caregiver needed to sleep on a pool chair the three days a week that the healer was in town. If this didn't shake up the energy in the villa enough, Dr. Sucralose got into a heated debate with Brutus that almost turned into a fistfight on the first night he was in town.

It didn't take long for Dr. Sucra to figure out that Jasper's game had fatal flaws. At the end of each week, Jasper and Brutus started a tradition that involved taking the Indonesian boys out drinking. Jasper shrugged off Heru's alcohol problems as a youth and firmly felt that a grown man should be able to celebrate a job well done. In addition to his negative tendencies toward alcohol, Heru is a Muslim that swore off the sauce because it conflicted with his religious beliefs. Dr. Sucra found this to be one of a few things that seemed a bit odd.

Dr. Sucra was a nice guy, but our relationship only lasted a few weeks. We had some *Soulful* conversations, but it wasn't long before he started coming to the Little One and me for advice on how to deal with Jasper's nonsense. We offered the doc the best *Assistance* we knew how to give. It wasn't our place to tell him what to do. *Being Compassionate* with his *Learning Process* helped him come to some pretty quick conclusions though. We answered all his questions to the best of our ability while he pieced things together on his own.

It wasn't cool to watch someone fall for the same alligator bait that we did. The experience was valuable for us because we got validation that the way Jasper handled himself was completely foul. We knew things were screwed up, but the outside-looking-in perspective helped us realize that we were doing a good job given the circumstances. We also saw Dr. Sucra cut ties with Jasper in an appropriate cutthroat manner. One day, he overheard Jasper claim to a client at the clinic that the sucralose documentary was his idea. The doc yanked him into a room, threw a fist full of money at Jasper for the bills he committed to pay, packed his stuff, and was on the next plane home.

The year at the clinic had a wide variety of ups and downs. Staying focused on maintaining an *Attitude of Gratitude* got interrupted only when we let it. Inconsiderate ignorance got under our skin every once in a while, and our old programming came bubbling to the surface. When our frustrations became obvious, Jasper used the discomfort we were feeling as ammunition to pull the healer away. His story about us being difficult is how he justified going in his own direction.

When we were able to live beyond our disappointment, the Bali experience had some incredible treasures for us. We shifted the film's focus to one that we were excited about creating. The story would reflect our *Love* and *Perseverance* to pioneer a better way. We set out to heal *Ourselves* and explore Eastern traditions that might fill in the gaps that the West is missing. There was something to be said about ancient traditions that have been around in the East for thousands of years. Our journey became about sharing with people the incredible power of the human *Spirit*.

We went out into the community and made *Friends* from all over the world. The island had healers scattered all over the place. There was every type of Eastern healing modality one could imagine, from witch doctors to *Chi* machines. I even saw a guy that claimed to be a high priest that was instructed by the Gods to beat bad spirits out of people with a sandalwood stick. The East had its questionable practices, just like the West. I did come across a few game changers that will be a part of my *Wellness Routine* for the rest of my *Life*.

I started conscious breathing years ago to help with stress and hypertension. In the jungle, Pak Heru sharpened my craft by teaching me how to meditate and activate my energy centers, called chakras. While in Bali, the Little One and I were invited to a meditation guru's house for tea one evening. He was a Grand Master that had been practicing meditation since he was a young boy.

He was able to access what he called the Akashic records. The records contained all the information that has *Been*, *Is*, and ever *Will Be*. During a reading of our past *Lives*, the guru was able to piece together our karmic lineage. We were told that this *Life* is an important time for us to *Lead an Awakening*. He told us that there is a consciousness shift on the horizon and that we needed to prepare ourselves to play a vital role in assisting it to happen. The guru had been conducting weeklong silent retreats for the last thirty years. He insisted that we came to the next one in two days' time.

It was all a bit much for me. The retreat was expensive, and I immediately wondered if the invite for tea was a cheap sales pitch. Then the guru said that I can pay whatever I had to offer. It had nothing to do with money, he explained. I came to him for a reason, and it was important that I *Accept* the training he was offering. Since the retreat was so soon, I only had a day to think about it. If I were serious about attending, the guru needed to make arrangements with his staff to ensure the accommodations were accessible.

It was a bit creepy how appropriate the timing was. I was in a rough patch emotionally, and the Guru read me like a children's book. He said that letting my *Being* occupy negative space was getting in the way of meaningful *Growth*. The Guru emphasized the *Value* in every moment and stressed the importance of maximizing our time on the island to *Learn*. The time for us to leisurely absorb life's lessons was coming to an end. Active *Leadership* is where our efforts needed to be focused for the future.

The retreat was in Ubud, which was about an hour away from our villa. Pak Heru approved of my weeklong absence from treatment, because he said advancing my meditation practice would amplify his treatments. Committing to the retreat was venturing even further into the unknown, which I seemed to be doing a lot of around this time. There wasn't room for a caregiver or access for my power wheelchair. Once we checked in, we were stuck there for a week. The only assistance we had was the hotel staff.

Once we were shown to our rooms, we were asked to cut off all communication with the outside world. Phone calls, e-mail, social media, and text messages were strictly prohibited for the duration of the meditation retreat. After we were given an itinerary for the week and a course introduction, we were served dinner and then a *Noble Silence* began. From that moment forward, we were not able to speak until the end of the week.

The sound of a gong started our day at four thirty in the morning. By five o'clock, we were in the meditation room poised for our first session. We meditated all day long, only stopping for meals and short lectures to guide our technique. There were about thirty of us from different places all over the world. Men and women of all ages and race had come *Together in Silence* to *Grow* their meditation practice. We were all there on a personal journey to observe the inner workings of our *Selves*, but we did it together, in rhythm, with a Master Guru.

I'd been building my meditation practice for years, so I didn't have trouble getting used to meditating for long periods of time. The difference was, I had never done it with so much focused intention before. I figured with each session things would get easier. It made logical sense to me that once we got used to the course routine, that getting deeper into meditation would be enjoyable. Logic definitely did not prepare me for what the week ahead had in store for me.

By the end of the first night, we meditated for about six hours intermittently throughout the day. When it was time for bed, I was absolutely exhausted. It didn't make any sense. All I did the whole day was sit quietly in a room with a bunch of people. How was this possible? I just chalked it up as another long day, and I slept that evening like a hibernating bear. It felt like the minute I closed my eyes, I was awoken by the gong to start the next day.

I woke up the next morning with so much anxiety that it felt like my heart was going to beat right out of my chest. I was extremely agitated, and my whole body ached like it had been thrown around in a car accident. Since we weren't allowed to speak with each other, there was no way to bounce our experiences off other people. Everything that I bottled up over the years had nowhere to go but to rise to the surface.

I had a tough time meditating the following morning. After our second session, I seriously contemplated if I wanted to continue with the retreat. While eating lunch, an avalanche of mental baggage completely consumed me. It felt like I was being suffocated. All my negative thoughts and emotions seemed to be haunting me all at once.

I thought to myself, "What was I doing making an already difficult situation even harder? Wasn't uprooting my life and moving to the other side of the world enough? Now I'm inconveniencing perfect strangers and making my *Wife's* job even tougher, and for what? So I can sit in a room with a bunch of strangers, trying to connect to the universe. This is dumb. I wanna quit. As a matter of fact, this whole trip has become bogus. I wanna go home."

Who was this guy squawking in my head like a lame duck? It couldn't be me, I've got my head wrapped around this. I don't give up; it's not part of who I am . . . right? I didn't know what was going on, but I wasn't about to back down from the challenge. I was too stubborn for that. The fact that it was hard meant that it was worthy of my effort. If I didn't *Believe* it was *Good* for me, I wouldn't have committed to doing it in the first place. I finished what was left of my vegetarian meal and was then carted off to the meditation room.

I made it through the day and then had a eureka moment while sifting through my thoughts at dinner. All the thoughts and feelings I was experiencing were deep-rooted fears that I had buried within my psyche. I became *Aware* of them once I cleared all the other garbage out of the way. So much information is downloaded during our day-to-day lives that our brain has to find ways to deal with it all. The way I reacted to previous peak experiences in my life is the only reference material I had to process things moving forward. If I found myself making the same mistakes, it was because I hadn't yet tweaked the mechanism that was causing the problem.

Burying the things that hurt causes an emotional imbalance that disrupts the harmony of *Life*. If a guitar has just one string out of tune, it completely changes the sound of the entire instrument. Meditating is a way to become *Aware* of what is out of tune with the body. Most people avoid thinking about their dramas instead of finding effective ways to deal with them. This causes an accumulation of bad energy that creates blockages in the meridian system. If these issues are not dealt with, they can mutate into serious physical and emotional problems.

It's almost like there are multiple layers that need to be processed in succession. The outside or superficial layers are all the things that are happening every day. Not only is there an incredible amount of information to process, the defense mechanisms running in the background can drastically complicate things. Just below that are thoughts and memories that we are aware of that help define our personality. Then there are all the thoughts and memories hiding in places we are not consciously aware of. These are usually the buried dramas that stand in the way of accessing our *Full Potential*. Below that is the *True Self*.

After the first day and a half of the retreat, I had consciously traveled *Deeper* into *Myself* than I'd ever been. As I did this, it was almost like I was experiencing an inventory review for everything I had going on in my brain. I became *Aware* that my circuitry was off, which resulted in some faulty programing. Since there was so much nonsense that I was constantly trying to process, I previously wasn't able to observe the root cause of all my drama. It was almost like I was a silent observer to a rolling credits version of my *Life*. Once a thought can be isolated and seen for what it *Is*, working through it becomes much easier.

I woke up the next morning feeling like a completely *Different* person. I felt light and energized. I had no trouble popping right out of bed at four thirty when I heard the gong. Once we made our way into the meditation room, it only took minutes for me to fall into deep meditation. Before I knew it, the Guru was softly notifying everyone that it was time for breakfast. An hour had passed in what seemed like seconds. With my mind clear, accessing my *True Self* was as simple as closing my eyes and focusing on my breathing.

The rest of the week was *Gratifying* in a way that's tough to put in words. I experienced an acute *Sensitivity* that made everything seem surreal. It was like I was seeing everything for the first time. The food tasted amazing. I felt the wind gently caressing my face when it blew across my brow. Everything smelled better and, in some situations, a lot worse. All the sounds of the jungle occupied their own unique space, and the way the sun reflected color off everything reminded me of the type of brilliance captured by a timeless piece of art.

Feeling this *Good* affected people around me in an incredible way as well. The first few days when everyone was traveling through his or her own train wreck, there was a solidarity vibe buzzing in the air. Once we all found a better version of our *Selves*, the rhythm of the whole group changed. Perfect strangers were going out of their way to help the Chicken and me up and down the stairs and in and out of our room. Even though we weren't able to talk, a positive vibration was radiating through everything we did.

On the final day, the *Noble Silence* concluded. When we could finally talk to everyone, it was like we were all long-lost *Brothers* and *Sisters*. Our age, race, and gender got completely tossed out the window. We spoke like extended *Family* gathering for a reunion. One of the guys that had been helping me up and down the stairs looked familiar, and I had been itching to speak with him.

When we were in the Sukabumi jungle, the Chicken and I saw a TV program about an Australian surf instructor who got into a bar fight in Bali. He got sucker punched helping a girlfriend into a taxicab and spent six months in a coma after the fight. He looked a whole lot like one of the guys that had been helping me up and down the stairs. When I finally got to speak with him, it turned out he was the guy from the TV show. We had a lot in common, including an out-of-body experience that involved seeing a *Light*. Now that he was back in Bali teaching surf lessons again, catching up with him after the retreat seemed like an interesting possibility.

The most significant *Lesson* I took from the retreat is very simple. I AM an individual *Soul* on an independent journey of self-exploration. The better I understand my *Self*, the easier it is to understand the world around me. Since the world around me is full of other people, their experience of *Themselves* is also part of my experience. So WE ARE experiencing the same thing, just from *Different* perspectives. You can't have one without the other. If we help each other out while developing our own understanding of *Life*, the collective experience is better for everyone involved.

The year at Jasper's wellness clinic fizzled as predicted. The business struggled to retain clients and never established any type of momentum. Excuses were aplenty, and the managerial outfit quietly pointed fingers. The treatment with Pak Heru continued until December, rendering minimal results. I'm not sure what happened. I was making significant progress in the Sukabumi jungle, then when we moved to Bali, everything changed. I have my assumptions as to why, but it doesn't really matter.

Jasper rented a villa with Brutus and his girlfriend and her two kids. One afternoon, they packed their stuff and moved to the other side of town. I received a text from Jasper with directions to the new location where Pak Heru would be working. He said if I still wanted treatment, I was more than welcome to come. And that's it. Jasper the friendly ghost disappeared in the same manner he showed up.

That's the thing about ghosts, there's really no way to predict their behavior. They're here one day and gone the next. You think you know what they're up to, but there's no telling what they're doing when you're not around. I guess it's worth believing in ghosts, because they're definitely out there. But letting them into your heart is a risky business. Having the intuition to know when to roll the dice is really the only way to hedge your bets. Jasper taught me that betting the house on something that might or might not be there tomorrow isn't worth the gamble.

We had minimal funds and nowhere to go. We saw a bunch of healers and got a ton of great footage from mystical Bali, but for some reason, the trip felt incomplete. When Billy69 got news of Jasper's disappearance, he asked what we were going to do. When we told him our situation, he said not to worry. He told us to stay as long as we would like as his guest. He would no longer accept our money for rent.

We met some incredible people in Bali, and we were treated like *Family* by Billy69. The Little Chicken and I fell in *Love* with the culture and befriended locals that we still maintain contact with. As I approached the final chapters of this book, I realized there was still something I needed to do. I didn't fly to the other side of the world to fall short of my goals. My plan was to make a full recovery and surf the waves of Bali. And that's exactly what I planned on doing.

At one point during the meditation retreat, I looked down at my hand. I saw years' worth of scars that I had acquired fighting and playing sports in my youth. I remembered how bad it stung when they happened and how long it took them to heal. Now they were *Totally Healed*, with only a scar to remind me of the memory.

That's all that was left on my spinal cord. Just a scar to remind me of how lucky I AM to *Be Alive*. I can say with confidence now that I'm *Totally Healed*. I might not be able to walk yet, but I'm sure science will come up with a fancy solution for that. Doctors and scientists are cheeky in that way. I'm just gonna throw it out there; our *Brothers* and *Sisters* in the East are up to some cool stuff. They have been for many years. Maybe a joint venture is the future of medicine. I sure *Believe* it is.

As for the surfing portion of my goals, I just so happened to know a guy that owned a surf school in Bali. Batty Matty, the Aussie surf instructor that I met at the meditation retreat, had become a good *Friend* of mine. We got along well after the retreat and shared a *Deep* connection due to the extraordinary stuff we experienced. His run-in with the *Light* was only a few years old. He was still struggling with the *Responsibility* that came with leaving then deciding to come back. When I mentioned to him that I wanted to get back in the water, his whole *Being* lit up like a Christmas tree.

Batty Matty wasn't the same when he woke up from his coma. The injury he sustained to his brain made him short-tempered, and it had a tendency to push people away. He saw through superficial nonsense after his brush with death and had a short fuse when putting up with other people's crap. When he woke up from the *Illusion* that was his life before, everything felt *Different*. Matty had trouble finding comfort in the same things he did before his scuffle at the bar.

Matty was the first foreigner to own a surf school in Bali. He had been running it for nineteen years, and like a lot of stuff, things just weren't the same. He was ready to move back to Australia but not until he gave one last epic surf lesson. He worked a few contacts and had a board shaped for the occasion. About two weeks after mentioning the idea to Matty, we had a custom board for a quadriplegic, ready to surf the Bali waves.

The morning I showed up to the beach, I felt a calm that was unusual, considering the circumstances. I was a paralyzed guy with minimal control of my body who was scheduled for a surf session with a guy I only met a few times. Oh, it's also worth mentioning, Matty had never done anything like this before. As far as I knew it, only two people confirmed they would be there to help me in the water. When I got out of the car, I was surprised to see *Families* scattered all across the beach.

At 8:00 AM on a random Sunday morning, Matty was able to rally close to thirty people to come join our surf session. When he told everyone what he was doing, entire *Families* showed up without asking any questions. He was so respected in the community that it wasn't even necessary for people to know the details. Matty and his surfer dude buddies rallied their wives and children to participate in something truly special.

When we were driving to the beach that morning, thousands of thoughts raced through my head. It had been such an *Unbelievable Trip*; it was hard to process that there was more for me to *Learn*. I didn't even know why it was so important for me to go surfing. I dreamed of making it happen, but things were much *Different* now, and I *Accepted* that. At home, there are coordinated surfing programs for people with disabilities run by trained professionals. If I was hell-bent on surfing, it made the most sense to do it at home. For some reason though, I felt like the waves of Bali had something *Miraculous* for me.

It really wasn't even about surfing. It was an *Opportunity* to reconnect with the ocean. In place of the fear I might have felt before, I was *Completely Open* to whatever was going to happen. I had *Faith* in the integrity of the moment. I knew the surf would be big and I didn't know who would be there to help, but I felt *Great* about making it this far. It was time for me to finish in a way that was acceptable to my standards. I knew I gave my best effort, and this was my final exam. I had to find a way to create *Value* with this *Opportunity*.

As I was being carried down to the water, one of the perfect strangers carrying me asked, "Are you sure you want to do this?"

With a sparkle in my eye and a grin on my face, I replied, "Of course I am. What's the worst that could happen?"

I was the reason we were all there on the fateful Sunday morning. I inspired those helping me to *Live* beyond what they thought was possible. Everyone gathered in *Communion* to *Transcend* an otherwise normal activity into something *Truly Special*. Nobody had any idea what they were doing, and the ocean conditions were pretty rough, but they looked to me for guidance. The moment the board hit the water with me on it, nothing else mattered. The common goal to push me into a few rippers was the only focus on everyone's mind.

The surfing experience itself was arduous. We were all pretty out of our element. The session lasted about twenty minutes, and we only caught a grand total of two waves. Something magic happened while we were out there though. At one point, I made direct eye contact with one of the guys helping me and instantaneously discovered my *Purpose*.

Once we made it back to the sand, everyone needed a few minutes to gather themselves. The experience was full-on. It took all seven of the guys in the water to give everything they had to keep me from drowning. It's one of the most logically unsound positions I have ever put myself in, and I had NO FEAR. During the session, when I caught a glimpse of the *Compassion* and *Determination* in the eyes of the people helping me, I knew why it was so important for me to surf the waves of Bali.

I was told by the *Abundant Being of Light* to find *Oneness* within *Myself*, to *Live* the example of what it means to *Be*, and to get to work on my *Purpose*. As the sun beat upon on my back and saltwater dripped down my face, I realized I had just accomplished all three things at once. If I went into the experience expecting an insane surf session, I would have left room for disappointment. By staying *Open* to whatever opportunity presented itself, I was able to receive the most important *Lesson* of my *Life*.

I realized that surfing without proper usage of my limbs wasn't the best idea. I could definitely find better, more productive things to do with my time. My hat's off to the quadriplegics who use surfing to create *Value* in their *Lives*. Staying true to a *Passion* that drives you often makes *Life* worth *Living*. But getting back into surfing isn't something that drives me to be *Great*. Reconnecting with the ocean in an effort to find a part of *Myself* that I had lost was the reason it was so important for me to surf the waves of Bali.

The process of finding *Oneness* within *Myself* meant I was *Living* an example of what it meant to *Be*. *Purpose* presented itself when I created *Change* through the *Process of Doing*. By *Believing* in a *Better Way*, I created one by never giving into the idea of failure. I found a way to help others simply by *Believing* that there is more to *Life* than what we currently understand. There was more to the Bali surfing experience than even I understood. It wasn't until I was transferred from the sand back into my wheelchair that I realized how powerful *Leading* by example can be.

Everyone that helped me in the water that morning was completely exhausted. The fact that they had participated in something truly amazing had their hearts and minds occupied with an entirely *Different* sensation. Multiple strangers quietly pulled me aside to say thank-you for letting them be involved in my experience. I thought I should be the one thanking them, but those who helped me where *Grateful* in a totally *Different* way. I had given them *Faith* in the incredible power of the human *Spirit*. If I could find it in myself to demand more out of my life, so could they.

I also helped restore Batty Matty's *Faith* that he wasn't alone. More people *Loved* and *Appreciated* him than he even knew. He did an incredible job making everyone happy over the years but wasn't aware of how *Grateful* people were for his efforts. When he woke from a coma, he was able to see *Life* for what it *Is*. The *Illusion* that was his life before had vanished, just as mine did. His friends expected the same Matty, but everything had completely *Changed*.

The absence of an *Illusion* made everything quite confusing. Carrying the burden of seeing things from a *Different* perspective comes with some serious *Responsibility*. It can be a frustrating process figuring this out. I *Believe* that's why Matty and I found each other— to help fill in the blanks that we couldn't do alone. I AM *Grateful* to consider Matty my *Friend* and I AM also *Grateful* that my *Life* unfolded the way it did. If it would have gone any other way, who knows how things would have ended up?

The way this story ends is in the same way it began. *Endless Potential.* The Little Chicken and I flew home to nothing more than a bed and television at my *Parents'* house. We forfeited everything we owned for an *Opportunity* to better *Ourselves.* In doing so, we created *Value* with our *Lives* that we can now share with others. Finding *Purpose* took flying to the other side of the world, only to realize the real journey can be experienced by turning inward. *Believing* that there is a *Better Way* motivated us to challenge the difference between wants and needs. The first step toward accomplishing any goal is *Believing* that it's possible!

THE END.
AND ALSO THE BEGINNING.

About the Author

D amien Minna currently lives in Orange County, California, with his *Wife* and *Family*. After spending three years in Indonesia, he returned to the States to pursue a coaching and speaking career. After experiencing a life-altering spinal cord injury in 2004, Damien has dedicated his life to one of *Purpose*. His passion for writing came from an itching desire to make sense out of life's crazy happenings.

He utilizes his communication and marketing degree to speak with groups of all different shapes and sizes. He offers *Inspiration* and *Motivation* in the form of one-on-one coaching sessions, small-group workshops, and large-audience lecture-style presentations. His intention is to shine *Light* on all the places that cast shadows upon the brilliance of our *Life* experience.

Damien strives to find balance in *Life* by applying the *Lessons* he's *Learned* on his personal journey of *Self-exploration*. He serves as an advocate and ambassador for multiple wellness movements and dedicates his time to projects aimed at bettering the human condition. He is a public speaker that uses *Belief* strategies to support those looking to find *Purpose* in their lives.

Hey, ahh…you're still reading. Right on! Wanna see some pictures? Go to http://www.Need2Believe.net for pictures that go with each chapter.